A VIEW OF SELMA.

Page 10.

UNCLE ROBIN,

IN HIS CABIN IN VIRGINIA,

AND

TOM

WITHOUT ONE IN BOSTON.

SECOND EDITION.

BY J. W. PAGE.

J. W. RANDOLPH,
121 MAIN STREET, RICHMOND, VA.
1853.

COLIN & NOWLAN, PRINTERS,
South-Eleventh Street, between Main and Cary.

CONTENTS.

PREFACE.

THE highly exaggerated accounts of the cruelty of Southern masters towards their slaves, to be found in Northern publications, having done great injustice to the South, call imperiously for truthful statements of the consequences and incidents of the relation of master and slave as it now exists in the Southern States.

The design of the author of the following work, entitled, "Uncle Robin in his Cabin in Virginia, and Tom without one in Boston," is not only to disprove those accounts, but to show that the evils of slavery, so glowingly depicted in the Northern romances, as far as they do exist, are (for the most part) brought upon the slave by the imprudent sympathy of the self-styled philanthropists at the North. The author has not written this work for literary fame; nearly the whole is in colloquy, among characters who make no pretensions to literature of the higher order, consequently, there has been no effort at ornament, above the plain, common style of social intercourse.

He is content that his plain, unadorned topographical descriptions should reflect no credit upon an imagination whose vividness has been chilled by the frosts of many winters; and, if successful in removing odium from a much slandered Southern community, and in throwing it back upon the latitude to which it belongs, his object is effected.

UNCLE ROBIN IN HIS CABIN IN VIRGINIA,

AND

TOM WITHOUT ONE IN BOSTON.

CHAPTER I.

THE RETURN HOME.

"You jus come from de greathous, Elce?"

"Yes, Robin, I jus dis minit from dare."

"Is Charles an' dem gals gittin' long pretty well, cleanin' and fixin' de house for massee and young missis? Masser tell me when he went away, dat he'd be back here de day after to-morrow, an I does want ebery thing mighty nice for him, when he bring he young bride home: Elce, you mus tend to dem gals and Charles, an' see dat dey wash all de windees; an' tell 'em from me, dat I won' be satisfied unless I can see my face in the furnitur plain enough to shabe by."

"I ain' gwine leave it to dem, Robin; I gwine see to ebery thing myself; I don' want my young missis, when she com home, to think we aint gentle-folks, an' aint use to havin' things like de quality."

"Elce, you can hab one nother cow to do pail; I gwine kill dat fat veal to-morrow night, so dat dey can hab good dinner prepared for 'em."

"Robin, I don' think you ought to kill dat veal now, cause I know when massa com home, he gwine hab mighty big weddin' dinner here, an he'll want dat veal for de dinner. I got plenty o' scovy duck and chicken, and Susan can git 'em very good dinner widout de veal."

"You right, Elce, we'll sav de veal, an I'll giv Susan one mighty nice pig for de dinner day after to-morrow."

"Pig! Robin, for a dinner for young bride! why, sartinly, Robin, you don' know anything 'bout de quality; pig right down tacky dinner."

"Why, Elce, I bin see my ole missis hab many pig for dinner, an I spose you'll 'low she was quality, an eberybody at dinner chuse pig."

"Robin, you gittin' ole now, an it bin som time sence you was boy waitin' in de house and see pig for dinner; quality mightly altered sence dem days, Robin."

"Well, Elce, I can't see why quality should 'spise any good thing de Lord giv um to eat, unless dey was Jew, an den dey would be right not to eat de flesh ob de swine."

"Robin, you may gib ober 'bout de pig; I ain' gwine to suffer pig to come 'pon dat table. I hope, Robin, dis young missis gwine be like our ole missis dat's dead and gone."

"Elce, I hope massa done chuse one young lady dat will som time or oder be like our dear ole missis; but she too young yit, Elce, to be anything like her now; it require heap o' 'flection to com up to her."

"Robin, I bin hear um say dat de folks in Pennsylvany

mighty fond o' black-folks, an I 'spose she's gwine make us fus rate missis."

"Well, Elce, I don' preten' to say oderwise, but 'taint always dat dem folks who make mos' fus 'bout der goodness is de best folks, der's some of de Pharisee lef in de worl' yit; our blessed Savior did'n drive um all out of de worl', *I* tell you. Elce, if I was gwine to hunt for one good, kind Samaratan, I would'n go out of ole Fugginny to look fur him."

"Well, Robin, I can't stay longer from my wuck at de house, massa will be here 'pon us in a hurry."

Elce was right in saying that the quality of Virginia was mightily altered from former days: at the period of the commencement of our narrative, there was scarcely a remnant of its aristocracy left; its time-honoured practices, however, still lingered in the recollection of some of the old servants: Robin's memory (for instance) went back to the day when a grinning roasted pig, with an apple in his mouth, was not only tolerated by the gentry as sufficiently genteel, but luxuriously-palatable, whilst the notions of Elce, his wife (a few years younger than himself), were formed upon the refinements of modern gentility, which repudiates the pig as decidedly vulgar.

We have high authority for saying that the only vestige then remaining of aristocratic ease and gentility, was to be found with some old negro man, who had seen and caught his master's manner, when making his *entrée* at a birth-night ball, or President Washington's levees. Robin, whom we shall hereafter call Uncle Robin, was too young to have caught the genteel bearing of those palmy days of Virginia; but his old master and mistress, themselves remnants of the aristocracy, had given him a certain ease of manner far above that of his contemporary fellow-servants. They found great difficulty, however, in teaching him the pronunciation of the Anglo-Saxon in its purity, and consequently, the reader will find his clear, strong views of things expressed pretty much in the corruptions interpolated by descendants from the African race.

Doctor Boswell (the young master for whose reception at home with his bride, the servants were anxiously engaged in making preparations) belonged to one of the oldest and most influential families of Virginia.

After completing his education at William and Mary College, he attended the medical lectures in Philadelphia, and received his diploma in the spring of 1848. While there, he became acquainted with Miss Ann Stephens, a beautiful and highly accomplished young lady from Norristown, Pennsylvania, and a mutual attachment being formed, they were married in the fall of 1848 at Norristown.

The Doctor being the only child of his parents (who were both dead), succeeded to an estate lying on the north-western side of the Blue Ridge mountain, on the river Shenandoah. His father had resided on the same estate, where he had reared a comfortable, commodious stone dwelling, on a beautiful height, commanding a view of the low grounds, the river beyond, and of the mountain on the opposite side. Being the owner of about forty slaves, he had built comfortable stone cabins for their accommodation, on the same height, in range with the mansion-house, the nearest of which was about two hundred yards distant. Great taste had been displayed by both parents in beautifying the grounds about Selma; the regular slope from the house to the low grounds was occupied by native poplars and elms, standing at such distances as to admit exotic evergreens, which had been collected with much care and expense from other climes, and here and there a native hawthorn, unconscious of inferiority, had claimed and maintained its right of soil by preoccupancy.

The green venitians of the dwelling-house, in contrast with its white stuccoed walls, the white-washed cabins, with their green baton shutters and doors, seen through the evergreens, gave to the *tout ensemble* a richness and softness of beauty, which filled the beholder with delight, as he ascended the slope from the flat to the mansion. It had been locked up during the minority of the doctor, after the death of his father and mother; but faithful Uncle Robin, by his assiduous care and attention, had prevented the least appearance of dilapidation. He had often said to Elce, "my young masser Johnny gwine com home when he gits he edication, an' he shill find ebery thing jist as he pa an' ma lef' it."

When the Doctor arrived with his lovely, interesting bride, the familiar arrangements, the freshness and beauty of Selma and its environs, brought so vividly to his recollection his lamented parents, that a momentary illusion may have presented them as still in existence and ready to greet his return to his much endeared home; 'twas but the dream of a moment, and he awoke to the reality of his indebtedness to the lingering affections of a coloured domestic for the preservation of those comforts and adornments which had been the work of by-gone days.

Mrs. Boswell and her brother, Mr. Henry Stephens (then a merchant in Norristown), were the only children of their parents, who had, until a few years before their daughter's marriage, been in affluent circumstances, and had brought up their children delicately, and without regard to any possible change which time might bring about in their situation. That change, however, did come, and, on the day before the wedding, old Mr. Stephens thought himself in honour bound to inform Doctor Boswell, that owing to a failure of one of the most extensive mercantile houses in Philadelphia, he was reduced almost to poverty. The doctor, a noble-hearted Virginian, was but little affected by the communication, further than feeling deep sympathy for the old gentleman and his wife. He earnestly entreated them to go and live with him in Virginia, which they consented to do, after they had arranged their matters for a final leave-taking of the place of their nativity.

As soon as it was known in the neighbourhood, that Doctor Boswell had arrived at Selma with his bride, there was much preparation made to offer customary greetings to the newly-married couple. Major and Mrs. Scott, the two Misses Scott, old Mr. Preble, his daughter, Miss Evelina, and his son, Mr. George Preble, were the first to offer congratulations; those two families being considered the top of the circle of that neighbourhood, were expected to make the first visit to all new comers, as they were generally allowed to be better acquainted with all those little considerations in the *beaumonde*, which make first visits strictly according to etiquette.

Mrs. Scott was a highly polished lady, having been well educated by her father Colonel Baytop, who was an officer of some note in the American Revolution, and who at the close of the war had settled in the county of Orange, where he raised an only daughter, and died shortly after her marriage.

Major Scott had received a tolerably good education, was a gentleman in easy circumstances, and was considered in his neighbourhood, a man of uncommonly sound views on all subjects, and was an oracle to whose judgment were submitted all difficult matters of controversy; although he had never been clothed with legal authority for their final adjustment, and was not entitled to the cognomen of Squire. The two Misses Scott were as different in appearance as two sisters could well be; Miss Julia was a brunette, with large dark-gray eyes, a regular set of features, and dark hair; her countenance was remarkable for its intelligence, and was the index to a mind of no ordinary stamp; she was engaging and interesting, without being a beauty. Miss Amelia was fair, with light-blue eyes, flaxen hair, homely features, and a countenance expressive of no intelligence; she was decidedly homely, without exciting much hope for amiability.

Mr. Preble was an old gentleman who had been left a widower; although himself a slaveholder, he had imbibed in early life, in the North (where he was born), some notions, which he himself could not well define, of something like impropriety in holding human beings in a state of servitude, but was nevertheless considered by his neighbours a very severe master. Miss Evelina Preble was lovely both in person and disposition. Her mind was well stored with useful knowledge; her principles were founded upon, and her conduct regulated by, the precepts of the Christian religion, acquired by a constant prayerful reading of her Bible, under the direction of her maternal maiden aunt, Miss Priscilla Graham, whose every aspiration for herself and those around her, was heavenly and heavenward. Mr. George Preble was a young gentleman of amiable disposition, volatile in his manner, by no means deficient in understanding, although he had not made the very best use of the opportunity afforded by a collegiate course.

"My dear, said Mrs. Scott (addressing herself to Mrs. Boswell), I hope you have come to Virginia with a determination of being happy among strangers;—but I will recall the word *strangers*, as I trust we shall be no longer considered such, and from this day forward you will look upon us as friends and old acquaintances."

"If I am not happy here, Mrs. Scott, I am sure it will be my own fault, for it seems to me there is everything calculated to make a reasonable being contented and happy; the doctor anticipates my every wish, and, besides having made every arrangement necessary for my comfort, he has promised me enjoyments derived from the best and most enlightened society, and I assure you I have good reason to believe that his promise will be fulfilled."

"Well, you must not expect too much from us, Mrs. Boswell; we are a plain people inhabiting this mountain region, but we generally do our best to make all who come among us feel comfortable and easy;" replied Mrs. Scott.

"I have no doubt of it, madam, that every effort will be made to make my time pass agreeably; and I hope to show, by my conduct, that those efforts are not thrown away upon one who is insensible to, and therefore unworthy of kindness."

"How are you pleased, Mrs. Boswell," said Major Scott, "with our mountain scenery?"

"Oh! I am charmed with it, sir. I am naturally of a romantic turn, and I shall never tire in admiring the grandeur of the scenery from our front door. Although the poet has said, ''tis distance lends enchantment to the view,' its nearness has more enchantment for me: there is something grand and sublime in its jaggedness and roughness, which is lost when it becomes an uninterrupted streak of azure."

"There is something in a near view of all the works of nature," said Miss Evelina Preble, "better calculated to exalt our admiration of the great Architect, than in the distant."

"That is very true," said Major Scott; "but did it never strike you, that there is something wonderful and grand in the fact, that the rough asperities of the mountain can be overcome and made smooth in the distance, by the power of the same Architect, in his formation and adjustment of the medium through which the rays of light pass to our vision?"

"I declare," said Miss Amelia Scott, "I don't see how anybody can like the mountain, either near or at a distance; I've been living all my lifetime in sight of the mountain, and I forget there is any mountain, for I rarely ever look at it."

"My dear daughter," said the Major, "I should be ashamed to acknowledge my indifference to the grand displays of nature, if I were you; I think I must carry you next summer to the falls of Niagara, to excite in you a taste for the sublime."

"O! father, do carry us both," said Miss Julia. "I'll promise you to be an exquisite in my admiration of everything grand and sublime. I won't say with sister, however, that I have not now a taste for those things; I have been admiring, from the window, this mixed mountain and water prospect ever since I came. I don't want to go to Niagara only to see the falls; I want to see some of the works of art: Philadelphia, New York, and other cities. We will go through Norristown, Mrs. Boswell, if you will go with us."

"Indeed, miss, I hardly ever expect to see Norristown again. My father and mother are coming in a few months to live with us, and then I shall have no desire to go back. My brother will visit us occasionally, and we have no other near relations in Pennsylvania. If Doctor Boswell, however, will agree to go and take me, I should be delighted with the trip."

"That is impossible, my dear," said the Doctor; "I have too much to do at home; you know it is said that a man can't wive and thrive the same year, and it would be certainly true with me, if I were to go journeying too for pleasure; no, my dear, you are now a Virginia farmer's and doctor's wife, and you must make up your mind to stay pretty constantly at home."

"Upon my word, Doctor," said old Mr. Preble, "you have begun in time; well, it is said, that whoever is harnessed in the honeymoon, has to wear it for life. How do you get along with our peculiar institution, Mrs. Boswell? I suppose you come among us with natural, instinctive, and acquired antipathies."

"I do not know," answered Mrs. Boswell, "that I have any natural or instinctive antipathies; but you may readily suppose that my education has been such as to produce a feeling adverse to what you call your peculiar institution. I am free to confess, sir, that my father and mother are both abolitionists, and that I have come to Virginia entertaining a strong feeling against slavery; indeed, almost with a horror at the thought of being in its midst; but, as I am doomed, you know, to wear the harness all my life, I must wear it, and obey my husband in all things, even should it be to tolerate slavery. It may be, that when I have become familiar with all its incidents I may pull tolerably well in that harness."

"Well, I don't know," rejoined Mr. Preble, "how it is, but I have been familiar with it here for nearly thirty years, and I am just as much opposed to it now as when I first left Massachusetts."

"I suppose, of course, you don't own slaves, Mr. Preble?"

"Why, madam, to tell you the truth, I do own a few: being in Rome, I think it but right to do as the Romans do."

"Certainly not, sir, when the Romans are leading us astray from the dictates of conscience."

Mrs. Scott, seeing the effect which this hit had upon Miss Evelina, proposed taking leave, as the carriages were at the door; the whole party left, after urgent entreaties that the Doctor and Mrs. Boswell should visit them.

"Well, my dear," said the Doctor, "how could you give old Mr. Preble such a rap? I was glad of it, however, for he is always croaking about the evils of slavery, and at the same time has no bowels of compassion for slaves; he neither gives them a sufficiency of clothing or food, and whips most cruelly. My father, who was a justice of the peace, kept him somewhat in check by threatening the law."

"Why, my dear husband, have you any law in Virginia to punish a master for cruelty to his slave?"

"Certainly, my dear; a man is not allowed to be cruel to his beasts; but as slaves are the only persons generally present, and as their testimony is not admissible against a white man, the law is rarely enforced against a cruel master."

"I have always thought it a shocking thing to prevent slaves from giving testimony against a white man; in our state the testimony of a black man is thought as good as that of a white."

"Well, my dear, as I have brought you to Virginia full of notions and prejudices against this peculiar institution of ours, it is my duty, and it is indispensable to your comfort here, that I should remove those prejudices as soon as possible. My first effort will be to reconcile you to what you call a shocking thing in our laws, and to show you how very shocking it would be (on the other hand), if slaves were allowed to give testimony against the whites.

"I must allow that there are evils inseparable from a state of slavery, such (for instance) as a depressed and lowered standard of morals; a general feeling of antagonism on the part of the slave towards the white man; which latter feeling, operating upon the low moral standard, which rejects the proper appreciation of an oath, would not only tend to insecurity of the life and property of the white man, but would injure the slave himself, if he were by law placed in a situation where there was constant temptation to perjury.

"Moreover, there is always, in every community, a class of whites whose moral standard is as low as that of the slave, but who, on account of their freedom, are more connected than the slave with the property transactions of life; and if, in contests between the whites relative to those transactions, the slave was admitted to bear testimony, what an advantage would the *villain* litigant have over the *conscientious* one, when there was so wide a field open for suborning slaves to perjury! A master's influence, too, over his slave might be made to bear very beneficially upon his own interest, and defeat the purposes of justice, if the slave could testify in his behalf; or he might be liable to injury from the testimony of a slave given under feelings of exasperation.

"It is entirely unsuited to the nature of slavery, to admit slaves as witnesses, for or against those who are connected with property transactions. If the slave were liable to be called to a court-house as a witness, where he might be kept for many days, what would become of the master's interest at home? What temptations also to vice would not be offered the idle slave at a public court-house; and above all, what chance would not occasional respite from labour at a public place give of success to the efforts of abolitionists to entice him for ever from servitude! We will dismiss the subject for the present; and if to-morrow is a good day, we will take a walk and see the condition of our servants."

CHAPTER II.

INSPECTIONS.—CONTRAST.—TAMPERINGS.

A BALMY morning late in the month of November (the season being what is called Indian summer), reminded Dr. Boswell of his promise to his wife, of a walk to see the condition of their servants; and having hurried over her labours at the tea board, she was in a short time after breakfast ready to accompany him. They made directly for Cabin Row (as it was called). The first cabin of the row was Uncle Robin's, who had been confined by slight indisposition ever since the arrival of his new mistress, and whom he had never yet seen. After asking about his health, the Doctor said to him; "Well, Robin, I have brought your new mistress to see you."

"I mighty glad to see you, missis," said Robin; "how you been do, madam?"

"I am very well, I thank you, Uncle Robin, and am glad to find you better."

"Thank you, missis, de Lord be praised, I feels myself considerable better dis mornin'; I's had a right tuff time of it, missis, since you bin com' home, else I'd bin to see you 'fore dis; walk in, missis, I 'spose you never bin in nigger cabin befo'!"

"I don't know that I ever was in a negro's cabin before, Uncle Robin, but I have been in a much worse house than yours; I am very fond of neatness and tidiness, and you seem to have everything neat and comfortable around you; I should think Aunt Elce was a very good wife."

"De Lord be praised, missis, she does suit me mighty well; you's bin see Elce, ain't you, missis?"

"O! yes, she's been several times at the house since I came."

"Where is she now, Robin?" asked the Doctor.

"Why, massa, bit ago, I see'd some sheeps on de young clober down in de fiel' 'pon de river, and I sends Elce to dribe 'em out, sir."

"How many children have you, Uncle Robin?"

"Only three, missis, dat gal Elce 'bout de house, my boy John, now at wuck in de fiel', and dis little boy Robin; whar is dat chile? Robin, com' here, boy, and see missis!"

Robin came from the little bedroom, where he had been hiding, and held his hand to his mistress.

"Keep back you' dutty han', boy! 'spose missis is gwine shake sich a black dutty han' as yourn?"

"If it was clean, Uncle Robin, I would not refuse to shake it because it was black."

"Oh! no, missis, I don't say dat; my ole missis dat's dead and gone, and is now wid de angels in Hebbin, never thought she'd be tarminated by shakin' han's wid de poo' niggers."

"Well, Robin," said the Doctor, "I hope this new mistress that I have brought you will be like your old one in every respect."

"Think so, masser? oh if she is, masser, I shall lobe her mo' 'an tung' can tell. When de Lord see'd fit to take my ole missis from me, I thought I neber should see any mo' peace in dis worl', and I did long so much to go wid my missis, but de Lord want me to stay here, and I did thought de Lord know'd bes', and I give up to de Lord, and tried to say, dy will be don', and de Lord healed de broken heart."

"I don't see any bed in your room, Uncle Robin," said his mistress.

"Why, we sleep, missis, in dat little room dar; dis room, my ole missis had built purpose for Sunday school and prayin' room, missis."

"I intend, my dear, to explain all these things to you hereafter, about the Sunday school, &c.," said the Doctor. "Let us now go and visit the other cabins. All the others you will find occupied by two families, one family in each room. This first room is Jim's and Dinah's; they are both at work in the field, and their children, when they are away, stay in the last cabin with old Aunt Juno, who takes care of all the small children, when their parents are at work from home. This next now, is Pheby's and George's; both doors seem to be open, we will take a peep into them."

"My dear husband, how very comfortable and neat they all seem to be!"

"The others," said the Doctor, "are pretty much like

those you have seen; we will pass on to the last, one room of which is occupied by old Aunt Juno, a native African. She is past work, and her only business (as I mentioned before) is to take care of the children."

"Well, Aunt Juno, how are you to-day?"

"Bad nuff, massa, dese chillons pesse me tu much, dey fights, dey fights ebery time, make Juner no fire, poo' ole Juner cole now."

"I'll have some fire made for you. Aunt Juno, here's your new mistress come to see you."

"How you do, missy? Juner berry glad see you, Juner ole now, can't see you berry well."

"How old do you suppose you are, Aunt Juno?" asked Mrs. Boswell.

"Why, missy, Juner seb-seb-sebinty; when Massa Braddec com' long here, Juner was big gal, missy."

"She is only a little out in her chronology, my dear," said the Doctor. "I have never yet seen a very old negro who hadn't something to say about Braddock; his march through Virginia seems to be a favourite epoch in their memories. There can be none left who remember that period; but many of those who are now living have some tradition, that there was such a person as Braddock; it is so with old Aunt Juno, for she can't be more than ninety years of age."

"Aunt Juno," said her mistress, "how many children have you to take care of?"

"Why, missy, hundred."

'How her arithmetic adds to my responsibilities!'

said the Doctor. "Why, Aunt Juno, there are not more than fifteen."

"Ah dem die, massa, dem die."

The Doctor had a fire made for her, and as they were about to leave, old Juno said:

"Missy, Juner wan' say som' 'tickler ting, missy, som' 'tickler ting."

"Say on, old lady."

"Missy, Juner wan' som' sugar, som' coffy, and som' tommer, missy."

"What does she mean by 'tommer', my dear?"

"I can't give you the derivation of the word; but the old negroes call wheat bread, 'tommer'. You will seldom hear a young negro use the word; it seems to be almost obsolete. She means that you must send her some flour with the sugar and coffee; and if you stay much longer, there will be various other little items added."

"If you are not in too great a hurry, my dear, I should like to ask her something about Africa."

"Well, you won't get much from her; but take that chair, and see what you can make of it."

"Aunt Juno, do you remember anything about your own country, Africa?"

"'Member, missy, yes, Juner much 'member. Juner big gal when Juner com' 'way; when dey put Juner 'pon dat big hous' 'pon top o' de water, whar Juner neber tun roun'."

"How did they catch you, and bring you there?"

"Juner farder gib Juner to one massa; Juner no' cry den, Juner be one conger, eat, eat Juner!"

"My dear," said the Doctor, "I have often heard her say the same thing, and I can only understand her, by supposing that the cannibal tribes of Africa selected beforehand those who were to be eaten, and that the selected ones were called congers; and that she was not sorry that she was taken away; because she was destined to be eaten."

"Do they eat each other now in Africa?"

"I suppose they do among some of the interior tribes, even now. At the time she speaks of, the tribes on the Gold Coast were mostly cannibals; but their intercourse with European nations since, and missionary efforts, have made them less savage all along the coast than they formerly were."

"Would you like to go back to Africa, Aunt Juno?"

"No, missy, Juner no go back, Juner no conger now; Juner no frien' dar now; Juner 'tay wid massa 'til Juner die."

"Where do you expect to go when you die?"

"Ole missy tell Juner heap 'bout hebbin, and Juner farder in hebbin, an' say, if Juner good, Juner go to hebbin when she die. She tell Juner 'bout one man die for Juner to car' Juner to hebbin; an' dat Juner mus' lobe dat man, an' Juner bin try lobe dat man; but mighty hard lobe when Juner no see um. Juner hope see um bimeby."

"My dear," said the Doctor, "I ordered George to get the carriage, that we might take a ride down the new turnpike this morning; and I see it now at the door. You must postpone any further enlightenment from Aunt Juno about Africa, and heaven, until another day."

"Missy, min' de 'ticklar ting."

"Good-bye, Aunt Juno; I will send you some sugar and coffee, and some tommer too."

"Tank you, missy; good-bye, missy, good-bye, massa."

"Drive to the new turnpike, George," said the Doctor, as he shut the carriage door. And turning to his wife he said: "Now, my dear Ann, I will complete the imperfect sketch of the character, sentiments, and actings of one, who is now a saint in heaven: I mean my dear mother. I have before told you that my maternal grandfather was a minister of the Protestant Episcopal Church, and was considered one of the first pulpit orators of the state; and what is of far more importance, was one of the most evangelical divines of his day. My grandmother was a lady suited in every respect to be the wife of such a minister. My mother (an only child) received her education at home, which was by no means an ordinary one, as her father was a man of learning, and instructed her in all the important branches of literature. There was a union of effort in forming her moral and religious character, which was as lovely as could have been hoped for, from such training.

"You may suppose that the individual who could obtain the heart and hand of such a woman must have had congenial endowments; and such a man was my father. After the house in which we now live was completed, he brought my mother to Selma, where they received an annual visit from my grandfather and grandmother during their lives; they died within a short time of each other, when I was about eight years of age. My grandfather had never owned a slave, though all the drudgery in his family had been performed by hired slaves. My mother, living in the midst of slavery, and having all her lifetime been waited upon by slaves, when brought to Selma was not ignorant (as you now are, my Ann) of its relations, and its consequences either for weal or for woe. After I became old enough to understand and enjoy her conversation, she often talked to me upon that subject; she said that very early in life, long before she was married, her mind had been much exercised upon it, that she had prayerfully consulted her Bible, and had come to the conclusion that it was not sinful in the sight of her Heavenly Father, for one human being to hold another in that relation; but, that there were duties and responsibilities growing out of it, the neglect of which was highly sinful. That the slave had a soul to be saved as well as his master; that if the master was inhuman, and regardless of the slave's bodily comforts, and denied him facilities for obtaining religious instruction, he (the master) perilled his own soul. By a strict performance of such duties, she thought slavery might not only be tolerated, but might be made to subserve beneficial purposes.

"She saw in the black free population around her, no promise of moral good from emancipation; and she came to Selma with a firm reliance on Providence for support, strictly to perform the duties of a mistress. My father's views being in accordance with her own, the old wooden cabins in which the negroes were then living, were exchanged for the stone ones we have just visited. Robin's cabin was arranged differently from the others; the chimneys running up in the middle of the others, make the two rooms of equal size; but in Robin's, one room is much larger than the other. My mother intended that large room for a sanctuary, where the negroes might assemble for Sabbath school exercises, and for preaching at such times as our parish minister might appoint for his plain lectures, adapted to their capacities, and for preaching by all other denominations of Christians, black or white. She soon established a Sabbath school, which she conducted herself, my father and some of the neighbours around assisting her. Robin was at that time a young man, waiting in the house. My mother finding him very truthful, tractable, and intelligent, bestowed more time and labour on his instruction than that of the others. She thought if she could qualify him as a teacher he would be of great assistance to her in the Sabbath school; and before her death, she found him sufficiently qualified to take the entire management of it. It was necessary, however, under the law of Virginia, that some white person should always be present, and take part in the instructions.

"My father and mother suffered their slaves to join any denomination of Christians for which they had a preference. Most generally, throughout this country, negroes who have made a profession of religion, have joined the Baptist denomination. Robin reads with considerable fluency, sometimes exhorts, and I believe he is a sincere Christian. There are some others on the plantation who make a profession of religion. Elce, Robin's wife, is, I fear, a hard case; but I trust Robin's prayers for her may be blessed. I have myself (as I have told you before) joined the Episcopal church; it was what my dear parents unceasingly prayed for, but they did not live to see an answer to their prayers, and a consummation of their hopes. I have determined, my dear Ann, to carry out the wishes of my parents in regard to our slaves; the Sabbath school shall be continued, and every effort in my power made to train them up for heaven; and I trust that I shall find in my dear wife that zeal for the souls of our slaves which shone so brightly in the character of my sainted mother. We are now at the turnpike, and there are the Irish shanties."

"What are they, my dear?"

"Shanty, my dear, comes from two Irish words, which mean an old dwelling; but with us, they mean what you now see before you: huts for human beings to live in. The women and children occupy them in the day, and the men who work on the public road, join them at night. As some of them are sick and may want medicine, we will get out and see them."

"Well, Jerry," said the Doctor, addressing himself to a man at the door of the first shanty.

"Och, Docthur, but I'm glad to see you, the day; the ould woman lies very ailing, she is."

"What's the matter with her?"

"She's got the agy and the faver, your honour, and I has to nurse and cook for the brats all the while. Come in, come in, and the leddy, if she isn't a fearing this stye, as it is, sure 'nough, of a shanty." It was a stye indeed; there lay the mother in one corner on a dirt floor, with nothing between her and the floor but an old worn out blanket, and half covered with something that looked like a black stained saddle-cloth. She was shaking with an ague. There were, in another corner, six children, half naked, and shivering as if they too had agues. The filth and stench was insupportable, and Mrs. Boswell had to make her escape to the fresh air as soon as possible; but the doctor, like a true son of Esculapius, stood his ground and administered medicine to the poor woman.

"Jerry," said he, "I am astonished to see your family in such a horrid situation. Why don't you get a bed for your poor sick wife to lie upon? A plain common tick, filled with straw, would make her much more comfortable; and there are your children, all naked; the winter's coming on, and if you don't give them some warm clothing they'll freeze in this open shanty."

"Faith, but there's little the danger o' that; they's used to it, do you see, Docthur; poor people's shildren, your honour, must be brought up hardy; many's the likes o' that in the ould counthry. I works very hard, your honour, for the ould mither and the brats."

Here the old lady raised her head, and cried in an unearthly tone:

"It's nothing a more but whiskey that's done it, Docthur, it is, it is."

"Don't mind what the ould woman says, Docthur, she talks the like o' that when the faver's in the brain, she does."

"I am afraid there's too much truth in what she says, Jerry."

"There's not the word of truth in it, your honour."

"Take this phial, Jerry, and after the ague is off, give her ten drops every half-hour; do you understand?"

"Faith but I do, Docthur; I'm up to the draps ony how, many's the one I've give the poor sick crater."

The Doctor joined Mrs. Boswell, and they went on to the next shanty; there stood Dennis Flinn at the door.

"Well, Dennis," said the Doctor, "how goes the world with you?"

"As to that, Doctor, I can't say much; the world goes over bad with poor folks, but we'll be better off anyhow than some of our nebburs; the brats are all up, and the ould woman's a going; there's Jerry's wife been tak down with the faver."

"I suppose you feel very thankful that your family has escaped."

"Why, as to the matter o' that, Docthur, they'll tak' it some other time; there's Patrick O'Nale, in the next shanty, he thought he was too strong for the agy, but it gave him considerable shake, it did; and there's Bet Flannagin, poor cratur', she's been nearer t'other warld than I'd like to be, onyhow."

"Wouldn't you like to go to a better world than this?" said the Doctor.

"When the praist says I'm ready, and my time's come. It's a long time since the praist was bye, and I've got considerable score to wipe off."

"Considerable score of what, do you mean?"

"Why, sins, your honour."

"And do you believe that the priest can wipe out your sins?"

"Yes, besure, your honour; jis tell him what you've been doin', and he'll wipe it out as sure as my name's Dennis."

"You didn't learn that from your Bible."

"Och! bother, your honour, I've no larning to read the Bible, and if I had, the praist wouldn't let me. The praist reads the Bible for all poor sinners, and they've no business with it onyhow, your honour."

"Have you never learnt to read?"

"No, your honour, in the ould counthry, the poor people warks so hard they've never a time for larning, no more."

"Don't you intend to send your children to school?"

"Och! no, your honour; when the children gets big enough they must go to work, as I have done before them; no time for larning, at all, at all."

"But suppose you were to send them to the Sunday school?"

"The praist says the Sabbath's a day of rest, your honour; and the like of us, who work hard all the week, should tak' rest on that day."

"My negroes work hard all the week, and go to hear preaching, and some go to the Sabbath school; why can't you do the same?"

"Now, your honour shouldn't compare your nigger slaves with white people, onyhow; we go when we plase, and stay at home when we please; and your honour knows there's a warld of difference between free people and slaves."

"If slaves have more learning than free people, more religion than free people, and have better houses to live in than free people, I think the difference is in favour of slaves."

"But, your honour, there's something in liberty better than the like of onything else in the warld."

"How many children have you, Dennis?"

"Four, your honour."

"Do you expect to keep your wife and children in this shanty all the winter? If you do, you should get some more plank and make a floor to your shanty, and stop those large cracks in the roof, and get warm clothing for them; they are almost naked now."

"When the money comes in for the wark, your honour, we'll try and do something o' that way."

"There's none a bit of it behind, the jug's tak' it all," said Mrs. Flinn, looking at a jug in the corner.

"Ah! Dennis, Dennis, that won't do; you ought to think of your wife and children."

"That's what I'm doin' all the time, your honour; and the more I thinks on the like o' them, the more nade there is for the jug, your honour."

"Suppose you were to die, Dennis, without having laid up anything for your wife and children; what would these poor creatures do after your death?"

"Why, your honour knows that the county would tak' care o' them; the ould woman would be sent to the house where they tends the poor, and the shildren would be bound out to trades, your honour."

"Well, Dennis, would it not be better to bind them out now before you die, and let them learn trades, and be taught to read?"

"Please God, my shildren shall never be taken from their poor mither and bound out to masters while Jenny Flinn's head's hot; no, my shildren shall never be made slaves onyhow," said Mrs. Flinn.

"If," said the Doctor, "the bare name of freedom is to you meat, drink, and wearing apparel, I will leave you to enjoy it. My dear, we will go to the next shanty and inquire how Patrick O'Neal is."

"How are you, to-day, Patrick?"

"Och! botheration, Docthur, I'm bad enough, bad enough; my head's in a flame, Docthur."

"You've been drinking too much, Patrick."

"That's jist what the owld 'oman said; I drank too much cowld water the morning, I did."

"But that is not what I meant; you've been making too free with the whiskey, Patrick."

"Now, your honour jist thinks so, because your honour knows how good it is to drive off the cowld when a body's shakin' and shivrin'."

"I now tell you, once for all, that if you do not leave off drinking whiskey, you'll be a dead man in a very short time, Patrick."

"Well, then, whiskey and I'll shake hands, Docthur, and be no friends any more, at all, at all, we won't."

"It is not worth while to give you any more medicine,

Patrick; I will not throw away any more physic or advice upon a patient who will neither take the one or listen to the other." In a low voice he said: "We will not go in here, my dear, it is worse than anything we have seen yet."

George, who had followed with the carriage, already had the door open, and the steps down; and when the Doctor and Mrs. Boswell had taken their seats, he turned back towards Selma.

"My dear Ann," said the Doctor, "I have carried you to-day among our slaves, and into the hut of the free white man. There are no words in our language more indefinite in their meaning than liberty and slavery; they are used for the most part as mere sounds: the one conveying to the mind everything that is precious and to be desired, the other, everything that is horrid and to be avoided, without any reference to the various modifications of each, to be found in different countries, and surrounded by different circumstances. You have seen, to-day, specimens of those modifications; and your good sense will determine whether the halo around the one, and the dimness around the other, are the unvarying characteristics of each; whether there are most of the true substantial blessings, which make life desirable, in the shanty of Dennis Flinn, or the cabin of Robin."

"My dear, I can't hesitate in assigning to the cabin of Uncle Robin a vastly greater amount of every procurement of real happiness in this world, than is to be found in the shanty of Dennis Flinn; but is not the estimate which is formed of the relative excellence of two conditions of life, from viewing the extremes of each, apt to be erroneous?"

"I do not allow that your estimate has been the result of a presentation of the extremes of each. To be sure, on our plantation, you see slavery in one of its best modifications; but you will see similar modifications of it on many, very many plantations in Virginia; and on the other hand, the Irish shanties do not present liberty in its most degraded modification; in the ould country (as they call it) it is infinitely worse."

The carriage was at the door; and Uncle Robin, who had felt himself better, had come down to see his master on business, and was ready to open the door when the carriage stopped. They got out, and Mrs. Boswell went into the house. But the Doctor, supposing that Robin (who was his foreman), wanted to see him on plantation business, remained in the portico.

"Masser," said Uncle Robin, "I want talk to you 'pon som' very serious business."

"Come along with me, Robin, down the garden walk, and I will hear what you have to say."

"Masser, you put me here as foreman 'pon you' plantation, and you specks me to tell you whatsomever I sees goin' wrong pun de place, sir. Now, 'bout two weeks gone, masser, one day 'bout twelve o'clock, I reckon, I goes to de new grown corn fiel' to see how de boys com' on puttin up corn, sir, and when I gets dar, Tom and Dick wos'n dar wid de oder han's. I stay dar least one half a hour, an dey did'n com.' You know, masser, dar's piece a wood ain't cleared in de corner of de fiel'. I creep 'long de fence 'til I com' near de wood, and who should I see, but Tom, and Dick, and one white man, settin down 'long side of one tree, dat had been blow' down; de man was ider readin' or talkin' to 'em; I couldn' see which. I waits dar for som' time, dey didn' see me; after a while I gits up and show'd myself. De boys den dey gits up and comes to whar I was; de white man gits up too, an I sees him put som'thin' in he pocket like one newspaper, an I sees him git over de fence into de road.

"Well, I didn' say one word to de boys. I thought, masser, though, I'd keep my eyes 'pon 'u ı well, masser, I bin think 'pon dis thing often sence, and I didn' know whether 'twould be woth while to tell you, or wait 'til I seed somthin' else in um, an I thought I'd wait. Well, sir, Elce com' home from de kitchen las' night 'bout nine o'clock, an she tell me she hear voice 'long de paff, and she stop and listen, an she hear Tom say to Dick: Der's no danger, Dick, we can get off esy 'nough; dat man you know, say, when we gets 'cross de 'Tomuck, it's all safe, an you know he teld us whar to cros'. Well, Tom, says Dick, I don' want to leave my daddy and mammy, but if you goes, Tom, I goes too. Well, Dick, is it one bargin? Yes, dat 'tis, clinched. Well, Tom, we'll wan' somthin' to eat. Never mind, Dick, I'll put you up to dat. Elce lef' um den, an if missis hadn' been wid you dis mornin, I'd bin tell you den, masser. I seed dat same white man in one carryall, dat day I car'd de wool to de factry."

"Say nothing about this to anybody, Robin, and tell

Elce not to mention it to a soul. I will think about it, and see what is to be done."

"Masser, I bin try my bes' 'pon dem boys, but dey too much for me, sir."

"Well, my dear," said the Doctor after reaching the parlour, "Robin has just made a communication which turns the dark side of the slavery picture; he has told me that two of my boys have laid a plan for getting off to Pennsylvania; and he thinks that they have been put up to it by some white person, with whom they were seen talking in the woods the other day. I cannot believe otherwise than that those boys have been tampered with by some abolitionist. I won't hint where I think he came from; but I hope for your sake, not from Pennsylvania."

"Oh! my dear husband, the Pennsylvanians wouldn't think of doing such a thing."

"You don't know, my dear, what the Pennsylvanians are up to, particularly in the matter of runaway negroes, whom they love so well. I have formed one determination, and that is, if any of my negroes run off, and are brought back, they shall never stay here. I can reconcile it to myself under such circumstances, and for certain other offences, to sell them off to the traders."

"Oh! my dear, the thought of selling a human being, and separating him from all his relations, is shocking to me."

"It is not so bad as you think, Ann. There are Tom and Dick, just as comfortably situated as they could possibly wish, both having on the plantation, parents, brothers, and sisters; determining to leave them, and be separated from them for ever; I do not see the great difference to their parents, whether it is my act or their act, which causes the separation: in every instance, however, it will be their act, and not mine; for I shall never sell unless they force me to do it by their own act."

On the following morning, as Dr. Boswell was about to take his customary ride over his farm, he saw three individuals approaching the house: one, he recognised as a neighbouring farmer, Mr. Green, another, Mr. Green's overseer, Mr. Glover, and the third, Mr. Johnson, a constable. After the usual salutations were exchanged, Mr. Green asked the Doctor to walk with him in the grove before the door, and informed him that he had come on business which was exceedingly disagreeable to him, and he supposed would be equally, if not more so, to himself. "I am come, sir, with a warrant from Squire Brown, to apprehend and carry before the Squire two of your boys, Tom and Dick, under a charge of having perpetrated burglary, by breaking open my meat-house, and stealing therefrom several pieces of bacon. My overseer, Mr. Glover, came upon them just as they were coming out of the house, and saw one of them with a bag, in which he supposed there was meat. There are five hams of bacon missing. They were too fleet for Mr. Glover, but he says he knows your boys Tom and Dick, and seeing them by moonlight, he will swear to their identity.

"The case is a very clear one, Doctor, and if they are taken before a justice, they must be sent on for trial before a called court, and will probably be condemned to be hung. I have thought, to prevent so disagreeable a termination of this affair, that I would propose to you to sell them off to a trader; and that if you would do that, I would drop further proceedings on the warrant; if not, the warrant will be put into the hands of the constable to be executed."

"I do not, Mr. Green, see any objection to your proposal. Those two boys, I have reason to believe, are making preparation for a trip to Pennsylvania; and your bacon, no doubt, was intended for that trip. Although I had some hint of their intention, I felt so great a reluctance to selling them, that I had determined to take no notice of the communication. Now, however, the case is altered by their having committed an offence which will cause them either to be hung or sent out of the country, and I shall be reconciled to the necessity of selling them."

"Your negroes, Doctor, treated as they are, I am confident, would have no disposition to leave you, unless they had been tampered with by some white person. There was a very suspicious character seen in the neighbourhood about a fortnight ago, a man in a carryall, pretending to offer some little matters for sale."

"I will, Mr. Green, send a note immediately to town, and request Mr. Bosher, the trader, to come down forthwith. There is some danger, however, of the boys making their escape before he arrives, particularly if they should find out that you and Mr. Glover are here."

"I don't know, Doctor, that we have been seen by any of your servants but old Robin; and I suppose he would never do or say anything which he thought contrary to your wishes. We will go away at once."

The Doctor, seeing Robin near the house, directed him to get a horse immediately, to take a note to Mr. Bosher. Robin was soon ready, received the note, and was on his way to town in a few minutes.

About three o'clock in the afternoon, Dr. Boswell directed Charles, a boy who waited in the house, to carry two chairs into the grove, intending one for himself, and the other for Mr. Bosher when he should arrive; and in a very short time he rode up, with Robin at a respectful distance behind.

"Mr. Bosher," said the Doctor, "I have sent for you on business, which is to me new, and extremely disagreeable. Two of my boys have been guilty of an offence for which I shall be forced to sell them, very much against my inclination."

"Well, sir," said Mr. Bosher, "my trade is that of buying and selling; and if we can agree as to the price, I will soon relieve you of them. I have a fixed price, sir, for tiptop young men, No. 1, that is, six hundred dollars; and if I like them, we will not be long in making a bargain."

"Robin," said the Doctor, "go after those two boys, and bring them here."

"We had better go where they are at work," said Mr. Bosher, "for if you send for them they might take the alarm and be off: if I once lay my hands on them I shall not fear their getting away."

Charles came with a message from his mistress, requesting the Doctor to come into the house.

As he entered the parlour, Mrs. Boswell threw her arms around his neck, and in tears said: "Oh! my dear husband, don't, don't sell those boys away from their parents; I can't bear it, indeed I can't. I almost wish I had never come to Virginia to witness such a heartrending scene. Oh! for my sake, let them stay."

"My dear Ann, it is forced upon me; I can't help myself. Those boys intended to leave their parents of their own accord; and now that they have been guilty of breaking open Mr. Green's meat-house, they can't stay here. If I don't sell them, Mr. Green will have them in jail before to-morrow morning, and they will perhaps be condemned to be hung; if not hung, they will certainly be transported. You must make up your mind, Ann, to bear what cannot possibly be avoided."

"Oh! horrid, horrid; I wish there was not a slave upon earth."

The Doctor unloosed her hands, which were clasped around his neck, placed her in a chair, and leaving her almost frantic, returned to Mr. Bosher.

"Well, sir, we will now walk to the potato ground, where those boys are at work." As they approached, he pointed out two very fine-looking young men in front of the gang, saying: "Those two are Tom and Dick, the boys we were talking about."

"They are fine-looking boys, sir. I suppose, Doctor, they are sound in every respect?"

"Perfectly so, sir, as far as I know and believe."

"Well, sir, I will give you your price. Boys, put down your hoes; (which being immediately done, he said), how would you like to go with me to a warm country, where negroes do nothing but eat and make cotton?" Both answered together,

"Not a bit, sir, can't go wid you any how; don't want leave masser for anybody."

"You'll have to go, anyhow," said Mr. Bosher (seizing both by the collar); "I have bought you, and you are now my property."

By this time, all the other hands had stopped from work, and a look of horror was on every countenance. The parents of Tom and Dick moved towards, and made a circle around their master, and with most piteous wail, they all exclaimed: "Oh! masser, you aint dun sell our boys sure 'nough?"

Dr. Boswell, with tears in his eyes, replied; "Yes, I have been forced to it. I have not only found out that your boys intended to run off to Pennsylvania; but that they have broken open Mr. Green's meat-house, and stolen his bacon; and, if they are not sold, they would in all probability be condemned to be hung."

"Well, masser, if dat's de case, let 'em go; it go mighty hard wid us to part from dem boys, but if dey bring it 'pon deselves, dey mus' 'bide by it. We always telled dem, dat dem white mens we see dem talkin' wid, wou'd bring 'em to trouble som' day or ruther."

"Dinah," said the Doctor, "you and Kate go and put their clothes in as small bundles as possible, and bring them down to the house."

The Doctor, Mr. Bosher, the two boys, and Robin, returned to the grove in the yard.

"Now that you have broken the ice, Doctor," said Mr. Bosher, "suppose you sell me some more? I haven't made up my number yet. What will you take for that man there?" (pointing to Robin, who had stopped some distance off.)

"*Take for him, sir!*" said the Doctor with vehemence; "why, sir, all the money in Mississippi couldn't buy him. I would just as soon think of cutting off my right hand, as of selling Robin."

"Well, sir, there's no harm done by asking the question; Robin anyhow is too far advanced in years for the Southern market; Southern planters prefer young negroes just grown up; children under six or eight years old, they wouldn't have at all."

"I suppose you find it a difficult matter to get as many as you would wish to buy?" said the Doctor.

"Oh! no, sir, we gets whole lots of runaways: whenever they are caught, they all come into our nets. Our trade would be completely broken up, Doctor, if 'twant for runaway negroes; and I think, sir, we have to thank the abolitionists for that; they entice them off, and we grabs them flying. I know a Yankee trader who gets whole lots in that way."

The Doctor could not stand the parting scene, and went into the parlour. Not finding Mrs. Boswell there, he followed her into her chamber, and found her lying upon the bed, weeping bitterly; he said not a word, but opened his desk and deposited the money he had received from Bosher.

Mr. Bosher took the boys off, and their parents in deep grief returned to their work. Robin followed them to the potato ground, and said: "Well, I trust dis gwine be a good lessin to de young people 'pon dis plantation; dey got one of de very bes' masters dat niggers eber had; and for him to be force' wid tear runnin' down he face to sell 'em cause dey misbehabe, is raly too bad. I knowd what 'twould com' to at last; dem boys bin too fond of leffin der work, and talkin' wid strange white folks, and see what it don com' to: dey been 'ticed to go off, and dey mus' den steal somethin' to carry 'long to eat."

"Robin," said Dinah, "I bin mistrus' my boy Tom for sum time; he ain bin like what he used to be for sum weeks; he bin sassy to he daddy an me, an a don' care sort of 'haviour 'bout 'im. Robin, I never did thought Tom would broke open house and steal; but, Robin, he did do dat sure as you an' I's alive. When I was rummaging for he clothes up in de loff, I fine a bag wid five piece o' bacon in it, and dar 'tis now, Robin."

"Dinah," said Robin, "dat bag musn' stay any longer 'mong you' stuff; 'twill bring trubble 'pon us all if it do. De Lord will punish us for dat accussed thing as he did de Isralites for de wedge o' gold. You mus' jus' go at once, and car' it to masser."

"Well, Robin, I was so 'stress' 'bout my boy, dat I didn' know what to do; but you's right, Robin, and I'll go dis minit and car' it to masser."

"Masser, here's Mr. Green bacon I fine up in my loff, when I bin hunt for Tom clothes."

"Dinah, that is proof positive enough that Tom broke open Mr. Green's smoke-house and stole his bacon. You were right, Dinah, in bringing it to me. Go into the chamber and see your mistress, and when you go back, tell Robin to get a horse and come to the house for this bag of bacon. It must be sent to Mr. Green."

"How you do, dis ebenin, missis?" said Dinah, as she approached the bed where her mistress was lying, with her face and head under the counterpane.

"Oh! Dinah, Dinah, what a shocking thing it was to sell your poor child away from you! I feel as if I never should be happy again."

"Well, missis, 'taint wufwhile, madam, to grieve so much. To be sure, I does feel mighty bad at partin' wid Tom, but he bring it all 'pon heself, madam. If he had been satisfied here, dis wouldn' bin happin. Tom had fine chance; good house to liv' in, good clothes to war', and Robin try he bes' to giv' him good 'struction in de Sunday school, madam, and he daddy and I giv' him good device out o' school; 'twas he own fault, missis. Masser wou'd never hav' sell him, if he hadn' brake open dat hous'."

"Do you think our boys did certainly break open that house and steal the meat?"

"No doubt on it, madam, I dun fine de bag o' meat up in my loff, an nobody but Tom could have bin put it dar, madam."

"One thing, Dinah, which made me take on so much

about it was, that I thought it possible they might have been innocent of the charge."

"Oh! missis, you may depend dem boys was guilty. I hope de Lord will pardon um, and bring um to see der wickedness. I does wish it cou'd bin so happen dat dey might bin stay here and git more 'struction from Robin, but de Lord chuse sen' dem away, and we mus' 'bide by his 'cision, madam; you sarvant, missis."

Mrs. Boswell, finding that Dinah was not so overwhelmed with grief as she expected, and that she bore the separation from Tom with commendable resignation, began to think that she herself had given way too much; and adjusting some little derangement in her person, consequent upon the violence of her grief, she repaired to the parlour, and found the Doctor reclining on the sofa.

"Uncle Robin wants you at the door, my dear," she said.

"Robin, take that bag of meat and carry it to Mr. Green, and tell him that Tom's mother found it up in her loft."

"My dear, I think you have grieved more for Tom and Dick than their parents."

"You must consider, my dear husband, that, although I have heard of this thing at a distance, it is the first time I have ever come in contact with it. Their parents, I suppose, have become familiar with it, from its everyday occurrence around them."

"My dear Ann, I find no fault in your exhibition of feeling; I like a soft heart, and I had much rather attempt to harden a soft one (if necessary), than to soften one upon which you could make no more impression than upon a millstone. Of all animals in creation, I think a female devoid of feeling and sensibility is the least engaging. It will be necessary perhaps to harden that little heart of yours, as our kind friends the abolitionists may make frequent drafts upon your sympathy. It is astonishing to me that they won't mind their own business, and let us alone, to manage ours as we think proper."

"My, dear, their *intentions* must be good; if they err it must be from mistaken philanthropy; they can have no other motive than a humane desire to better the situation of these poor creatures."

"They have sense enough, my dear, to know that every effort they make to entice a slave from his master, injures not only those enticed away, but all the others. The laws regulating that kind of property are made more stringent, their privileges are abridged, and they are rendered unhappy by being made dissatisfied with their situation. Even those who are successful in making their escape, in most instances, exchange comfort and ease for a life of wandering to and fro, without the means of support; and of abiding inquietude and apprehension, lest they should be recaptured. And, when recaptured, they are in every instance subject to all the horrors of sale, so pathetically depicted by abolition writers.

"Their motive is miscalled, when denominated mistaken philanthropy; there can be no mistake about it. They know very well, that in fact they themselves are the very bitterest enemies of those whom they pretend to

5

succour. Their true motive is to be found either in a vain desire to set themselves up as philanthropists, or to agitate for political effect; which latter is the most prevalent motive, if we form our judgment from the characters who lead and control the masses. It is a most preposterous notion, that corrupt politicians, working their way to inglorious preferment, are vicegerents of heaven, commissioned to do away an institution which has existed throughout all ages, even in a theocracy. Its presumption can be equalled by nothing but its folly."

"Well, Robin," said Mr. Green (as Robin rode into the yard), "what have you in your bag?"

"Your bacon, sir. Tom mammy fine it in her loff, and masser tell me to bring it to you, sir."

"Carry it round to the smoke-house, Robin; and I'll get the key."

After he had opened the door, he said:

"Now, Robin, empty the bag, and we will compare it with this bacon. I cut my hams somewhat different from most people."

"No mistake, masser," said Robin, "dis your bacon; nobody else in dis neighbourhood cuts der hams in dat way, sir."

"I think it probable, Robin, that having to break open this house last night, and being seen by Mr. Glover, prevented your boys from going off. I have just heard that two of Major Scott's boys, and two of old Mr. Preble's, went off last night, and I suppose it was all planned that they should go off together."

"Very like, sir, very like. I s'pose, masser, old Mr.

Preble won't try to git he boys back, cause he always sayin' what bad thing slabery is?"

"Let him alone for that, Robin; George Preble and two other young men went off in pursuit, as soon as it was known that they were gone. I haven't heard whether Major Scott employed anybody to go after his. These abolitionists, Robin, when they own negroes, are the very worst masters in the country. I shall be very glad to hear that old Preble's negroes get off; he gave one of those boys a cruel flogging, some days ago."

"Well, masser, I don' know how 'tis; dey always pityin' poor niggers, and 'suadin' dem to run off, and still, when dey have um, dey mighty bad to um; and when dey git um way back dar north, dey let um go almos' naked, and let um almos' starve."

"The fact is, Robin, they don't care half as much about negroes as we do, but they take pleasure in teasing and vexing us about them; and that's the whole secret of the business."

"'Tis mighty unchristian, masser, for dem to do so to der nabbers; de bible say we should do to oders as we wish dem to do to us; and I's sure dey wou'dn' like you, masser, to take der property."

"I had forgotten to ask you, Robin, whether you saw Mr. Bosher?"

"Oh yes, sir; he did cum 'long wid me, and dun take dem boys off, sir."

"I was very sorry, Robin, to force your master to sell those boys, as I know he is much opposed to selling negroes. They are going, however, to a country where the labour is very light; and you know, Robin, it is the master's interest, everywhere, to take care of his slaves. It is certainly a great deal better for them, than if they had gotten off, and gone to a free state, where they would have found it very difficult to get work enough to support them comfortably."

"Dem boys, masser, whether der situation is better or wus, have deselves only to blame; der's no people better off dan my masser's servants. Masser, now I think on it, will you let you people know dat de Reverend Mr. Grattan gwine preach to de black people, nex' Sunday ebenin, in my cabin?"

"Yes, Robin; and I will try and make them go. What time do you hold your Sunday school? I should like some of my little ones to go, if you will take them in."

"Well, masser, as for dat, I don' know; we got heap o' young ones o' our own dat go; and you see, masser, I's almos' de only teacher: Dinah does help me little. I hopes my young missis will help after while; and der's Miss Ebelina Preble, she promise com'; and if we kin git dat much 'cruit to our teachers, masser, I'll let you know, and you kin sen' some o' your'n. Der's your boy Jim, sir, would make fus' rate teacher, if he would com'."

"Well, I will speak to Jim, Robin, and I think he will be inclined to go, as he is religious, and I hope inclined to do good in that way."

"Sunday school, properly tended, masser, mighty good thing for de souls of young folks. Well, masser, can't stay any longer from my masser's business; your sarvant, sir."

"Good-bye, Robin. Tell your master that I am very thankful to him for sending the bacon."

When Robin had put away his horse, he went to the house to see his master.

"Well, Robin," said the Doctor, "I suppose Mr. Green was very glad to get his bacon again?"

"Yes, masser; he say he mighty thankful to you for sen'in' it. He telled me, masser, dat two o' Major Scott's boys, and two o' old Mr. Preble's dun gon' off; and dat Mas' George Preble dun gon' after um, sir."

"I hope no more of ours will take such notions into their heads. You should take every opportunity of talking to them, Robin, and telling them that the design of these abolitionists is not to do them good; that the inevitable consequence will be, that they will be hunted like wild beasts, that their lives will be endangered, and that, as soon as they get into a free state, they will find that their pretended firiends won't do for them what they promised. They have plenty of white people there to labour for them, and they won't employ the blacks. There is our neighbour, old Mr. Preble, who pretends to hate slavery, and as soon as his negroes run off, he is the very first to send after them."

"Masser, I don't fear any more of ourn will go off. I does give um, sir, line 'pon line, and precep' 'pon precep'; we dun got rid now o' de only two 'pon dis plantation I had any mistrus' of. Whar you wan' dem taturs put, masser?"

"In the barn, Robin, for the present; see that they are removed to the cellar before the hard frosts come."

CHAPTER III.

WORKING FOR SERVANTS.

"THIS, my dear," said the Doctor, as they were about to sit down to breakfast on the following morning, "is the day that old Mr. Frazer promised to come and cut out the negroes' clothes. I have had a fire made in the end room, and have directed all the girls, who are tolerably expert with the needle, to come and work on the coats and pantaloons. I hope you will take them under your direction, and be a second Dorcas in turning out garments for the poor and needy."

"I have had," she replied, "but little experience in making garments for men; but of late years, I have made my own clothes, and with a little instruction from Mr. Frazer, I hope I shall be at least able to know when the girls are going on properly with their work; and I shall engage in it, I assure you, with much pleasure. I shan't be entitled, however, to the credit given to Dorcas, for her many garments were all made with her own hands."

"If Dorcas, my dear, had been surrounded by blacks as you are, I suppose she would not have suffered them to remain idle when she was at work herself; and there not being any abolitionists in those days, I presume she would not have objected to slave labour. That squeamishness is the refinement of modern days."

Charles then informed his master that Mr. Frazer was at the door, who had entered before he was announced.

"Good morning, Mr. Frazer. That, sir, is my wife; a lady with whom you will become better acquainted during the progress of your work."

"I take pleasure, sir, in offering Mrs. Boswell my congratulations."

"Thank you, thank you, sir."

Mr. Frazer had been once a merchant tailor, and was easy and genteel in his manners. Of late years he had injured himself by intemperate habits, and had now a little shop at the cross-roads, not far from Selma.

"It's very cold this morning, Doctor; I am chilled all over."

"Warm yourself by the fire, Mr. Frazer, and then take a seat at the table, and my wife will give you some hot coffee."

"Coffee is very good, Doctor, but when a body's thoroughly chilled, there is something better than coffee to take off the chill."

"I belong, Mr. Frazer, to the temperance society, and only keep spirit for medicinal purposes, and of course can't offer it to you, unless you put yourself on the sick list."

"Well, Doctor, to tell you the truth, I do not feel very

well this morning, I am full of pains, and you may put me down on the sick list."

"If that is the case, I presume I should have to charge you a little more than your day's work would come to, Mr. Frazer."

"I believe I will turn to the table, sir, and take some hot coffee. Have you and the madam heard the news, Doctor?"

"I don't know what news you allude to, but I suppose, of course, yours will be tailor's news."

"Any news coming from me, sir, would, of course, be tailor's news. Did you hear that the abolitionists had persuaded off two of old Mr. Preble's boys, and two of Major Scott's, and that George Preble, Tom Kizer, and Ralph Commins had gone after them."

"That is tailor's news, Mr. Frazer, literally and figuratively, for we had heard it before; to be sure we had not heard that they were enticed off by the abolitionists, we only conjectured so."

"It must be so, Doctor, it can't be otherwise. How can these negroes, who have been in the corn-field all their lives, hardly ever off their master's plantation, make right straight for Pennsylvania, and know exactly where to cross the river, and what route to take after getting into Pennsylvania, unless they get instruction from white people?"

"It would seem so, indeed, Mr. Frazer."

"Well, then, did you hear that fourteen others had gone off from the neighbourhood of Middletown and Front-Royal, and that they were overtaken in Pennsylvania, and made battle, and that one of the negroes was killed, and that the others were all caught and sold to the soul-drivers?"

"No, we had not heard that."

"That is only tailor's news, then, because it comes from a tailor.—The ladies are generally pleased to hear something about courtships and matrimony, and I've got a little scrap of that for Mrs. Boswell's ear. They say our Parson is very fond, of late, of visiting at the cottage; don't you think Miss Evelina Preble would make a first-rate parson's wife?"

"Indeed she would, Mr. Frazer," said the Doctor. "If he had asked me to choose a wife for him, Evelina Preble would have been the girl, of all others. We had not heard it before, but I sincerely hope it may be so."

"Why, as to that, Doctor, there's no knowing. They say the old man don't like it; the Parson has not enough of the wherewithal, but one would think, that as he has but two children, it would make but little difference whether Miss Evelina married a poor man or a rich one; but I tell you he's mighty fond of the main chance; and though he talks so much about our peculiar institution, if he don't love to own negroes, and pride himself upon the number that he has, my name's not Joel Frazer. If he has got any abolition feeling about him, why did he not let his boys go, and not send George after them? mind what I say, Doctor, if George catches them boys, if they don't go to the traders, you'll see. Now, there is Major Scott, who don't think it any harm to hold slaves; he won't take any step to get his back, I'll warrant you."

"Yes, he will, Mr. Frazer. I have conversed with Major Scott upon that subject, and he thinks it a duty he owes to the community in which he lives, to take all proper measures to recover his slaves when they run away; for, whenever any of them are successful in making their escape, it encourages others to make the like attempt. Therefore, he thinks it wrong to encourage his neighbours' negroes to go off by his neglect. Now, Mr. Frazer, if you have emptied your budget, we will go to work upon something that will keep negroes warm at home this winter. Ann, my dear, we shall not be ready for you for some time; not until the first coat is cut out."

The Doctor and Mr. Frazer then went into the room prepared for the work. They found the girls ready, and the men at the outer door waiting to be measured.

"Mr. Frazer," said the Doctor, "here is a roll of linsey; what do you think of its quality?"

"This is first-rate, Doctor."

"Mr. Frazer, I wish you to be particular in cutting their garments full large; I dislike very much to see their limbs confined in tight clothes. I give them frock coats, extending a little below the knee. The pantaloons, also, must be large and easy. Now I must leave you, Mr. Frazer, to your work, and I must go to mine."

When Mrs. Boswell supposed she had given Mr. Frazer time to cut out the first coat, she went into the room where he was at work, and, with his assistance in fixing the different parts, she set the girls to sewing, and took a sleeve for herself. Mr. Frazer could never give his tongue holiday while his shears were at work, and said,

"Madam, you seem to take very readily to slavery, considering you are not used to it, and that you come from a state where they think it all wrong."

"Why, Mr. Frazer, as I have cast my lot among them, I must make the best of it, you know."

"Madam, I don't see how anybody can think it wrong; it's very plain from Scripture that the Lord don't think so, and why people should set themselves up to condemn what he has established, I never could well understand. It's a good institution, madam; I almost wish I was Dr. Boswell's slave. Here am I, madam, with a large family of young children, and if I was to die, I do not know what would become of them. Now, if I was Dr. Boswell's slave, I wouldn't have a care about them, because he would take better care of them than ever I could, even if I was to live until they grow up."

"But, Mr. Frazer, there is something sweet in the idea of liberty; of having a will of your own, not controlled by that of another person." It must be remarked, here, that Mrs. Boswell, being unaccustomed to such company, was not aware that her last observation was not well suited to the ears of slaves.

"I assure you, madam, there's mighty little sweetness in liberty with poverty along with it; and it seems to me that if all the bad wills in the world were controlled by the good ones, it would be the very best arrangement for the human family. If the Doctor, for instance, had had the control of my will, and had directed all my actions, I would have been a thousand times better off in soul and body than I am now. I do believe, madam, that there is more real happiness among the slaves in this part of the country than among the poor white people; and, if the abolitionists would only let them alone, they would never be for changing their situation. There is proof positive of that, madam, in the fact, that notwithstanding the exaggerated statements made to them of the horrors of slavery here, and the sweets of liberty in the free states, that so few of them, comparatively, can be induced to make the attempt to get off. Don't you think, Mrs. Boswell, that the Lord will bring these abolitionists to judgment, for the many murders they cause to be committed in the efforts to catch runaways, whom they have enticed off; and for the many heart-breakings occasioned to these poor creatures, by sales to traders of those who are caught?"

"Certainly, sir, if such are the consequences of their mistaken philanthropy, and they know from experience that such consequences will result, they must expect the vengeance of Heaven, if they don't desist."

"It is a mighty curious sort of philanthropy, madam, mistaken or not mistaken, which causes them to instigate the black man to butcher the white; the black man himself can't believe otherwise than that they have some improper motive in doing so; it is so contrary to his own instincts, which teach him to love best those of his own colour." Mr. Frazer's tongue wagged on all the while, and Mrs. Boswell was much edified as to neighbourhood matters, and was evidently surprised when the three o'clock dinner-bell rang so soon.

"How do you come on, Mr. Frazer?" asked the Doctor, as the former entered the dining-room.

"Oh! very well, sir; I shall, I think, get through by night."

"How would you like to put yourself on the sick list, before dinner?"

"First-rate, sir, but for those big figures of yours. I think, Doctor, Mrs. Boswell will make a fine wife for a Virginia farmer."

"She plies the needle well, does she? knows all about managing negro girls, by this time? has she boxed any of them, yet?"

"No, sir; I don't think Mrs. Boswell will ever be very much given to boxing negroes."

"I don't know how that may be, Mr. Frazer; northern ladies are very apt to be good disciplinarians. What do you think of it, my dear?"

"I hope I never may be tempted to box one of those girls, but Kate was right provoking to-day with her work."

"And didn't your little fingers burn, my dear, to give her a slight little box? frequent provokings will be very apt to bring them in contact with Kate's jaws."

"I don't know how it would be if she was a white girl; Mr. Frazer thinks we northern people do violence to natural instincts, and love the blacks more than the whites. Perhaps, if Kate was white, the burning of my fingers would soon be cooled by contact."

"Indeed, Mrs. Boswell," said Mr. Frazer, "I did not mean to class you with the abolitionists; and if anything

I have said can be construed into such an indignity, I beg pardon, madam."

"If you had classed her among them," said the Doctor, "your excuse is to be found in a geographical line. It is too true, sir, that she comes from north of Mason and Dixon; but I'll promise you, Mr. Frazer, she will be a whole soul Virginian after a while."

"No doubt of it, sir, no doubt of it," said Mr. Frazer, as he left the room to go again to his work.

"Mr. Frazer, in intellect, seems to be a man very much above his calling in life," remarked Mrs. Boswell.

"Yes, my dear, he is a man of very strong mind, and some little cultivation. He has in a most eminent degree, however, a fondness for collecting and retailing news. Poor fellow! I don't know how he gets along; he is intemperate in his habits, has a large family to support, and a very delicate, sickly wife."

"If he stays here to-night, my dear, would it not be well to hint at the subject, and give him a little advice in regard to his habits of intemperance, and persuade him to join a temperance society? I sincerely wish he could be reclaimed, for he seems to have some very correct views; and if he could be induced to give up that horrid practice of drinking, what a blessing it would be to his family!"

"My dear, I have had many conversations with him upon that subject, and obtained from him many promises; but it is a habit not easily given up. However, if an opportunity occurs to-night, I will as delicately as possible throw out some hints; and may be what has heretofore fallen like seed sown by the wayside, may now reach a better soil of his heart, and spring up and bring forth good fruit. At any rate, there will be no harm in making the experiment; and if we can induce him to become a son of temperance, I shall give all the credit to her who first suggested the effort."

"The satisfaction in seeing him reclaimed, would be of more consideration with me than any little credit which might attach to my humble effort in effecting his reformation."

Mrs. Boswell then left the room to attend to some household matters; and the Doctor said, in an audible soliloquy, "I have the very best soil to operate upon; and if Ann does not resemble my dear mother in all things, it will be the fault of her instructor."

Mr. Frazer, finding that he could not finish his work in time to get home, told the Doctor that he would have to tarry the night with him; which information was particularly agreeable, as it afforded the opportunity of saying a word in season, for the benefit of a family in which he felt much interest.

When the supper table was removed, Mrs. Boswell, after some little instructions from Mr. Frazer, resumed her work upon the linsey garment.

"Doctor," said Mr. Frazer, "I think I feel better to-night than I have done for months past; the exercise before breakfast, and the agreeable chat with Mrs. Boswell and yourself, seem to have given me very different feelings from what I generally have at this time of the evening. It may be, because I have left my cares, the old woman, and the little ones at home."

"Mr. Frazer," said the Doctor, "I could let you into the secret of continuing and preserving those good feelings, if you would put yourself under my direction. And I will take this opportunity of speaking to you in a plain, friendly manner, upon a subject, it is true, that we have conversed on frequently before, not in the hearing, however, of any other individual than ourselves; but I hope the presence of my wife at this time, will not increase the reluctance which you have generally manifested; as I can assure you that she feels as deep an interest in the welfare of your family, as I can possibly have.

"Your candour and regard to truth, will, I know, cause you to plead guilty to a charge which I have often before brought against you, and which I mean now to renew: of habits of intemperance. You know from your own experience at home, and from your observations abroad, how entirely destructive those habits are of domestic happiness. You know that the softest heart, and the very best natural feelings, are entirely changed and made obdurate by the intemperate use of ardent spirits; that the individual who is kind and affectionate to his wife and children when sober, becomes, when under the influence of liquor, a ferocious brute, yea, a madman: and that the objects of his affection when sober, are most apt to become the subjects for his violence to operate upon when intoxicated. You know how difficult it is for a poor man to earn, by his labour, a support for a large family, even when all his time is given to labour, and all the earnings of his labour are devoted to that object; but when a great portion of his time is lost in intoxication, and much of his earnings expended upon liquor, you know full well that the consequences to the family of that man must be ruinous; that he is setting an example to his children of immorality and vice, which may be transmitted through many generations; that he is impairing his own health, and finally brings himself to a drunkard's grave, with the sin of suicide added to the mass of iniquity which has been accumulating for years; and perhaps with the dreadful thought upon his mind at dissolution, that no drunkard can inherit the kingdom of heaven.

"To you, Mr. Frazer, who must acknowledge that such consequences do flow from intemperate habits, I now offer a sure and certain remedy in the temperance pledge, if you will take that pledge, with a fixed determination of never violating it. I will propose you to the meeting of our society, on Friday night next, and I know that you will experience benefits which I am unable to describe."

"Well, Doctor, I acknowledge the truth of everything you have said, and I have long wished to join your society; but I have been prevented by the fear that I could not stick to the pledge. I will promise you one thing, that I won't taste another drop of ardent spirits between this and next Friday morning, and by that time I can see how it will work; and if I think I can safely take the pledge, I will go with you and have my name registered as a son of temperance."

"Oh! Mr. Frazer," said Mrs. Boswell, "I am delighted to hear you say even that much!"

"I have no doubt, Mr. Frazer," said the Doctor, "that those uncommonly pleasant feelings, which you say you have to-night, are owing in a great measure to your having abstained from ardent spirits to-day. If I had put you upon the sick list this morning, and at dinner, you might now have felt very differently; particularly if my attention had been drawn off from the quantity my patient might have been inclined to take at a dose."

"Well, Doctor, I have made the promise—don't run me too hard. To change the subject, sir, did you know that Mr. Crump was going to move to California? and, because he can't carry his negroes there, he's going to sell them all to Mr. Bosher, the trader? Now, sir, if that was a slave state, he would carry all his negroes, and keep them together; but, as he can't do that, they will be carried to New Orleans; and husband and wife, parent and child, brother and sister, will all be separated. These abolitionists are always croaking about a subjection to separation being one of the greatest evils of slavery, while they themselves are producing that very state of things which causes the greatest amount of those same evils; and every application of the Wilmot proviso (as it is called) will increase them."

"That certainly will be the effect, Mr. Frazer, if the slave-owners of the south are denied the right of carrying their slaves to the new states. Those who go must sell them to the traders, and the horrors of separation, so glowingly depicted, must be increased a hundred fold. But that is only one of many evidences that they are constantly injuring those people for whom they profess a much sympathy. Mr. Frazer, it is now getting nearly bed-time; you will join us in family worship? Have you ever introduced it into your family, sir?"

"I am astonished, Doctor, after the conversation we have had to-night, that you should have asked me that question. Can you suppose, sir, that a man of intemperate habits would ever be in a fit situation to summon his wife and children around a family altar, and ask the blessing of God upon them?"

"I beg pardon, sir, for having inadvertently asked the question; but I hope, Mr. Frazer, you will ponder upon your own answer to my question, between this and Friday next, and let it come in aid of what I have said, to bring you to a proper determination."

After prayers, they all retired to bed; and Mr. Frazer, finishing his work early the next day, returned home. Mrs. Boswell and the girls were busily employed that day on the coats and pantaloons.

CHAPTER IV.

SABBATH SCHOOL.—GEORGE'S RETURN.

On Sunday morning, Miss Evelina Preble, having taken an early breakfast at home, walked over to Selma, and found the Doctor and Mrs. Boswell at their breakfast.

"I have come, Mrs. Boswell," said she, "to help Uncle Robin to-day, in his Sabbath school. You must go with me, and we will each take a class; and, as I was afraid to walk by myself, I have brought our man Lewis, who reads very well, and, if Uncle Robin likes, he can be of some assistance. I also brought some of the little ones as scholars."

"I am very glad, Miss Evelina, that you have come; and, although I have but little experience in Sabbath school teaching, I will accompany you with a great deal of pleasure, and do the best I can in instructing the little things."

"Have you received any tidings of George, yet, Miss Evelina?" asked the Doctor.

"No, Doctor, and indeed I am very uneasy about

George; he went on a very dangerous mission, and one, independent of its danger, I never could approve of. If I had had a voice in the matter, those boys might have had every chance of getting off, as it was their desire to go."

"I have thought pretty much as you do, Miss Evelina; but old Major Scott, who is a very considerate man, has convinced me that it is a duty we owe our neighbours, and the society in which we live, to take every proper measure to recover them when they run off."

"You and Major Scott, Doctor, and most other slave-owners, may entertain that opinion with perfect consistency, but my papa has his peculiar notions about what he calls our peculiar institution. If I had the same views upon the subject that he has, I would not own a slave for any consideration. George and myself differ with papa; we don't think it wrong to hold persons in slavery, but notwithstanding that, I have always thought, that when they make the attempt to get off, I would give them the chance, rather than be obliged to sell them if recaptured. My papa thinks it wrong to hold them in slavery, but brings up his old adage about Rome and the Romans in justification of his doing so."

"I never could exactly understand your papa's views upon the subject, Miss Evelina; there is certainly an inconsistency about it which I could never reconcile. I suppose, however, he means, that living in a society where it is tolerated, that if it is wrong (as he believes), he only participates in a general wrong, which cancels individual responsibility. Such a system of ethics would completely obliterate the distinction between right and wrong, each individual in a crowd of wrongdoers having the same plea of justification."

"Well, Doctor, to tell you the truth, I am not casuist enough to unravel it. This one thing I know full well, that the relation of master and servant imposes certain duties upon the master which it is highly sinful to neglect."

"Ladies," said the Doctor, "I hear Robin's bell; it is time to go. I will go with you, and if Robin's classes are not too far advanced for me, I will lend a helping hand."

They found the children, some of the grown negroes of the plantation, and some of the neighbouring children already assembled and seated on benches; the males on one side, and the females on the other. Robin, after very respectfully receiving his master and mistress and Miss Evelina, and providing them with seats, gave out in a clear, audible voice, the hymn commencing,

> "Jesus, that condescending King,
> Is pleased to hear when children sing."

He raised the tune himself, and most of the children and grown persons united with him in singing it. After it was ended, he offered up a very solemn, impressive, and comprehensive prayer for the teachers, the children, his master and mistress, his fellow servants upon the plantation and throughout the neighbourhood; for Africa and her children in every clime, and for the spread of the gospel throughout the world. When the prayer was ended, he asked his master to take the first male Bible class; to Miss

Evelina, was assigned the first female Bible class; Mrs. Boswell preferred taking the lowest female class, which was taught orally. Dinah took the intermediate female class, and Robin and Lewis took the other two male classes. The exercises continued about two hours, and were closed with an appropriate hymn and prayer from Robin. When the school was dismissed, the Doctor and his party returned to the house, and every one left the cabin but Robin, Elce, and Mr. Preble's Lewis.

"Uncle Robin," said Lewis, "I s'pose you bin hear 'bout our two boys goin' off?"

"Yes, Lewis, I bin hear somethin' 'bout it."

"Well, Uncle Robin, I don' think masser ought to bin giv' dat boy sich a whippin'; but masser, when he begin, does whap powerful."

"Lewis, I don' like hear you talk dat way 'bout you' masser. De Scripture tells us, you know, dat as de son honour he father, so ought servant to honour he masser."

"Uncle Robin, I neber see dat in de Bible."

"Elce, han' me down dat Bible, here; you kin read it you'self, Lewis. Turn to de fus chapter Malachi, 6th vus."

"Uncle Robin, dis vus don' say 'cisely what you say it did; it don' say suvant *mus'* honour he massér, but say suvant *does* honour he masser."

"Well, Lewis, when de Lord make he Proffit to talk of what de people do, if 'taint right he tell um so, and if he don' tell um 'taint right, you may be sure he 'prove of it. Now same thing when our Saviour tell massers how to act to der suvants, and suvants how to act to der massers.

He don' say you shall have suvants, or you shall have massers, but he certainly does 'prove of it. S'pose I was say to my boy John; John, when you play bandy, you mus' play wid one straight stick, instead of one crooked one, don't I giv' my boy John liberty to play bandy, dough I don' tell him he mus' play?"

"Well, Uncle Robin, I believe you is right, and I ain' gwine talk so 'bout my masser enny mo'."

"I was surprised at not seeing yourself and Mrs. Boswell at church, to-day, Doctor," said the Reverend Mr. Grattan, after he had made his respects to the ladies, upon entering the parlour about three o'clock.

"Why, sir, although we were not at church, I hope we have not been unprofitably employed this forenoon. The ladies and myself have been teaching the young idea how to shoot, in Robin's Sabbath school. To tell you the truth, sir, I did not propose to my wife to go to church, thinking that she would not like to be gazed at by so many strangers."

"My dear sir, I don't suppose people go to church to gaze at others; I'm in hopes they go for a far different purpose."

"You know, sir," replied the Doctor, "the poet has said: '*veniunt spectatum, veniunt spectantur ut ipsæ.*'"

"Such an object as that," replied Mr. Grattan, "might move a heathen congregation to assemble, but certainly not a Christian one."

"The poet," said the Doctor, "confines his remark to one class only of a congregation, as he has put *ipsæ* in the feminine; the ladies, I suppose, can tell us whether there are any church-going females, who desire to see and be seen."

"I presume," said Miss Evelina, "that in all congregations there are males and females, who are not indifferent to admiration for themselves, and who look about to admire others also; but members of the church, and those out of the church who are serious, it is to be hoped, go for Christian edification, and the comforts which are to be derived from the services of the sanctuary.

"But, Mr. Grattan, I have not yet made *my* excuse for not going to-day. I had often promised Uncle Robin to come and assist him in his school; and this morning was so sweet a one, that I thought I should never have a better opportunity for complying with my promise. It has just occurred to me, that I may (in part), have been the cause of the Doctor and Mrs. Boswell's not going."

"No, indeed, Miss Evelina, we should not have gone if you had not been here."

"Doctor," said Mr. Grattan, "I don't see why this same excuse may not be pleaded again, as Mrs. Boswell will be a stranger whenever she makes her first visit to church."

"No, I assure you," said Mrs. Boswell, "it shall never be pleaded again."

Dinner was then announced. Mr. Grattan and Miss Evelina took seats opposite to each other, and the Doctor and Mrs. Boswell, on comparing notes afterwards, thought some sly glances were exchanged.

After dinner was over, Mr. Grattan proposed that they should all go with him to Uncle Robin's cabin, where he was to preach to the servants. When they got there, they found the cabin completely filled by servants from all parts of the immediate neighbourhood. Dr. Boswell and the ladies, not wishing to disturb the negroes who were all seated in the cabin, took seats on the steps before the door. Mr. Grattan gave out a hymn; the tune was set by Uncle Robin, and taken up by almost the whole congregation. After a short prayer, Mr. Grattan preached a plain discourse, suited to their capacities, upon the duties of servants to masters, and to their fellow-servants, from Ephesians, vi. 8: "Knowing that whatsoever good thing any man doeth, the same shall he receive of the Lord, whether he be bond or free." It did really seem that there were very few in that black congregation who came there with any other desire than to be instructed and edified,—such was the profound silence and deep attention. After another hymn, prayer, and benediction, they returned to the house.

Miss Evelina was preparing to go home, but Mrs. Boswell told her that she would carry her the next morning in her carriage, if she would stay. She consented to do so, and they found no difficulty in persuading Mr. Grattan to do the same.

"You have a Sabbath school, Mr. Grattan, for the blacks, have you not?"

"Yes, sir, we have a very flourishing one, held near the church every Sabbath morning. The young members of my church are very kind to the blacks in that respect, punctual in their attendance, and very competent to perform the duties of teachers; and I hope are doing much good."

"I suppose you preach on some plantation in the neighbourhood every Sabbath afternoon?"

"Yes, sir; nothing but very bad weather prevents me. Sometimes, however, I have but thin congregations to hear me; particularly upon those afternoons when Baptist ministers preach in the neighbourhood. You know all the negroes, almost, in this part of the country, who profess religion, are Baptists; indeed, throughout our state it is the case. I am told it is not so much so in South Carolina and Georgia. In those states there are many Episcopalians, Methodists, and Presbyterians among the negroes. Some ministers there give their whole time to the blacks; and the masters are said to afford great facilities for religious instruction. I think if teachers in our Sabbath schools would make the children commit to memory portions of the liturgy of our church, we should have more of them to join it.

"The Episcopal liturgy seems to me to be peculiarly adapted to persons of their description, who are not capable of forming prayers for themselves. When they become better acquainted with it, by committing it to memory, the prejudice which now exists against our forms would wear off, and we should see them more frequently at the Episcopal communion."

"I have thought, Mr. Grattan," said the Doctor, "that that prejudice is encouraged by the conduct of masters. They are driven to church by their servants, and those servants are suffered to remain outside, during the whole time of service, laughing and talking, and perhaps doing worse. Being suffered by their masters to do so, it produces an impression upon their minds that the Episcopal worship is only for the gentry, and that it is a matter in which they have little or no concern, and, finally, their indifference degenerates into contempt. I know of no more legitimate exercise of that authority which the master has over his servant, than to compel him when at the temple of the Lord to enter its walls, and to pay a decent respect to the services. This is not (as some would call it) compelling people to become religious, but is only inhibiting a disregard of the means of grace. If they were even informed that it was the wish of their masters that they should enter the church when the services commence, I believe they would generally do it. My negroes have been told that you would give us prayers and a lecture to-night in this room, and they know it is my wish that they should attend; and I shall be much surprised if they are not generally present."

Seats were arranged around the parlour for the negroes, and those who were on the plantation were most of them present. Mr. Grattan gave them a plain lecture upon the importance of a serious consideration of a future state of happiness and misery; and closed with prayer.

Mrs. Boswell the next morning performed her promise to Miss Evelina, and in going to the cottage, they called at Major Scott's, where the party, including the Doctor and Mr. Grattan, were very cordially received. It fell to the lot of Mr. Grattan to entertain the ladies in conversation; while the Doctor and the Major were engaged in one on a sofa in a distant corner of the room.

"I think I have mentioned to you, Doctor, my views upon the subject of the recovery of runaways. I have so far carried out those views as to have offered a reward of two hundred dollars each, for the apprehension of my boys."

"Has nothing been heard yet, Major, from George Preble?"

"Not a word, sir; his father is very uneasy about him, and, I think, not without cause. George is a very fine-hearted young man, and though he was armed, I don't think he would make a violent attack, but he is very fearless, and I apprehend would expose himself to danger. Those boys of Mr. Preble's, I am told, are very desperate fellows."

"Have you any just grounds for suspecting, Major, that your boys were tampered with by abolitionists?"

"Why, sir, I believe they have emissaries constantly passing through this country. I cannot believe that my boys would have gone off unless they had been enticed. You know, Doctor, very well, how I treat my negroes; they are just as comfortably situated here as I am, they have good houses to live in, good winter and summer clothing, a plenty of the best food. They are required to do constant, but very easy work; and I never whip, except for some flagrant fault. Neither of those boys were ever flogged; they have left parents to whom they have always appeared to be much attached. Under such circumstances, sir, I cannot believe otherwise than that they have been persuaded off. There was a suspicious-looking white man, about a fortnight ago, seen to leave his carryall in the road and get over into my field, and enter into conversation with those boys. If those people would but let us and our property alone, how much better it would be for the master and the slave both."

"They won't let us alone, Major, until they incite our slaves to insurrection, and bring upon the slaves themselves, all the horrors consequent upon such a state of things."

"I do not apprehend, Doctor, any further injury from the wicked designs of abolitionists, than the occasional loss of property. I think it no want of charity, however, to believe that those Northern abolitionists wish to produce insurrection; but from the utter impossibility of success, I do not believe that the slaves will ever attempt it. They have been taught such a lesson in the few attempts which have been made in Virginia, that it would be perfect madness for them to entertain the least hope of success. The insurrection about Richmond, many years ago, and the one of later date, in the county of Southampton, resulted in the execution of every individual who was proved to be in any manner implicated.

"They have sense enough to see that they have not the means of acting in concert, to effect such an object. But few of them can read or write, and if written communications were sent from one part of the country to another, they could not be read by those for whom they were intended. They would be intercepted in the post offices if sent, and result in the apprehension, conviction, and execution of those who sent them. They would be constantly betraying each others' secrets to the whites, and telegraphic communications would in a few minutes make them known throughout the state. If they have any reasoning powers (and we all know they have), they must see the utter impossibility of effecting anything by insurrection, than their own destruction; and therefore (as I observed before) I have no apprehension that they will ever attempt it."

About this time Miss Amelia Scott took Mrs. Boswell from the parlour into her mother's chamber, where she was introduced to a very decent-looking mulatto woman in the following manner:—

"Mrs. Boswell, this is my Mammy Betty; she has been begging me ever since you came, to bring you in here to see her."

"I am very much pleased to see you, Mammy Betty," said Mrs. Boswell.

"My gal, here, bin talk so much 'bout you, madam, sence she see you tother day, dat I bin monstrous ansious to see you, madam; I wos at you hous to de meetin' yiste'day, but you went 'way so soon I didn' bin had chance to see you, madam."

"I wish I had known, Mammy Betty, that you were there; why did you come away without going to the house to see me?"

"Madam, I understoods you had comp'ny, and I didn' wish to 'trude, madam."

"It would have been no intrusion, Mammy Betty; you

must never come there again without coming to the house to see me."

"No, madam, I neber will."

"Mrs. Boswell," said Miss Amelia, "this old Mammy Betty of mine is a precious old creature" (at the same time throwing her arms round the old woman's neck and giving her a kiss.)

"Ah, Missis," said Betty, "you don' know how dis chil' and me does lobe one another; dare's no body in dis worl' dats so good to me as my 'Melia, and I hopes she and I'll neber be parted as long as breath's in dis body."

"Mammy Betty, you must expect Miss Amelia to get married sometime or other, and then you may be parted."

"Please God, madam, I'll go wid my 'Melia whereber she does go, madam."

"If you will believe me, Mrs. Boswell, I would not marry any man upon earth who would not let me take mammy along with me. If I ever have a chance to be married, I'll make that a condition."

"As the old lady loves you so much, and you love her, I think you would be perfectly right to make it a condition, Miss Amelia, and nobody but a brute of a husband would wish to separate you."

"Did you bring you mammy 'long, Missis, when you com' to Selma?"

"Mammy Betty, where I came from white people don't have black mammies; we have no slaves in Pennsylvania."

"Ah! sure 'nuff, dat de place whar our boys all run to; a'nt it, madam?"

"I suppose some of them go there, but not all."

"I bin hear um say dey mighty kine to black people dar, madam."

"Well, Mammy Betty, I suppose they are not kinder than your master and Dr. Boswell are to theirs."

"Dey couldn' well beat dem in dat, madam; my masser and Dr. Boswell mighty good massers, madam."

"Good-bye, Mammy Betty; it's getting time for us to be going to the Cottage."

"Good-bye, missis; I'll com' to de great-house to see you, nex' time I go to meetin' at Selma."

"Do, Mammy Betty."

As they passed into the parlour, the servant, who had been sent to the post-office that morning, returned, and handed to Miss Amelia a bundle of newspapers, which she carried to her father. His attention was first directed to the advertising column of a Cumberland newspaper, in which he saw a notice of four negroes of Virginia having been pursued and overtaken in the neighbourhood of Cumberland; that they made battle, and that Mr. George Preble, the owner of two of the slaves, had received a ball in the shoulder, from a revolver discharged by one of his own servants; that Mr. Preble's two negroes had been apprehended, and were now in jail in Cumberland; that the other two (said to belong to a Major Scott, in Virginia) had made their escape into Pennsylvania. The Doctor saw from his countenance that he had met with something unpleasant, and followed him into the passage. Miss Julia and her mother followed, closing the parlour door which opened into the passage. Miss Evelina Preble was so pleasantly engaged in conversation with Mr. Grattan as not to have observed what was going on. Major Scott was reading the account, when Mrs. Scott and Miss Julia entered the passage.

Miss Julia heard enough—she fell in a swoon. Major Scott and the Doctor carried her and laid her on the bed in her mother's chamber. Mrs. Scott, not knowing exactly what she was about, emptied a pitcher of water on her face; she so far revived as to open her eyes. The Doctor gave her some drops in a wine-glass of water; and after consciousness was restored she burst into tears, exclaiming "Oh, George! George! poor George!" Mrs. Scott, herself in tears, consoled her by telling her they must hope for the best; that the Doctor had assured her that a wound in the shoulder was rarely ever fatal. The chamber door was closed, and it was determined that it should be kept secret from Miss Evelina, until she arrived at the cottage. Mrs. Boswell and Miss Amelia left the parlour, and were informed of the news, Miss Evelina all the while so absorbed in conversation with Mr. Grattan as not to suspect that anything extraordinary was going on. It was arranged that Miss Amelia should go with them to the cottage, to be with Miss Evelina. A difficulty arose how Miss Evelina was to leave without seeing Mrs. Scott and Miss Julia. Dr. Boswell told her that "Miss Julia had been taken suddenly unwell, that her mother was with her, and that he did not wish her to be disturbed."

It may be thought somewhat strange that Miss Evelina, so uneasy as she was about her brother, had not asked Major Scott if there was any news relative to George;

but it is very doubtful whether she saw the bundle of papers handed to the Major; and if she had, she probably would not have calculated upon their containing news about her brother, as Major Scott she knew took only the Intelligencer and Recorder,—the Cumberland paper having been sent him upon that particular occasion.

When they arrived at the Cottage, Miss Evelina was handed last from the carriage; and the servant, who had been there to open the carriage door, having the desire which belongs to all negroes, to communicate news good or bad, said, "Have you bin hear, Miss Evelina, dat Mas' George bin mighty badly wounded?" She shrieked, and fell into the arms of Dr. Boswell, insensible, who, with the assistance of her father (who met them at the door) carried her and laid her upon her own bed. By chafing her temples, she was soon restored to consciousness; and the Doctor took the earliest opportunity of telling her that her brother was wounded in the shoulder, and that there could be no danger of the wound being fatal."

"Oh! where is he, what has become of him?" she exclaimed.

"We are not informed," said the Doctor, "but from the nature of the wound, I think it probable he will be able to travel in a carriage, and he may be now on his way home."

"Oh! papa, do send our carriage for him, he may not be able to procure one where he is."

Old Mr. Preble was not a man of much sensibility; he was not, however, entirely devoid of natural affection for his children, but his countenance was never relaxed into an outward expression of sympathy.

"'Tisn't worth while to be in a hurry about it," said he; "George will be here sometime to-day."

"Oh! but, papa, he may at this very moment be lying in some miserable hut, wanting attention from kind friends, without even a physician to dress his wound. Do let me go to him; and if Doctor Boswell would go with me, what a comfort it would be to him."

"If," said the Doctor, "your father thinks proper to send the carriage, and you are to go, I will go with you, with a great deal of pleasure."

"Oh! papa, do, do, let us go at once?"

"Evelina," said her father, "if you were to go, you would be very apt to miss George. There are several roads leading to the neighbourhood of Cumberland from here; he may take one route, and you another: he may get here and want the aid of a physician, while the Doctor is hunting for him in the mountains. You had better wait a few hours at any rate."

She covered her face with her hands, and sobbed aloud.

Miss Priscilla Graham, who seldom left her own room, hearing of Evelina's situation, was assisted down stairs, and stood by her bed-side.

"Oh! Aunt Priscilla, Aunt Priscilla, what shall I do; what shall I do? Poor George!"

"My dear Evelina," said Miss Priscilla, "I am astonished to see you give way so much. You know, my dear, that George is in the hands of the Lord, and that he can take better care of him than we could, if we were with him. I think, my dear, you are acting sinfully, in putting so little trust in the Almighty. I had supposed that under all trials, and under all earthly afflictions, you were prepared to say, 'Thy will be done.' I have always thought, my dear, that it was sinful to be violent in our expressions of grief, even for the *loss* of friends; to be sure, we can't help feeling, and it is right to feel upon such occasions; but when those feelings are boisterous, they evince a distrust of, and dissatisfaction at the decrees of Providence, unbecoming a Christian, whose confidence in the Almighty should never for a moment suffer diminution."

"My dear aunt, I hope the Lord will pardon me for having indulged even a momentary suspension of entire trust and confidence in Him. I know that he can and will take care of George; and I trust that I am content to leave him in His hands. But the Lord requires of us, aunt, that we should do our part towards those in pain and affliction; and I think it my duty to go to him."

"It is your duty in this matter to obey your earthly parent; and if he should overrule your going to George, your Heavenly Parent will accept your will to do so, as the performance of your duty to Him."

They were interrupted by a noise in the further corner of the room, and upon looking round, Miss Priscilla discovered George's old mammy Phillis on her knees, with her head on a chair, weeping violently.

"Phillis," said Miss Priscilla as she approached her, "you should not give way so much to your feelings. You have heard what I said to Miss Evelina; and it is as much your duty as hers, to show your trust in God by quietly submitting to his providences."

"Missis," said Phillis, "I knows 'tis my duty to submit, but when I thinks 'pon my poo' George cover'd wid he blood, my poo' George who I nussed, who bin so kin' to me, I can't help cryin', missis, dat I can't."

"Well, Phillis, I hope and trust it is not so bad with George as you suppose. Your master seems to think he will be at home to-day."

"I pray to de Lord, madam, it may be so."

While this conversation was carried on in Miss Evelina's room, the Doctor, Mrs. Boswell, Miss Amelia Scott, Mr. Grattan, and old Mr. Preble, were in the parlour. A young gentleman who had been taking a walk when the party from Selma arrived, returned, and was introduced by Mr. Preble, as Mr. Benson, from Boston. Mr. Benson, who was the son of a Boston merchant, had, at a northern college, contracted a friendship for George Preble, and had arrived at the cottage the day before, when Miss Evelina was at Selma.

"Your first visit to Virginia, I presume, Mr. Benson?" said the Doctor.

"Yes, sir; I have long wished to see Virginia, and have taken the opportunity of a leisure moment from business, to visit my old chum, George Preble."

"We have heard bad news of George, to-day, Mr. Benson," said old Mr. Preble.

"Why, what's that?" said Mr. Benson, rising from his chair.

"We have seen it mentioned in a Cumberland paper,

which I read since you left the house, that George has been fired at by one of those runaways I told you he was in pursuit of, and that he received a ball in his shoulder."

"Whereabouts is he, Mr. Preble? suppose I go immediately in pursuit of him?"

"If he does not come in a few hours, Mr. Benson, the Doctor and my daughter will go in the carriage after him."

Lewis, the servant of whom we have spoken before, opened the parlour door, and informed his master that there was a carriage coming up to the house. The Doctor, Mr. Benson, and Mr. Preble went immediately into the portico, the ladies and Mr. Grattan to the parlour window.

"That must be George, sir," said the Doctor; "that carriage does not belong to this neighbourhood; it is certainly a strange carriage," addressing himself to Mr. Preble.

"The horses," said Mr. Preble, "look like Squire Brown's, but I think they are rather dark for his; don't you think so, sir?"

"That is not Squire Brown's carriage, sir, nor is it any carriage belonging to this part of the country."

In a few moments it was at the door, and George Preble presented himself at the window, with his arm in a sling, his coat buttoned under his chin, and an empty sleeve hanging over his wounded shoulder. The smile upon his countenance dispelled at once all alarm for the wound he had received.

Mr. Benson was the first at the carriage door.

"Why, Bob," said George, "where in the world did you come from? I'm rejoiced to see you."

"You may be sure I am glad to see you, George, as I have come so far for that express purpose."

The greetings were all very affectionate, and the Doctor, taking George's sound arm, led him into his sister's room.

Miss Evelina sprang from the bed, and was about to throw her arms round his neck, when he cried out, "take care of my game arm, Lina:" he kissed her, and passed on to his aunt, who had taken a seat at the foot of the bed.

"George," she said, "I am truly thankful to the Lord for having restored you to us;" and kissed him.

"And here's my mammy, too," said George; "she must come in for her buss;" and, indeed, the sound was echo to the sense.

"De Lord be praised," said she, "my boy dun com' back."

Miss Evelina prepared herself for going into the parlour with George. Miss Priscilla Graham was assisted up into her own room, and in that sanctum, on her knees, she returned thanks to her Heavenly Father.

When Miss Evelina went into the parlour, her eye caught Mr. Grattan's; she blushed, from what cause it is difficult to say.

Old Mr. Preble put some question to George, which gave rise to a relation of his adventure.

"We happened by accident, sir, to take the very route to Cumberland that the boys had taken, hearing occasionally of them, from persons who had seen at a distance four men who looked like negroes, sometimes in the road, and sometimes in the fields. On Friday morning, we found we were not far from them. A white man had seen four persons crossing a field, about a half-hour before, making towards a cabin in a skirt of wood, two hundred yards distant from the road, which we were told was occupied by a free black man. We made immediately for the house, and when we got near, heard several voices inside. I ran up, and getting in at the front door, found our four boys, a white man, and the free black man, sitting at breakfast. As soon as the boys saw me, they rose from the table; and, as they attempted to make their escape through the back door, I caught one of Major Scott's boys by the collar; and, as I held him, I heard the white man say, 'Fire!' and immediately a ball from a revolver, in the hands of our boy Jack, struck, and passed through the fleshy part of my shoulder.

"After being wounded, I let go the boy I had hold of, and he ran by Tom Kiser and Ralph Cummins, who seemed more anxious to attend to me, than to catch the boys. I told them to let me alone, and go after the boys. They overhauled our two, who gave themselves up; there being two revolvers pointed at them. I had told Kiser and Cummins not to shoot unless in self defence. The white man disappeared as suddenly as if he had gone into the ground. I asked the free man who he was, but he pretended he had never seen him before; and said that he had come to his house only a few minutes before the boys. We carried them to Cumberland, and put them in jail. I got a physician there to dress my wound, hired a hack, and left on Friday afternoon. Some notice, I understand, of this affair appeared in the Cumberland paper of Saturday morning, but I was in hopes to have gotten home before you had seen it."

"Well, Mr. Benson," said Mr. Preble, "these are some of the fruits of our peculiar institutions. But for slavery, sir, we should never hear of these shocking occurrences. You are happily free, sir, from such."

Mr. Benson nodded assent.

"It is a self-evident truth," said the Doctor, "that, but for slavery, Mr. Preble, we should never hear of runaways; but these shocking occurrences are not the legitimate consequences of slavery. They are produced, sir, by an unpardonable intermeddling on the part of northern abolitionists with our property; producing dissatisfaction among those who otherwise would be contented with their situation, inciting them to resist the authority of their masters, even at the peril of their masters' lives.

"Shocking occurrences are, moreover, common, sir, in every society, whether slavery exists or not. We hear of the unlawful use of the revolver as much in the free as in the slave states."

"Doctor, you and I never could agree upon that subject; you think slavery right, and I think it decidedly wrong."

"If we were both judged by our actions, Mr. Preble, it would be supposed that we both thought alike. We both hold slaves; and I had much rather hold them, thinking that I had a right, or that it was not forbidden, than to own them, thinking at the same time that I had no right."

"Being here amongst them, Doctor, being surrounded

by them on all sides, and experiencing all the evils, it would be a hard case for me to be denied the benefits."

"Then you do allow that there are benefits resulting from slavery."

"Why—sir, why—yes, sir; your slave labour drives away all white labour, and if I did not own slaves, I could get no work done at all."

"As for that, sir, you might employ the free blacks; there are plenty of them."

"Oh! sir, they are all good for nothing; I would not be pestered with them."

"If we were to set all our slaves free, sir, they would be just as good for nothing as those that are now free, and more so; for the more free ones there were, the more worthless they would be."

Mr. Preble was luckily relieved from the argument, by Lewis coming to the door, and saying that "*one man* wanted to see him in the yard."

He went out, and found Mr. Bosher sitting upon the steps. Without asking him into the house, he took a seat by him on the steps.

"I see from the paper, Mr. Preble, that you have two negro men in jail in Cumberland, and I'm come to see if I can't buy them of you. What kind of men are they?"

"Young men, sir; the one twenty, and the other two-and-twenty; as likely men as are to be found anywhere—quite sound in every respect. My price for them is six hundred dollars each, and the purchaser pays the jail fees."

"That's tough, Mr. Preble; six hundred dollars is as

much as I can possibly afford to give, without the jail fees."

"You can't have them for less, sir; that's my price. I will keep them in jail until I get that price, no matter how long that may be."

"Well, sir, I came to buy them; write the bill of sale and an order to the jailor, and I'll pay you the money."

He went into the house, leaving Mr. Bosher on the step. While he was in, Dr. Boswell saw Mr. Bosher from the window, and, wishing to inquire about the boys he had sold him, he went into the portico.

"Well, Doctor," said Mr. Bosher, "I told you we grabbed them flying. I have just caught two in the Cumberland jail."

"Have you bought those two boys of Mr. Preble?"

"Yes, indeed, sir; and the old man, though he is an abolitionist, knows how to sell niggers, I tell you! He has made me pay him more than I have given to any one else. I suppose, however, he must have a little more than others, for conscience sake."

"How do the boys come on that I sold you, Mr. Bosher? do they appear satisfied?"

"Oh! yes, sir; they are as merry as crickets."

Mr. Preble returned with the papers, and told Mr. Bosher he had directed the jailor to deliver the boys whenever the jail fees were settled.

"You needn't been so particular, sir, for he would not give them up until he got his fees."

Dr. Boswell and his lady intended their visit as a

morning call; but the incidents of the day had detained them so long, that they agreed to stay to dinner.

When the gentlemen returned to the parlour, they found Mrs. Boswell and Mr. George Preble, in conversation together, Mr. Benson and Miss Amelia, Mr. Grattan and Miss Evelina. Old Mr. Preble, as he entered, cast a look of evident dissatisfaction towards Miss Evelina and Mr. Grattan; to the latter he had not addressed one word of conversation during the day.

Mrs. Boswell, in an under tone, said to Mr. George Preble: "Mr. Preble, it's really worth while to be in trouble, or receive a slight wound, to try the attachment of our friends towards us. We have had, to-day, strong evidences of yours, for you. The announcement of your perilous situation, like to have been attended with serious consequences."

"My sister Lina, madam, I believe, loves me very much. She is easily overcome by any sudden relation of disaster happening to any one."

"I don't mean your sister only, Mr. Preble."

"You certainly can't mean Aunt Pris, for she so entirely realizes the hand of Providence in all events, that she could look undisturbed upon a world in conflagration. Oh, you mean my old mammy, good old soul; every twinge that I feel, pierces her to the heart."

"No, I don't mean either of *them*. Of all your female acquaintances in the neighbourhood, out of your own family, who do you suppose, Mr. Preble, would feel most sensibly any evil that might happen to you?"

"Why, madam, that is a hard question to answer. I

don't know that anything happening to me, would give more than ordinary pain to any female acquaintance I have out of my own family. Miss Amelia, there, having come here to-day, in consequence of hearing of my mishap, has certainly evinced more concern upon the subject than any other female but yourself."

"The anxiety of another, Mr. Preble, may have been so intense, as to have prevented her from undertaking such a trip."

"If you mean, madam, that Miss Julia Scott has been kept at home to-day by the intensity of her anxiety on my account, you have relieved me of a world of inquietude, resulting from an apprehension of her indifference."

"If I had not supposed, Mr. Preble, that there was such an understanding between Miss Julia and yourself, as to quiet all apprehension of indifference towards you, it is a subject that I would not have ventured on."

They were summoned to dinner, and immediately after dinner, Mr. Grattan, the Doctor, and Mrs. Boswell, took their leave for their respective homes.

The road to Mr. Grattan's led through Major Scott's farm, and as he passed near the house, he concluded to alight and inform the family of George's safe arrival. To relieve at once the anxiety depicted upon Julia's countenance, he hurriedly said, "I have good news for you; George has arrived at home, with only a very slight wound in his shoulder; the family are all in good spirits, and old Mr. Preble has made quick work with his runaway boys, having already sold them to Mr. Bosher, the trader."

"It is just what I expected," said the major, with all

his pretended abolition notions; he is just as keen for putting them in his pocket when an opportunity offers, as anybody."

Julia was somewhat disconcerted at her father's remark, and observed, "Papa, you have determined to do the same, if yours are caught."

"There is a great deal of difference, my dear, in my selling negroes, and Mr. Preble's doing so; he pretends to be a thorough-going abolitionist; thinks it, as he says, decidedly wrong to hold human beings in slavery, and yet, when any of his slaves attempt to resume the liberty which he pretends to say they have a right to, he is more prompt in his efforts to recover them than almost anybody else, and sells them with as much indifference as he would sell a horse, or any other chattel. I, on the other hand, my dear, have never pretended to hold abolition views. If the master does his duty towards his slaves, he has authority from Scripture, in my opinion, to hold them in that relation; and I think my duty as a citizen requires that I should make an example of those who abscond. If my boys are recovered, I shall sell them, but it will be with great reluctance; and the sin of doing so, if any attaches, must be transferred from my skirts to their abolition advisers.

"I have never yet heard your opinion, Mr. Grattan, upon the subject of slavery. I will have your horse taken, and you will stay with us all night."

He left the room to give the order, and when he returned, the conversation was resumed by Mr. Grattan, who said that he seldom expressed his opinion upon the subject of slavery, unless requested to do so.

"I consider, Major, that all our views, upon every subject whatever, are derived from revelation. Out of, and beyond revelation, all is dark and obscure. In looking into that book which reveals to man the will of his Creator, we find governments established; and besides the relation of the governed and the governors, we find that of parent and child, and authority given to the parent over the child, as long as the dependence of the one upon the other lasts. We find the institution of matrimony, and authority given to the husband over the wife. We find, also, the relation of master and servant, and authority given to the master over his servant, without limitation as to the time of its continuance.

"The question arises, what is our duty in regard to those relations? whether it is to destroy or continue them? The only plea for their destruction, is the presumptuous one, that the rules revealed for their regulation are imperfect and faulty. The Jacobins of France have in former days attempted to take from the parent authority over his children, and to confer on children liberty uncontrolled, and unsuited to their tender years. Fourierism, and other isms, would destroy the sacred ties of matrimony, and abolitionism the relation of master and servant. But vain are the attempts of man to destroy those things which God has established. It were better that his efforts were confined to a strict application of the rules revealed for their government, than that they should be fruitlessly expended in a vain attempt to destroy. The improper exercise of authority over the child by the parent, or over the wife by the husband, or over the slave by his master, affords no plea for the destruction of those relations, but furnishes evidence of that wisdom which foresaw the necessity for those divine precepts revealed for their regulation. An awful responsibility, however, rests upon those who disregard those precepts, and act in those relations as their whims, conceits, and passions move them."

"Do you think, Mr. Grattan," said Julia, "that George did wrong in going after those boys?"

"Certainly not, Miss Julia. In the first place, I presume, he was obeying his father's orders; and, independent of that, he was right in not intrusting a business of that sort to the entire management of those who might have been less prudent than he determined to be. He went armed, but with a fixed determination not to use the arms except in self-defence; and even after he was wounded, he cautioned those young men who were with him not to fire, unless to protect their own lives."

"I have seen it mentioned, somewhere," said the Major, "that a party of slaves, who had run away from their masters in Kentucky, after remaining some time in Canada, had gone over to Africa, to become citizens of the republic of Liberia. Do you suppose, Mr. Grattan, that Governor Roberts would knowingly receive runaway negroes as citizens of that republic?"

"Undoubtedly not, sir; it would be his duty to send them back in the same vessel which had carried them to Africa. Can you suppose anything more foreign from the intention of Southern philanthropists (who planted the colony of Liberia for the reception of coloured persons then free, and who were to become so by emancipation), than that it should recoil upon themselves, produce insecurity in their slave property, by becoming an asylum for runaway negroes? The very idea, sir, is a slander upon the republic of Liberia; a direct charge of ingratitude and breach of faith."

Major Scott, whenever a minister of the Gospel tarried with him the night, summoned his slaves to join the family in prayer, and to hear any words of instruction which the minister might be inclined to give. They were nearly all present; and Mr. Grattan gave them a few words of exhortation, and a prayer.

When Dr. Boswell arrived at home, he found a note from Mr. Frazer, informing him that he was afraid to trust himself, and therefore declined taking the temperance pledge, and hoped that he and Mrs. Boswell would excuse him for exciting hopes which could not be realized.

The incidents of a country neighbourhood are so few, that the reader would not be interested in the occurrences of the following two months, except that, during that time, George Preble got entirely well of his wound; that his friend Mr. Benson stayed with him for some weeks, which they spent together mostly at Major Scott's; and rumour said that they were both engaged to the young ladies,—George of course to Miss Julia.

CHAPTER V.

EXQUISITE SENSITIVENESS.

At length the day arrived on which the Doctor was requested (by letter received from his father-in-law, Mr. Stephens), to send his carriage to the depot for Mrs. Stephens and himself. As it was a permanent move, the Doctor naturally concluded, that, in addition to the carriage, a wagon would be necessary for their baggage; and Uncle Robin was sent with a two-horse wagon. Before they arrive at Selma, we must introduce the reader to the character of each. Mr. Stephens was a man of moderate capacity, of business habits, very industrious, and of so strong, robust a frame, that he could endure much hard labour. His disposition was what would generally be called amiable. Mrs. Stephens had been brought up delicately, was of tall, genteel appearance; her temper, naturally quick, had been soured by a change in their circumstances, from affluence to a state, not of actual poverty, but of very moderate means of support. She was extremely sensitive upon the subject of slavery, and had imbibed, to a very great extent, the prejudices against the South and its peculiar institution, so common in Pennsylvania. Nothing but a desire to be with an only daughter, could have induced them to take up their residence in Virginia, for he, too, had similar prejudices. Such being the case, they were coming to Virginia, expecting to enjoy but little happiness in their new abode; and Mrs. Stephens may be said to have determined to be dissatisfied with everything Southern.

Uncle Robin and George were at the depot sometime before the cars arrived. The carriage was placed opposite the platform where the passengers were to get out. After the cars had stopped, Robin saw a gentleman and lady making their way to the platform, and he and George went up and saluted them.

"Are you Dr. Boswell's domestics?" said the lady.

They looked at each other, not exactly understanding the meaning of a word which they perhaps had never heard before. She repeated,

"Are you Dr. Boswell's domestics?"

"We he sarvants, missis," said Uncle Robin, who saw her turn up her eyes and repeat something to herself; and in the abiding devotion of his own feelings, and the simplicity of his Christian heart, he concluded that she was returning thanks for her safe delivery from the perils of a railroad car; but he learnt afterwards, that she was kindly commiserating his own and George's situation, and ejaculating with uplifted eyes, "*poor creatures.*" George heard distinctly the same words repeated several times before they reached Selma.

Mrs. Boswell met them at the carriage, and exclaimed: "My dear father and mother, how delighted I am to see you!" and threw her arms round the necks of both.

"Oh! my dear child," said Mrs. Stephens, "do carry me into your chamber and let me lie down; I am almost exhausted."

Mrs. Boswell assisted her to the bed, and brought a smelling-bottle, which she took and held in her hand, remaining some time with her eyes closed. The negro girls were seated around the room, employed in knitting. When she again opened her eyes, she caught a view of them, and exclaimed in a voice audible enough for them to hear, "*poor creatures!*"

Mrs. Boswell at first thought her mother had been overcome by the fatigue of her journey, but that exclamation satisfied her that there was some other cause for her nervousness. She ordered the girls to go to the garden and assist Uncle Robin in some work he was to go at there, as soon as he had put away his horses.

"Oh! mamma," she exclaimed, as soon as the girls left the room, "how sorry I am to see you so much distressed at sight of our slaves. I had hoped that you and papa had come to live with us, and partake the happiness which we all enjoy upon this plantation; indeed, mamma, you are entirely mistaken about slavery. It is nearly three months since I came here, with not a few prejudices against it, but those prejudices have been entirely removed by seeing for myself what slavery really is. I have never, anywhere, seen more satisfaction and happiness than appears to prevail among the slaves throughout this neighbourhood, with the exception of a few who are said to have been enticed off by persons from our state.

"As to myself, I feel of much more importance in the world than I have ever felt before, surrounded by persons who look up to the Doctor and myself for religious instruction, and for all the temporal comforts calculated to produce happiness. I have been most pleasantly engaged in superintending the making of coats, waistcoats, pantaloons, and stockings for the negroes, which they all now have on, and the girls are now employed in knitting a second pair of stockings for each. Mamma, be pleased not to let them hear you call them poor creatures again; it can do no good, and is only calculated to make them discontented with their situation."

"My dear," said her mother, "it is bad enough for me to be constantly exposed to see human beings in a state of slavery, and it will be much worse if I am to smother my feelings; I can't do it, my dear; and if I do produce discontent among them, it will be only hastening what I have so much at heart, their emancipation."

"I assure you, my dear mamma, it will not have that effect, but will only convert their present contentedness into dissatisfaction and misery."

"Uncle Robin," said Kate, when he joined them in the garden, "a'nt missis' ma crazy?"

"What mak' you think so, gal?"

"She look up to de celin' an' say, poor cre'tur's."

"I seed her look up when she 'rive at de depo', an' repeatin' somethin' to herself, an' I thought she mought be prayin', but George tell me jus' now, he hear her heap o' times say, poor cre'tur's, as dey com' 'long."

"Maybe, Uncle Robin, she lef' som' nigger gals home she couldn' bring 'long, and when she see we gals, it mak' her think o' dem."

"'Ta'nt dat, Kate."

Uncle Robin had sense enough to know that there were no slaves in Pennsylvania, and began to suspect the real cause of those exclamations, but he had prudence enough to keep his thoughts to himself.

"Uncle Robin," said Kate, "I hope dey ane gwine put me to wait 'pon dat ole 'oman; I dun fraid o' her reddy."

"Shure, chil', she ane gwine hu't you."

"I don' like her looks anyhow, Uncle Robin."

"If missis tell you to wate 'pon her ma, gal, you mus' do it, an' make no fuss 'bout it."

The care of the room assigned to Mrs. Stephens, was, sure enough, given to Kate, and when they came up to their room at night, Kate was at her post. The awful words, "poor creatures," reached her ears, just as Mrs. Stephens entered. Kate sidled off to the door, and flew down stairs like lightning.

"I declare, Mr. Stephens," said his wife, "I can't stand it; I was fearful before I came, that it would make me very nervous, but it is a great deal worse than I apprehended. I cannot be waited upon by these 'poor creatures.'"

"Well, my dear, we are here among them, and it can't be helped; there are no white servants in this country that I know of; however, if you will agree to clean out the room and make up the bed, I will bring water and attend to the fires, and we shan't want any waiting upon by slaves."

"You know very well, Mr. Stephens, that I never was accustomed to wait upon myself; I never made up a bed or cleaned out a room in my life."

"It must be done then by slaves, my dear; there's no help for it."

"It will kill me, Mr. Stephens, if I am constantly to witness the drudgery done by these 'poor creatures.'"

The next morning after breakfast, the Doctor and Mr. Stephens were walking out, the latter said to the Doctor:

"My wife, sir, has a most unconquerable antipathy to slavery, and I very much fear, from the nervous situation into which she has been thrown, by seeing it all around her, serious consequences to her health."

"I have heard her," replied the Doctor, "several times, when the servants came into the room, ejaculate, 'poor creatures,' but I thought it would wear off in a few days; I never for a moment apprehended serious consequences. It does seem to me, Mr. Stephens, that this whole abolition feeling has originated in, and is kept up by, the diseased, sickly sensibilities of females, and I am astonished that men of reflection, men in high standing, too, in the nation, should so far lend their aid to such sensibilities, as even to endanger the perpetuity of this Union. I hope, sir, that you have come among us, with a determination to conquer such feelings, if you have them, and to unite with my wife and myself in our efforts to reconcile Mrs. Stephens to the state of things which she finds in the land, where she has cast her lot for the future. You have come here, I know, under very erroneous impressions of what slavery really is, in Virginia, but when you have become better acquainted with it, I will venture to predict that your preconceived notions will be changed. It will be more difficult, however, to deal with the deranged sensibilities of Mrs. Stephens."

"What was that building intended for, Doctor?" said Mr. Stephens, as they passed a good-looking two-story house on the plantation, about a half mile from the dwelling-house of Selma.

"That house, sir, was built by my father, a short time before his death, for a widowed sister of his. She died about the time it was finished. Her children were taken by their paternal relations, and the house has been locked up ever since."

"A thought has just struck me, Doctor, which I will make known to you at once. How do you think it would do for my wife and myself to occupy that building? I have ample means to furnish it well, and it is possible that we might hire two or three white servants in the neighbourhood to wait upon us. If you could attach some land to it, I could find profit and amusement in cultivating it, as I am able to endure any kind of hard labour. I think with another grown hand I could make a comfortable support."

"I certainly, Mr. Stephens, can have no objection to your proposal, other than the great disappointment it would occasion Ann, at not having her mother with her in the same house."

"My dear sir, it will be so near, that Ann and her mother may be together every day, and I know that Ann will have much more pleasure in her mother's society when her mother is removed from the sight of slavery."

"Very well, sir," said the Doctor, "if it is agreeable to the ladies it will be perfectly so to me; and it seems to have happened very apropos, that this morning, as overseer of the poor, I received an order of Court to bind out two children of a father and mother who are unable to support them, and who must themselves go to the poor-house. One of the children is a boy about fourteen years of age, and the other a girl of twelve. If you determine to remove to that house, and will sign the indentures, you shall have them until they are of age."

"If, upon seeing them, I like their appearance, that arrangement will suit exactly."

They returned to the house, the ladies were consulted. Mrs. Stephens was delighted with the plan; Mrs. Boswell was at first very much opposed to it, but she saw something in her husband's manner which induced her to believe he favoured it, and she acquiesced without farther opposition. It was determined that they should all go to old Mr. Crosby's the next day, to complete the arrangement about his children.

On the following day they were at Mr. Crosby's by eleven o'clock. Robin had carried the two-horse wagon for the children. Mr. Crosby's house was an old log cabin, in that region of country called the Pine Hills. Although not an old man, he walked with great difficulty, in consequence of a fracture of his thigh-bone, caused by a fall from his horse a few years before, which rendered him entirely unfit for any out-door work; and an affliction in his eyes, by which his sight had been impaired, had put a stop to his in-door work at his trade, which was that of a shoemaker. His wife had supported the family, after his eyes became worse, by her wheel; but, a few weeks before, she had been taken sick, and they were then dependent upon charity. The Doctor had so arranged it with another overseer of the poor, that the father and mother were to be taken to the poor-house, on the day that their children should be taken from them; and they found Mr. Conway's wagon ready to carry them there.

"Do you know me, Mr. Crosby?" said the Doctor, advancing towards him.

"No, sir, I don't know you—can't see."

"My name is Boswell, Mr. Crosby."

"You be Dr. Boswell, that lives down in that big house 'pon the river?"

"The very same, sir. Mr. Crosby, the overseers of the poor have determined to send you and Mrs. Crosby to the poor-house; and Mr. Conway has come with his wagon to carry you there."

"And what's gwine to become of my children, Doctor?"

"I am directed by the court, Mr. Crosby, to bind your children out until they are twenty-one years of age; and I have brought my wife's father, who lives upon my plantation, to see them; and, if he likes their appearance, he will take them."

Mrs. Crosby, upon hearing that, screamed, "Oh! they going to take my poor dear children away from me! what shall I do? what shall I do? My poor Sally never was from me one night, in her life; and now they going to take her away, and I shall never see her again."

"Why, Mrs. Crosby," said the Doctor, "she will be only about five miles off, and you will see her frequently. I will lend John a horse, and he can take Sally to see you at any time."

"Oh! I shall die, I shall die, if they take my poor children away from me."

"It is a case of necessity, Mrs. Crosby; the old man can't work, and you can't work; the children are too young to support you; it is better to take them, than that you should all starve here together. I will promise you, Mrs. Crosby, they shall be well treated."

"I had a great deal rather starve here with my poor dear children, than to be separated from them. Oh! Doctor! Doctor! don't take my poor children from me."

The mother and children were all screaming; she clasped her arms round them, and exclaimed, "They shan't go! they shan't go!" The old man hobbled up to the bed, and told her 'twould be best for them all that the children should be bound out.

"Oh! you cruel father! you cruel father! you shan't take my darlings from me."

Mrs. Boswell was in tears; Mrs. Stephens looked very composed, until Robin and George came into the room to tear the children away from their mother; when they passed her, she exclaimed, "poor creatures!"

The children were taken out and put into Robin's wagon, and the screams of the poor mother were heard until they got out of the reach of her voice.

When they got home, Mrs. Boswell and the girls set about making clothes for the two Crosbys.

The gentlemen were attending to cleansing and airing the house; and it was arranged that they should go, the next day, to town, to procure furniture.

When the Doctor and Mrs. Boswell were alone that night, he said:

"My dear Ann, you must have observed from my manner, when this plan was proposed, for your father and mother to go to housekeeping, that I rather favoured than disapproved of it. I was a silent observer of your mother's conduct after her arrival here; and I was pained to see her extreme sensitiveness whenever she came into the presence of our slaves; because, I knew that such conduct would keep you for ever uneasy, and was moreover highly calculated to do great injury to the servants themselves. The constant application of the term 'poor creatures' to them, might at last make them believe that they really were poor creatures, notwithstanding that their many comforts around them were evidences to the contrary. For those reasons, I must confess, that I was very well pleased when your father made the proposal.

"It has, moreover, given me an opportunity, to-day, to show you that the evils of separation, and the severance of endearing family ties, are by no means confined to a state of slavery, but are common to all classes of society. I was very forcibly struck, too, with that genuine sympathy manifested by yourself for real suffering, in contrast with your mother's perfect indifference for that which is real, and her affectation of it, for that which is only imagined. She listened to the wailings of a truly bereaved mother with perfect composure, while the presence of George and Robin (two happy beings) could draw forth the unmeaning exclamation, of 'poor creatures.' That was, my dear, a veritable picture of abolitionism; sitting with destruction-dealing look over the desolations it had occasioned to the white man, and shedding tears of sympathy over the imagined sorrows of the negro."

Dr. Boswell and Mr. Stephens on their way to town, the next day, had to pass by Mr. Frazer's at the cross-roads. Mr. Frazer was standing in his yard as they were passing, and hailed the Doctor with,

"Did you hear the news, Doctor?"

"No; what news, Mr. Frazer?"

"Why, sir, they have caught an abolitionist at last.

A fellow in a carryall came to Squire Brown's last night and asked for quarters; the Squire consented that he might stay, and after he had taken his supper, he went to the stable and got into conversation with the Squire's hostler; asked him if he didn't want to be free, and told him if he would go off, that he would help him to get to Pennsylvania. The servant (who is a very trusty negro), said but little, but rather induced him to believe that he would go. After the man went back to the house, the hostler saw his young master Tom in the yard, and told him of the conversation at the stable. Tom told him to say nothing about it to any one, but that when this man went up to bed, he must go along with the candle, and when he got into the room, he must begin and say something about going off. Tom and another white man (who was working for his father), went up before bed-time, and hid themselves under the bed. When the negro boy and this fellow came up, a conversation took place similar to the one at the stable; the whole of which was heard by Tom and his companion, who immediately left their hiding-place, seized the fellow, and carried him before the Squire, who sent him to jail forthwith." Mr. Frazer's story being finished, the Doctor left him.

While they were absent that day, Mrs. Stephens walked into the garden, and the following conversation was held with Uncle Robin, who was at work there. As she passed him, she made an inclination of the head to him, and with eyes turned up, exclaimed, "Poor creatures!" Uncle Robin waited until she returned down the walk, met her, and very politely said, "Missis, I's feared somethin' press 'pon you' mind mighty; I's hear you say heap a times, poo' creturs; now, missis, if you any way 'strest 'bout we niggers, I should like, madam, to 'lieve you' mind; we ain't de poo' creturs, madam, you thinks we is, we got good masser here, we hab good clothes, plenty to eat, no whippin', plenty opportunity to go an' hear de word o' God preached, madam; an' jus as happy here as masser or anybody else, madam."

"But you are slaves, my friend, kept in bondage by a master who has no right to hold you as such, and you are kept ignorant of your real happiness."

"Why, missis, bein' content here, madam, I don' think it wuff while to 'quire 'bout my masser' right to hav' me as he slave, but if I did, madam, de word o' God does give him 'thority, de word o' God does tell me to serve an' 'bey my masser; and, madam, if people does think dey's happy, 'tis jus' same thing, madam, as bein' happy. I a'nt, missis, as you say, ignant of my rale happiness, my rale happiness up yonder, madam," (pointing up to the heavens.)

"But you haven't the liberty, my friend, of working when you please, and going where you please, and doing whatever you please; you are a slave, and bound to obey the will of your master, and as long as you are so bound, you can't enjoy what I would call happiness."

"Now, missis, jus' le's see; s'pose I was free, I'd do maybe jus' like dem free blacks I sees ev'ry day; dey do little wuck, an' dey gits little money, an' dey goes to de grog shop an' spends it all; dey don' clothe demselves or der children; ebery bad thing done in de country falls 'pon deir shoulders, whether dey 'sarve it or not; now, madam, is dat what you call happiness? Which de happiest, madam, dem people, or we, who live here wid masser? and missis, you go to our cabins, madam, an' den go to dem

Irish board hous' dey call shanty, an' cum back an' tell me which you think got mos' happiness, dem folks, or we. Missis, we de foot to war de shoe, and if de shoe don' pinch us, madam, I don' see why it should pinch oder people, madam."

"Well, my friend, I see you don't know what's good for you, and I will leave you to reflect upon what I have said."

As she left, Uncle Robin said to himself:

"I wish missis would 'flect little 'pon what I bin say."

Mrs. Boswell was for several days very busy in fixing her father and mother's house, which was made very comfortable, with the best of furniture, carpeting, &c., and they at length took possession of Fredonia, as the old lady called it. The Doctor and Mrs. Boswell dined with them the first day, and they were all very much diverted, except the old lady, at the awkwardness of John and Sally. Mrs. Boswell had proposed to the Doctor to let Charles go over to give them some instruction, but he replied:

"No, my dear, if you want me to enjoy myself to-day in the land of freedom, let us have no adulteration of it by the presence of these 'poor creatures.'"

Old Mr. Preble visited them in a few days, and he and Mrs. Stephens held a long conversation upon the subject of slavery, upon which they agreed theoretically, the old man cautiously avoiding any mention of being himself a slave-owner.

Mr. Stephens hired a white man, Mr. Brock, to work with him on the plantation, as John Crosby had been taken by his wife for the house. He also hired a free black woman to cook, by the name of Rachel.

As the spring advanced, he laboured hard in preparing

for a crop of corn, and was seldom in the house except at meals. He often found John and Sally in tears, and old Rachel apparently not in the best of humours. Upon one of those occasions he happened to ask John what was the matter, in presence of Mrs. Stephens.

"Madam did beat me, sir," said John.

"Yes, and I didn't give you half as much as you deserved, sir; you are the most vexing and perplexing little scamp that I ever had anything to do with. Mr. Stephens, you must, indeed, get me a cowhide; I can't get along with John, or Sally either, without one; they will worry me out of my life."

"My dear, you must have a little patience with the children, and they will get along better, after a while."

"Patience, fiddlestick! You are, Mr. Stephens, and always have been, the very worst hand to manage servants I ever saw. Isn't it calculated to spoil them completely, to hear you always preaching up patience to me? If you won't get me a cowhide, I will get Mr. Brock to cut me some hickories. These children, as you call them, must be kept in order, and taught obedience, Mr. Stephens."

"My dear, I don't know when I shall have time to go from home to get you a cowhide; Mr. Brock can get you plenty of hickories, if you have need of them."

"Need! I have need of them every hour of the day, Mr. Stephens."

"Sally," said Mr. Stephens, "carry Mr. Brock his dinner; I must be off to my work."

That afternoon Mrs. Boswell sent Kate over to Fredonia with a jar of sweetmeats for her mother; and when Kate returned, she asked her what her mother said.

"She say thanky, madam."

"Was that all she said, Kate?"

"I didn' hear her say nothin' else, madam, but call me poo' cretur; an' I's sure I an't so poo' cretur as dat gal she got dar; she look poo' 'nough, goodness knows!"

George Preble, whom they had not seen for some weeks, rode over to Selma that afternoon. He was in fine spirits, and seemed to have something of a pleasing nature to communicate, as soon as they would give him an opportunity.

"I hear some good news about you, George," said the Doctor.

"Ah! what's that, Doctor? I find I have been talked about wherever I go; but a man who has been wounded in a rencounter with a negro, must expect his ears to burn."

"There are other rencounters, George, which cause neighbourhood gossippings, in which if a man gets wounded he's not apt to recover so speedily as you have done from your shoulder-wound."

"I don't clearly understand you, Doctor."

"They say, George, that you have been pierced in the heart, by a little archer called Cupid; and that not being able to bear the pain alone, you have caused him to pierce somebody else."

"Do, Mr. Preble," said Mrs. Boswell, "tell us all about it; we have heard something about you, and should be delighted to hear from your own lips that it is true."

"Well, Mrs. Boswell, as I am somewhat indebted to you in this very matter, I will tell you that I am positively engaged to Miss Julia Scott."

"I knew it would be a match, Mr. Preble; I was confident that Julia's fainting, when she heard of your wound, proceeded from some other feeling than ordinary sympathy."

"I declare to you, madam, that I had not at that time addressed Julia. To be sure, I had given her reason to believe that I intended it; your hint on that day brought me to the determination of doing it at once."

"If I had known there was no engagement between you, I should not have given you the hint, Mr. Preble."

"Why not, madam?"

"Because I should have thought I had no right to betray to a gentleman the secret of a lady's heart, before he had obtained it from herself. I had no doubt at the time but that you were then engaged."

"Well, madam, there's no harm done; I am very much obliged to you, and I don't suppose Julia is very angry about it."

"What has become of your friend Mr. Benson?" asked Mrs. Boswell.

"He returned home some weeks ago. Perhaps you would like to hear whether a report which is in circulation about him is true? and, as it is all over the neighbourhood, I might as well tell you at once that he is engaged to Amelia."

"Upon my word, they made quick work of it."

"I think, Mrs. Boswell, that short courtships and short engagements are best."

"I am glad to hear you say so, about engagements, as it gives promise of an early wedding, and I am very fond of weddings."

"Well, my dear," said the Doctor, "that is a plain hint for an invitation."

"Mr. Preble says I brought it about, and if so, I have a right to claim a bid to it."

"Certainly you have, madam, and your right shall not be withheld from you. Doctor, I have received an invitation from a relation of my mother, to come to San Francisco and join him in a very profitable business he is engaged in there. I have mentioned it to Julia, and she is willing to go; my father is anxious for me to go; Aunt Pris and Lina oppose it most violently; I want your advice upon the subject."

"What do Julia's father and mother think of it? I should suppose that they would not even consent to your marriage, if they thought you would carry Julia to such a distance. What will they do, George, after both their children are taken from them? you say Amelia is going to Boston."

"Well, sir, if they oppose it very strenuously, I will abandon all idea of going; I would not give up Julia for all California, and Mexico to boot."

"You had better weigh the matter well, George, even if they consent; you will have enough here, and I do not like the thoughts of your going away, to such a distance, as there is no earthly necessity for it. There is another matter, George, in which I feel considerable interest, and I hope you will not think me too inquisitive, if I ask you how it goes with Mr. Grattan and Evelina. I think very highly of both, that they are well suited to each other, and I should like to hear that their love matters were as well adjusted as yours and Mr. Benson's."

"I don't know much about it, Doctor; if it suits them, I am very well disposed to their union. My father, I fear, will be opposed to it, from hints he occasionally drops, of the necessity of having something to make the pot boil. I dare say Lina hasn't much objection, and Aunt Pris no doubt thinks that that match has been registered in heaven a long time ago. Mr. Grattan is a very pious man, and a very sensible one, and I think Lina was intended for a minister's wife."

"I wish, with all my heart," said the Doctor, "that it could be brought about, and I see no reasonable ground for objecting. Mr. Grattan, as to worldly matters, is pretty much like other young ministers, and we see that they all get along very well; besides, your father is very able to assist them."

"Yes, my father's very able, but you know he don't like to part with his property, Doctor. Aunt Pris has something considerable, and I suppose Lina will get all that, except her negroes. They are as dead a shot for Liberia as ever pointed that way."

"Oh!" said Mrs. Boswell, "I do feel very much interested in that matter; I wish it could take place; suppose we all try to prevail upon Mr. Preble to give up his objections, and let them be married at once?"

"My dear, it is a delicate business to meddle with; I neither like match-making nor match-breaking. Matrimony, you know, is at best a lottery, and those who draw blanks are the first to blame those who persuaded them to buy tickets."

"Yes," said George, "and I can tell you, it is best to let the old man alone; he will go his own way, and the more you persuade him the more obstinate he becomes. If I thought I could do anything with him, they should very cheerfully have my services."

"George," said the Doctor, "you talk of going to California; don't you know you can't carry your negroes there?"

"I have no negroes, Doctor, to carry there. My old mammy Phillis couldn't be kept back by a regiment of soldiers, if I go. She would be free when she gets there, but I should like to see the mountain of gold that could induce her to leave us after getting there."

"But, George, your father-in-law could spare you at least ten negroes; and if he gives them to you, what will you do with them if you go to California?"

"If I could carry them with me, Doctor, and keep them all together, I would; but as I can't carry them, if the old man gives me any, I must sell them. I would not sell negroes who had not misbehaved, to traders; I would sell them in the neighbourhood in families, even at a sacrifice. That is one of the evils resulting to the South, from California being a free state. We Southern people who go there, must either make a sacrifice in selling them at home, or we must do what is revolting to humanity, sell them to traders, who will scatter them all over the extreme Southern slave states, without any sort of regard to natural ties. I wonder the abolitionists don't think of that when they are eager to apply the Wilmot proviso to all new states, and are at the same time abusing the South for cruelty, in separating husband and wife, parent and child, and all other connexions."

"George," said the Doctor, "abolitionism is a humbug,

an idea, expended in the isolated word slavery, without any reference to what it is, what are its incidents or its consequences."

"Well," said George, when he was about to leave, "you must keep in mind the first day of June."

Mr. Stephens walked over from Fredonia. As soon as he entered the house, his daughter and the Doctor discovered something in his countenance like trouble and inquietude.

"Doctor," said he, "I am in a terrible fix; Brock has left me, and I can't get along with my planting."

"What was the cause of his leaving you?" said the Doctor.

"He has been growling and grumbling for some time, I understand, because he did not eat with us at the table; and last Saturday night, I wanted my boots cleaned for Sunday, and sent them to him; he sent them back, positively refusing to do it, and said that white people wa'n't accustomed to do such mean work, that I had better send them ovor for one of Dr. Boswell's niggers to clean."

"It is very different with us, Mr. Stephens, from what it is in your state. With you there are only two classes, the labouring whites and those whose circumstances put them above labour. With us, there are three classes, those above labour, the labouring whites, and the slaves. Your two classes are just as far removed from each other in social intercourse, as the two extremes of ours. The labouring white man, with us, occupies a grade between those extremes, and he is watchful and jealous to maintain that grade, and takes umbrage at any real or imagined effort on the part of the highest grade to sink him to a level with the lowest. When you get better acquainted with that class of whites here, you will be able to get along better with them. I sometimes have white men to work for me, and if they are decent, I have them at my table at meals."

"I should have no objection myself, Doctor, but my wife won't agree to it; and we have been in the habit of sending Brock's meals to him in the entry. Is there no other white man in the neighbourhood you could recommend to me, Doctor?"

"Let me see—let me see—Yes, there is a man living close by, who sometimes hires himself by the day, week, or month. Charles, take my horse and ride over to Mr. Looney's, and ask him to come over here immediately. Tell him I want see him on some particular business."

"My dear daughter," said Mr. Stephens, "you seem to get along with your domestics, here, with very little trouble."

"Papa, I find it the easiest thing in the world. These girls that you see about the house have been trained to do certain work; and all the trouble I have, is to fix for them parts of the work, which they find difficult to do, without instruction. They are tractable and obedient, and I find very little need even for scolding."

"You are very fortunate, my dear, to be so situated."

"Papa, I wish you would prevail upon mamma to come over here to see me; I am there almost every day, and she has not been here since you moved."

"My dear, your mother in her new establishment has a good deal of fixing to do. Those children too, get along very badly, and worry her a good deal; you ought to go every day, Ann, to see your mamma."

"I sincerely wish mamma was back here, papa, and that we could be constantly together; it does seem so strange, that you and she should live on the same plantation with an only daughter, and not in the same house; and then, papa, I am afraid you will injure your health by hard work, which you are not accustomed to."

"My dear, I feel happier when I am at work, than when I am idle, and I think work agrees very well with my constitution. You know how excitable your mother's nervous system is in certain situations; you must be satisfied at the separation, and make her time as agreeable as possible, by coming over at all times of the day."

"Good-evening, Mr. Looney," said the Doctor, to a stout, robust-looking man, as he entered the room; "how do you do, Mr. Looney?'

"I'm up and a-going, sir," said Looney.

"Here is a gentleman, Mr. Looney, who lives upon my plantation, who is preparing to make a crop of corn, and wishes a white man to assist him in his work."

"Well, sir, I'm just that man, sir, who can do any sort of plantation work, and if the gentleman will give me my price, and will treat me well, I'll work with him till Christmas, if he likes. There's one thing, Doctor, I ginerally stipulates for; some of you gentlefolks have a way of treating poor white folks like niggers, by sending them to the kitchen to eat; now, I can't stand that, Doctor; I'm a free man, and thinks myself as good as any other free man going."

"I would certainly not send you to the kitchen to eat, Mr. Looney," said Mr. Stephens, "but my wife is very particular and neat, and doesn't wish her carpet to be soiled by the feet of persons coming from work in all weathers, we generally send the meals of those we employ to work, into a small room adjoining the house, where you would also sleep."

"Well, sir, if I can't eat at the same table with gentle-folks, it's no go with me, sir. Good-evening, gentlemen; and you, too, madam," (turning to Mrs. Boswell).

"He's a rough chap, that," said the Doctor; "I fear, Mr. Stephens, you will find it a difficult matter to get another white man; I can't think of any other in the neighbourhood. How would it do to take my man Billy? he is an excellent hand, and you are very welcome to his services. If you take him, you know you could keep him out of sight of the house, as there would be no necessity for his going nearer than the kitchen."

"You are very kind, Doctor, and the necessity of the case is such, that I will take Billy, and be very thankful to you for him."

"Papa, I have heard the Doctor say that he has more negroes on his plantation than he has use for, and he was sorry that circumstances prevented his offering you the services of both field hands and house servants."

"The Doctor is very, very kind, my dear, but you know it would not do to have them in the house; your mother would never consent to it, I know."

"Well, papa, I hope to see the day when mamma will think very differently upon the subject of slavery than she now does."

"It may be so, my dear, it may be so. You must come over, Ann, early to-morrow, and spend the day with your mother."

"If it is a good day, I will, papa. Good-bye, my dear papa."

"I will send Billy over early in the morning," said the Doctor, as Mr. Stephens took his leave.

"Well, Ann, this thing is working just as I expected. Your father and mother, too, will find that slaves are the only servants they can get along with in comfort in this country. Your mother will have more trouble with those two little Crosbys than you would have with a hundred blacks such as ours. I must say to you, Ann, without any intention of wounding your feelings, that I very much fear there will be a necessity for taking those children from her, and for putting them somewhere else. You know, my dear, that I am under a promise to their parents to see them well treated; and, independent of that, my duty as an overseer of the poor requires that I should take care that they are not abused. From what I have seen and heard, my Ann, I am fearful that your mother is not as kind to them as she should be. This excessive sympathy for slaves seems to me to close all avenues to the heart for kindly consideration for the indentured white servant."

"What in the world would she do, my dear husband, if they were taken away from her? and then the mortification of having it known throughout the country that they were taken away because of bad treatment! nothing that could happen would give me more pain. I hope, my dear, for my sake, you will put it off as long as you possibly can. Perhaps, after they become better acquainted with the work they are put to, there will be an alteration in mamma's treatment of them. I think when I go over to-morrow, if I see any appearance of their having been badly treated, I will give mamma a gentle hint upon the subject."

"You had better be cautious, my dear, or you may make it worse. There are very few persons who can bear being interfered with in matters of that kind. Most people would at once conclude that sympathy expressed for persons in their situation had been elicited by misrepresentations on their part; and such an idea would increase rather than diminish severity."

Mrs. Boswell spent the following day with her mother; but seeing nothing particular about those children than a melancholy cast of countenance, declined saying anything to her mother about them. The old lady was more composed and cheerful than she had seen her since her arrival in Virginia; but strenuously resisted all her daughter's importunity for a visit to Selma. Not a word was said by her about Billy, and Mrs. Boswell concluded that her father had kept him out of sight. The old man, however, took the opportunity, afforded by Mrs. Stephens's absence from the room, to say that he was, so far, very much pleased with Billy; that he seemed to understand work, and to do it with good-will and cheerfulness. He had made a lucky escape, he thought, in not employing that rough fellow, Looney.

"Papa, from what I have seen since I came here, he is a pretty good sample of the white labourers in this country, I would think."

"If so, my dear, I would greatly prefer Billy to any of them. If I had employed that fellow, Looney, he would have given me much trouble, and perhaps would have left me when my work was most pressing, and would probably have been impertinent all the time. Billy, on the other hand, seems very tractable and humble."

"I sincerely hope, papa, that you will continue to like him, and that after a while you will find out that slavery is not so terrible a thing as most of our Pennsylvania people think it is."

"I have no time now, my dear daughter, to argue that matter with you. You must come over and see us every day, and bring my kind friend the Doctor with you sometimes."

"I have no doubt, papa, he will often come over with me with much pleasure. Don't let me keep you from your work, papa; good-bye."

CHAPTER VI.

CALIFORNIA SOCIETY.

GEORGE PREBLE and Evelina were in the constant habit of sitting from supper to bed-time, in their Aunt Priscilla's room, and on his return from Selma (the evening of his visit there), he found Evelina with his aunt. She had supped, and had carried George's supper up stairs, to be kept warm by Miss Priscilla's good fire.

"Lina," said George, "I am just from Selma, where I spent an hour or two in very agreeable conversation with Dr. and Mrs. Boswell; they are charming people, ain't they?"

"Yes, they are, indeed, George; I don't know two better people in this word than they are."

"Come, Lina, that's too extravagant; where's Aunt Pris and Mr. Grattan?"

"You know, George, Aunt Priscilla is excepted by the general rule, which puts present company out of the operation of a remark of that kind."

"And by what rule is Mr. Grattan excepted?"

"I did not say that Mr. Grattan was excepted at all, George."

"Now, Lina, I know you don't think the Doctor or Mrs. Boswell either, as good as Mr. Grattan."

"They are each as good, or better than the other in their particular sphere, George. The Doctor is a better physician and farmer than Mr. Grattan, and Mr. Grattan is a better minister than the Doctor, and Mrs. Boswell in her sphere is as good as she can be."

"Ah! Lina, that's just a quibble; you meant to say at first that you did not know any better moral people. Now, I know you think Mr. Grattan better than either of them."

"Why, George, I do think Mr. Grattan has more piety than either the Doctor or Mrs. Boswell, but I love them so sincerely that I may be too extravagant in their praise."

"I just understand you now, Lina, you praise the Doctor and Mrs. Boswell because you love them so dearly, and Mr. Grattan, because you think so and so of him. I will venture to say for Mr. Grattan, that he would rather you would think less highly of him, and love him a little more."

"Aunt Priscilla," said Evelina, "I've dropped a stitch in my knitting; I wish you would take it up for me."

"My dear," said Miss Priscilla, "you know I can't see to do that in the day, much less at night."

"Lina," said George, "as I made you drop the stitch, hand me the knitting, and I will take it up."

"You made me drop it, George—how did you make me drop it?"

"Why, by talking of Mr. Grattan and love, Lina."

"Aunt Priscilla, do make George eat his supper, and hush his nonsense, will you?"

"My dear, it is more than I can do, to make George stop talking nonsense; his supper is very much in my way, and if he don't eat it shortly, I'll make Mary take it out."

"I 'll save Mary that trouble, aunt." He took up his supper, went to the table, and soon despatched it.

"Lina, if you hadn't been so near making me lose my supper, I would tell you what I heard said about you this afternoon."

"If it hadn't been for me, George, you would not have had that supper, for I brought it up for you."

"Well, deary, as you brought my supper, and are now in a good humour with me, I will tell you, that I heard Doctor and Mrs. Boswell say some very kind things about you."

"George," said Miss Priscilla, "you know that I don't like Evelina to be told of what people say in her praise. We are all frail creatures, and are too prone to think too highly of ourselves; and when, to the estimate we put on ourselves, is added the flattery of others, it is apt to produce a self-complacency, incompatible with that meekness and lowliness of spirit which ought to adorn every Christian."

"Aunt, the kind things I spoke of, were only expressions of kind wishes for Evelina's future happiness. Would there be any harm in telling her that?"

"It depends entirely, George, upon what was to contribute to her future happiness. For instance, if her friends wished her to be rich, and a very fine gay lady of the world, by being told of such wishes, young ladies generally might be induced to hope for those things for themselves, when they hear that in the opinion of friends those things constitute happiness. I do not, however, fear such consequences to Evelina; I flatter myself that her views of real happiness are such that she would not seek it in such trifles as those."

"Suppose, aunt, I were to tell Evelina that her friends wished her future happiness to be derived from a union with a pious evangelical minister; what would you think of that, aunt?"

"George, I can't say that I would object to such a communication as that; Evelina already knows that such wishes are perfectly in accordance with my own, and that it is the first wish of my heart that her future destiny should be interwoven with that of an evangelical minister of the Gospel."

"Lina, dear, don't cry; aunty won't make you marry a minister, if you don't want to." Evelina was actually in tears, at thought, however, of her father's opposition.

"George, if you don't hush," said Evelina, "I will tell Julia Scott not to marry such a harem scarem boy as you are."

"Ah! deary, Julia Scott won't mind what you say. Julia knows that I am a very sedate body, and that Mr.

George Prebles are not to be met with every day. I am going over to-morrow morning to the Major's to broach to him the subject of California."

"George," said Miss Priscilla, "I was really in hopes that you had given over that extraordinary notion of yours of going to California. If Major Scott consents to your taking Julia off to California, he must have pretty much the same opinion of you that you seem to have of yourself."

"Well, aunty, why not? everybody seems to think well of Mr. George Preble."

"I am sure I would not let Evelina go to California with Mr. George Preble, or Mr. George anybody else," said Miss Priscilla.

"No, aunty; Mr. Grattan's name isn't George. Suppose, however, she was going with the Reverend Mr. John Grattan; would you object to it then?"

"I would not like Evelina to go to California with anybody, George."

"Now, aunty, if he was missionary to Greece, China, or Africa, what would become of your zeal in behalf of the heathen, if you were to object to Lina's going to assist him in his missionary labours? I know you would let her go then; and why not let her go with him to California, where they want missionaries as much as they do anywhere upon the face of the earth."

"It will be time enough for me decide that question, George, when an occasion occurs for its decision; but you don't pretend to be going to California as a missionary."

"In one sense I do, aunt; my mission is to collect gold dust."

"That is a mission, George, for destroying, instead of saving souls; and it grieves me to think that my sister's son should be engaged in so unholy a mission as that."

"It is not necessarily unholy, aunt. I can go there, and be very industrious, and very moral, and set all the people there an example of uprightness of conduct; and come back here with a few hundred thousand of the shiners; and what harm have I done to myself or anybody else?"

"You acknowledge, George, that it is a vicious community, by saying that there is great need of missionary labours there. Now, if you go there, you will expose yourself to temptation, to sin, and iniquity in every shape and form; and it is much more probable that you will follow the multitude to do evil, than that the multitude will follow your example to do good. Moreover, if you escape the contaminations of the place, in those few hundred thousand of shiners, as you call them, which you might bring back, there is an onerous weight of the mammon of unrighteousness, sufficient to sink your soul to perdition."

"Everybody, aunt, seems to be trying to collect some of these shiners; how many do you think it safe to possess, so as to keep one's soul out of perdition?"

"It would be safe, George, to possess so much, and no more, than what you would make a good use of. As the quantity increases, so increases the danger of improper use. With the increase of the quantity there is also an increased desire to accumulate, increased affection for that which is accumulated, and increased estrangement of the affections from those things which belong to our everlasting peace."

"Well, aunt, it seems to me that the more I had, the more good I would do with it."

"You may think so, George, now that you are out of the possession of wealth, but the general experience teaches, that its possession contracts rather than expands the desire of doing good."

Their conversation was interrupted by the striking of the clock, which announced the arrival of Miss Priscilla's hour for retiring.

George Preble and Mr. Benson had both obtained the assent of Major and Mrs. Scott to their marriage before Mr. Benson returned to Boston; and George, the day after the conversation in his aunt's room, went over to the Major's, and sought a private opportunity of informing him before his marriage, of his intention to go to California for a few years. He was apprehensive if he delayed making the communication until after he was married, that he might be charged with having taken an undue advantage of his wife's parents. He determined to abandon the idea of going, if their opposition should be so very decided as to put at hazard his marriage with Julia.

"Major Scott," said George, "I am come to inform you of my plans after my union with your daughter. I have, within a few days past, received an invitation from a connexion now residing in California, to come and join him there in a business he represents as being very profitable. He thinks that if I will connect myself with him, and remain in California about five years, that at the end of that time I may return to Virginia a wealthy man. I have mentioned it to Julia, and she says that although it will give her great pain to leave her parents, she would not throw any obstacle in the way of an adventure which might be profitable to myself and family."

"George," said Major Scott, "although it will be as severe a shock to my wife and myself as could possibly come upon us, if, after carefully weighing this matter, you are brought to a positive conviction of its beneficial results to yourself and your family, we must acquiesce, and determine to bear the separation from our daughter with becoming fortitude. I will take this opportunity of informing you of my intended distribution of my property during my life. I have thirty negroes, which I have divided into three lots, in families, one of which is intended for you, one for Mr. Benson, and the other, with my farm, I shall retain for the use of my wife and myself as long as we both live. After our deaths, of course, Mr. Benson and yourself will divide the whole. If you determine, George, to go to California, what will you do with your lot of negroes? you know you can't carry them with you."

"I have thought of that, sir, and if I go, I can't do otherwise than sell them; but I will not sell them out of the county, and shall inhibit the traders from buying, if I should not be able to sell them privately."

"Under such circumstances, George, you must expect to sell them at a sacrifice; but I admire your kind feelings, and shall be reconciled to such a sale as you propose. Mr. Benson is similarly situated, and I presume would sell in the same way."

"Why, sir, if Benson were to carry out his abolition feelings, he would set all his free; but I do not think he will do that; he certainly cannot, with any degree of consistency, refuse to adopt the mode of selling which I propose."

"I should hope not," said the Major; "if he were to sell them, so as to separate members of the same family, it would cause great anguish to my wife and myself."

"If he does that, sir, my opinion of him will be very much changed; I have always thought, however, that this abolition movement did not proceed from real sympathy for slaves, but from a desire for agitation, and from a disposition to meddle with matters that does not at all concern them. This will afford an opportunity of testing Benson's real feelings upon the subject, where his pecuniary interest is to be affected by a true and bona fide exercise of benevolent feelings towards the slave."

Mrs. Scott then came into the room, and was told by the Major of George's contemplated visit to California. She appeared much agitated, but her heart was too full for any expression of dissent, and she employed herself at work, in profound silence. George joined Julia, whom he saw in the garden.

"Well, Julia," he said, "I have broken the ice, and informed your father and mother of my intention to take you to California."

"Have you made up your mind positively to go, George? I thought you would have taken longer time to consider of it."

"I can't say, Julia, that my mind is positively made up and settled, but I think the chances are in favour of our going, particularly as your father seems reconciled to it. I fully appreciate, Julia, the sacrifice which you are willing to make for our mutual benefit, and the return which I feel myself bound to make you for so much confidence, and so ready a desire to consult my wishes, and to act in accordance with them, will be found in an increasing effort on my part to promote your happiness."

"George, I feel very confident that you will make that effort, and I think I shall have a right to claim it, after having made the greatest of all sacrifices I could possibly make to gratify your wishes; exchanging a home endeared to me by the presence of devoted parents, for one in a far distant land, among strangers, where, if reports are true, the prospects for comfort, ease, and happiness, are anything but flattering."

"I have no doubt, Julia, that those prospects are brightening every day, and that we shall spend five years very pleasantly in Francisco."

"It may be so, George, but I shall remain sceptical until experience has taught me otherwise. What do your Aunt Priscilla and Evelina think of your going?"

"Oh, as to that, Aunt Pris thinks that if I go anywhere beyond the reach of her lectures, I'm a doomed man, and Evelina has some little matters of her own to engross her thoughts."

"I thought nothing could divert her thoughts from you, George, for she has always appeared to me to be the most devoted sister I have ever known."

"I believe Lina loves me very sincerely; but you know, Julia, there are two kinds of love; the one a sort of natural feeling, and the other—what shall I call the other, Julia?—an indescribable something, that throws nature all a-back; a little monopolist, ain't it? that shuns the rivalry of nature's—do help me out, Julia, in my awkward description; you know something about it, don't you?"

Julia blushed, and ran into the house.

CHAPTER VII.

DEATH IN A CABIN.

AT the early dawn of a beautiful morning about the middle of May, Dr. Boswell was aroused from his slumbers by Aunt Dinah, who had come to the house to inform him that old Aunt Juno was very ill. He hurriedly dressed himself, and went to Aunt Juno's cabin. He found her apparently without disease, but so much prostrated that he concluded she could not live many hours, as he had no hope of a reaction of her system, in consequence of her extreme old age."

"Do you feel any pain, Aunt Juno?" said the Doctor.

"Juner gwine—Juner gwine—Juner no pain, massy."

"Why do you think you are going if you have no pain?"

"Juner feel so—so bad; massy—Juner sent for."

"Sent for; by whom do you suppose?"

"Juner Farder in hebbin; dat Farder old missy tell Juner 'bout."

"Are you willing to go to your Father in Heaven?"

"Yes, massy, Juner glad—Juner gwine—Juner gwine meet dat Man old missy tell Juner 'bout—say die for Juner—Juner be happy in hebbin—Juner no farder here; no moder here; no broder here; no sisser here."

"But you have kind friends here; haven't you?"

"Yes, massy, missy good; massy good; Robin good;

Dinah good; all good to Juner; but Juner can't 'tay—Juner mus' go, massy."

"I am glad to find, Aunt Juno, that you are willing to go, for I think you will be taken from us in a very short time."

"Tang God, massy—Tang God Juner gwine—Juner no wan' 'tay here."

When the Doctor returned, he found Mrs. Boswell waiting breakfast for him.

"My dear, he observed, I think old Aunt Juno is not long for this world. She seems to be going out like a candle in its socket. I am much pleased to find that she is aware of her situation, and that she is perfectly willing to go. She is a child of God, snatched from heathenism by his grace vouchsafed to the pious labours of my dear mother."

"My dear husband, what a beautiful thought it is that a poor African, once condemned to be eaten by cannibals, should be now on her death-bed, in a Christian country, surrounded by Christian friends, and rejoicing in the assurance of eternal salvation, procured by the death of her Saviour!"

"Yes, my dear, it might carry consolation to the bosom of a Wilberforce, mourning over the horrors of the African slave-trade." After breakfast Mrs. Boswell took her work, and repaired to Aunt Juno's cabin, where she intended to spend the day, provided her lamp of life was not extinguished before the day closed.

"Aunt Juno," she said as she approached her bed, "how are you now?"

"Juner mighty glad see missy 'fore she go'—massy say

can' las' long, missy—Juner never feel so 'fore, missy—Juner cole—Juner heart cole, missy—Juner gwine."

"I am very glad to hear from your master that you are so willing to go, Aunt Juno."

"Missy, Juner can't 'tay here—Juner got no farder here—Juner farder up yonder, missy—Juner glad go to Juner farder—Juner gwine see dat Man die for Juner—Juner see ole missy dar—Juner no wan' 'tay here, missy—can missy ting for Juner?"

"What shall I sing, Aunt Juno?"

"Dat Man, missy—dat Man die for Juner."

"Is it this, Aunt Juno?—'Jesus can make a dying bed.'"

"Dat um, missy, dat um."

Mrs. Boswell sung it for her, and while she was singing, Aunt Juno lay with her eyes closed, and her hands clasped upon her breast. When the hymn was finished, Mrs. Boswell, thinking she was dozing, did not disturb her. In about half an hour she became restless, and Mrs. Boswell asked her some questions, to which she returned no answer. Poor Aunt Juno was speechless. Dinah was sent for the Doctor, who arrived at the cabin just in time to close her eyes in the sleep of death.

The Doctor sent for Robin, and gave orders for a pine coffin. By this time many of the women had assembled at the cabin, and were directed to see the corpse decently laid out, and to remain with it, which last order was unnecessary, as the negroes upon some of the plantations in Virginia, whenever the death of a grown negro occurs, are in the habit of keeping wake, singing hymns as a requiem to the dead.

The next morning the corpse was carried to Uncle Robin's cabin, where several funeral hymns were sung, and an address delivered by a coloured minister of the neighbourhood, from the text, "Blessed are the dead which die in the Lord, from henceforth," &c. After the services were ended, the corpse was carried to the plantation burial-ground; and in the grave of Aunt Juno was mingled the dust of two continents.

The gloom and melancholy which pervaded the mansion house at Selma, that afternoon, was broken in upon by the arrival of Mr. Frazer; and it was fortunate for Mrs. Boswell that she had retired to her chamber, as her presence would not have restrained a person always so anxious to retail news as he was, from making to the Doctor a communication which was calculated to give her much pain.

"Doctor," said he, "I have a message for you from old Mr. Crosby, whom I saw to-day as I passed the poor-house. The old man made me promise to deliver it this very afternoon. He says that he was told by Mr. Brock, who lived a short time with Mr. Stephens, that his children are dreadfully abused there; that he himself got several hickory switches for Mrs. Stephens, and that she *does* lay on upon them at a *powerful* rate; that you promised him they should be well treated; and that it is, moreover, your duty as overseer of the poor, to see that they are not abused. He says, if you don't put a stop to it, that he will go to the court-house, if he has to walk, and employ a lawyer to make complaint to the court, and petition that they shall be taken away from Mr. Stephens, and bound to some one who will treat them better."

"Well, Mr. Frazer," said the Doctor, "you can tell Mr.

Crosby that I will inquire into this matter; and, if his children have been badly treated, I will prevent its happening again."

"Doctor, how is it that abolitionists have so much affection for black people, and are so cruel to whites, when they have anything to do with them?"

"Is that the case, Mr. Frazer?"

"Certainly it is, sir, when the black people don't belong to them; but when they get to owning slaves, they are cruel enough to *them*, too. There's old Mr. Preble whips more in six months than you would do all your lifetime."

"It is very unaccountable, if it is as you say it is, Mr. Frazer."

"My dear Doctor, there's no doubt of it. I've known several Yankees to own slaves, and to be the cruellest masters agoing: and show me negroes under a Yankee overseer, and I'll show you scars enough."

"Doctor," he continued, "ain't it a pity that old Mr. Preble should refuse to let his daughter marry that nice parson, Mr. Grattan? they say it's all off."

"I have neither heard that it was off, or on," said the Doctor.

"Ah! Doctor, you don't live at a public place like the cross-roads. People are always stopping there and telling me things that I dont care about hearing. It's strange what a propensity some people have of talking about other people's matters; they come to my house sometimes, sir, so full of neighbourhood news, that if I didn't listen to them, and let them out with it, I do believe they'd almost burst."

"Some people have that propensity, Mr. Frazer, in a very high degree, and seem to be not conscious of it."

"Just so, sir, just so! I've seen people, before now, who gossip about everything in the world, and blame their neighbours for doing the same thing. It seems strange that people shouldn't know themselves better. Oh! Doctor, I'd like to have forgot,—did you hear that there are to be two weddings over at Major Scott's, in about ten days? George Preble is to marry one of the young ladies, and a Yankee from Boston the other."

"Yes, I did hear something of that, Mr. Frazer."

"Well, now, sir, if *I* were the Major, I wouldn't let *my* daughter marry a Yankee, anyhow. And there's Tom Roach's daughter, they say, is going to marry a man who will carry her off to Florida. Parents who let their children go so far off, can't have the same affection for them that *I* have for *my* daughters. When *they* get old enough to be married, I'll let these foreigners know they must keep away from *my* house."

Mr. Frazer, finding but little encouragement in the Doctor's manner for him to go on, took his leave.

The case of the young Crosbys, presented to the Doctor by the message from the old man, was the most difficult and perplexing that he had ever had under consideration. He felt great reluctance to mention it, either to his wife, her father, or her mother, and yet his duty required that something should be done, and done immediately, to prevent a public exposure of the cruelty of his mother-in-law, consequent upon an application to the court for removing those children. He determined, however, that he would consult with Mrs. Boswell on the subject, as her assistance would be necessary in any approach to the old lady by way of remonstrance. He immediately went into her chamber, and proposed a walk over to Fredonia. Mrs. Boswell was always ready for a vist to her parents, whom she loved with an ardent affection, although she was not blind to the disagreeable traits of her mother's character.

"My dear," said he, when on their way to Fredonia, "I have received a message from old Mr. Crosby, about your mother's ill treatment of his children; and he threatens, if she does not treat them better, he will petition the court to take them away. I am very much at a loss to know what course to pursue. What do you think had best be done?"

"Doctor, we should, in the first place, endeavour to ascertain, with certainty, whether they have been badly treated, and if so, I should not hesitate to remonstrate with mamma, tell her of Mr. Crosby's determination, and point out the disgrace it would bring upon us all to have a public exposure."

"But how can it be ascertained, my dear, whether there is truth in Brock's statement?"

"If there is any truth in his statement that they are severely whipped with hickories, they must certainly have marks upon them; and if I can possibly get an opportunity, I will examine Sally, and you do the same with John. It will be a very disagreeable business even to let the children know we suspect such a thing; but the necessity of the case requires some action on your part, and I can think of no other mode of proceeding."

"My mind can suggest no other, my dear. If an opportunity offers, we will make the examination, and if we find that they are not scarred, we will say nothing to your mamma about it; and if they are, we will postpone until to-morrow, saying *anything* to her."

Mrs. Stephens met them very kindly, and carried them into her chamber. Sally was employed at her knitting, and John rubbing the furniture.

"Mamma," said Mrs. Boswell, "did you hear of the death of old Aunt Juno?"

"Yes, my dear, I heard of the poor old creature's death."

"Oh! mamma, I wish you could have witnessed her triumphant death. She was not only willing, but anxious to go; and seemed to have an assurance that she was going to heaven to be happy."

"Poor creatures! it is well they can find a resting-place at last. Their trials in this world are heart-rending, but the Lord will reward them in the next, where they will be exalted far above those who are their oppressors here."

Dr. Boswell and his wife exchanged looks, but neither of them spoke. It was unnecessary for them to make a close examination of John and Sally. It was too evident, from the marks of the lash upon their faces and hands, that Brock's statement was true.

"Mamma," said Mrs. Boswell, "have you ever seen a native African?"

"No, my child, and I hope I never may. The very idea of their being forced away from their parents and friends, and brought to this country and sold to cruel masters, makes me shudder. The Lord will take vengeance upon people who do such things."

"Well, mamma, I am no advocate for the African slave-trade, but it does seem to me that it was infinitely better for Aunt Juno to be brought here and taught the Christian religion, than to have remained in Africa to be eaten by cannibals."

"I had much rather, child, be eaten by cannibals than be a slave."

"Rather be eaten by cannibals! mamma, and not know what will become of you after death, than be a Christian slave, and know that when you die you will go to heaven, and there be happy for ever with your Saviour?"

"My child, do not talk to me any more about those matters. You know I detest and abhor slavery, and that I never can speak of it with any degree of composure."

"Mamma, I fear I have been remiss in my duty in not speaking more to you on that subject than I have; your happiness here depends upon your rightly understanding the nature of slavery as it exists in Virginia. You have come here to live with us, with prejudices founded upon very erroneous notions as to what slavery really is, without examining into it, and judging for yourself since you have been in Virginia. You have given yourself up to a fixed idea, attached to the word only, without any apparent wish on your part to divest yourself of that idea, or to see whether it is correct, and sustained by an acquaintance with the workings and incidents of the relation of master and slave. In Pennsylvania you were surrounded by persons who had imbibed the same false views that you have. In your circle there of connexions and friends, there is a sympathy in common for the situation of those persons whom you call, 'poor creatures,' and an expression of such feelings of sympathy was met by corresponding feelings.

"Here, however, it is different. You stand alone upon that subject, you meet with no corresponding sympathy; if it is indulged by you, it must prey upon your own mind alone, and will be a source of constant inquietude. I have no doubt, mamma, that your removal from our house in consequence of indulgence of that sympathy, has already occasioned you much vexation. You left *there* servants who had been well trained to the performance of the duties assigned them; perfectly satisfied and happy in their condition, willing to administer to your every comfort; and you have come to this house to be waited upon by two individuals, who, for the time that you have them, are as much in a state of bondage as our negroes; who are entirely unacquainted with the performance of the services you require of them, and whose awkwardness, and perhaps obstinacy, must be a source of unceasing vexation.

'You must excuse me, my dear mamma, for saying that I discover evidences of that vexation upon the persons of those children. With all filial reverence and affection, my dear mamma, I would put this question to you: who is most censurable, he who holds slaves for life, who treats them as friends, furnishes them with all things necessary for their comfort, is lenient towards them for faults common to all human beings; or he who holds white persons in a state of bondage for a term of years (children taken away from fond parents), and corrects them severely for every positive offence, and even for every exhibition of awkwardness.

"Mamma, I am forced by circumstances to speak plainly to you upon this subject. By hiring white men to work for you, you have subjected all the occurrences in your family to be exposed to this whole community, perhaps with much exaggeration. The man papa hired to work with him, and who has left him, not with the most friendly feelings, has circulated throughout the neighbourhood, that you were excessively cruel to the two little Crosbys, which report has reached the ears of their parents, and the old man threatens a public exposure, by applying to the Court to take them away from you." (It is proper to mention here, that before those remarks were made by Mrs. Boswell, the young Crosbys had been sent out of the room on some errand, by the old lady.)

"My dear," said Mrs. Stephens, "I only wish I never had come to Virginia. Here I am avoiding all sort of connexion with what they call their peculiar institution; and because I take white people to work for me, and correct them when they deserve it, my name is carried high among them, and I am called a tyrant. The truth of the matter is, they do not wish anybody whipped but slaves. I wonder, if a master was to whip one of those *poor creatures* to death, if half the notice would be taken of it, that is taken of the little necessary whipping I give John and Sally?

"Ann, I must get your father to carry me back to Pennsylvania. I can't stand Virginia any longer. As long as I do stay, however, I will keep John and Sally, and correct them whenever I think they deserve it; and if old Mr. Crosby thinks he can take them away from us, he is very much mistaken. The indentures are signed, and they are our property until the time runs out. As to your saying, Ann, that by hiring white servants we expose to the public whatever happens in our families, is not the master subject to the same exposure from his slaves? When those *poor creatures* have a chance to get away from home, they have plenty of tales of woe to communicate to those they meet with abroad."

"There, mamma, you are entirely mistaken. The slaves generally love their masters, and I am told that the reputation of the master is as dear to the slave as his own, and that he will defend his master, his mistress, or their children, whenever anything bad is said about them."

"You say, Ann, I have got nobody here to join me in sympathy for those *poor creatures*. There's old Mr. Preble, a good, benevolent old man, who thinks and feels exactly as I do."

"Mamma, you are just as much mistaken in that, as you are in a good many other things. Mr. Preble talks a great deal about the evils of slavery, but would you believe that Mr. Preble owns slaves himself?"

"I never would have believed, from Mr. Preble's conversation, that he owned a slave; but I suppose being here, and being surrounded by them, he is obliged to own them in self-defence."

"Mamma, I wish with all my heart you would adopt that mode of self-defence; I think it just as necessary for you, as it ever was for Mr. Preble. But I could not seriously advise you to that course either; for if anti-slavery views are formed upon principle, and are a matter of conscience, I would never advise a departure from them from mere expediency."

"You needn't fear, Ann, my adopting that course; I wouldn't be a slave-holder for the universe."

Mr. Stephens, whose labours had ceased for a time in consequence of his corn-planting being over, had rode out that afternoon, returned, and come into the room just as Mrs. Stephens made the last reply to her daughter.

"Indeed, my dear," he said, "I am sorry to hear you

make that remark, for I had hoped those notions of yours were giving way. I entertained them to some extent when we left Pennsylvania, but I must confess my views of slavery are somewhat changed since I have seen what it really is."

"You men, Mr. Stephens," replied his wife, "are as changeable as weathercocks. The fact is, you have no fixed principles upon any subject. I suppose working with this *poor creature*, Billy, has converted you. If I had had my way, Billy never should have come here to work." She then left the room.

The Doctor and Mrs. Boswell looked with astonishment at each other, supposing, as they had done, that Billy's working there would be kept secret from the old lady.

"How did you like Billy, Mr. Stephens?" said the Doctor.

"Why, Doctor, "I never have worked with any hand who pleased me more than Billy; he did his work well, was constantly in place, and seemed always cheerful and good-humoured."

"I did not expect you to send him homo after you had done planting; you can have him again at any time that you may want him."

"I've been to the cross-roads, Doctor, to get Frazer to do a little work for me. What a great talker he is! he told me more news than I have heard before since I have been in Virginia. He said he had seen you this afternoon."

"Yes, he was at my house just before we left home. You could not have been long with him."

"Not more than a half-hour, but you know he could tell a good deal in that time."

"Did he tell you, Mr. Stephens, what carried him to my house?"

"Yes; he said he had carried you a message from old Mr. Crosby, and I was very sorry to hear, Doctor, that that fellow Brock has been telling tales about my family."

"Indeed, Mr. Stephens, I am very much concerned at it, especially as old Crosby looks to me for redress of the grievances he complains of. I told Ann, and she has told her mother. We both thought something should be done at once to keep the man quiet. Mrs. Stephens seems to think that he can do nothing, although he should apply to the court, as they are regularly bound by indenture; but she is mistaken. The court can, for good cause shown, cancel the indenture and bind them to others. If the treatment complained of is not repeated, however, the thing will drop, and we shall hear no more about it. I wish you would endeavour, Mr. Stephens, to prevent a repetition of it."

"I will, Doctor, certainly; and I think I may say there will be no more complaints about severe treatment."

"I sincerely hope there may not," said the Doctor.

"My dear," said he (as they were going home), "you were rather more hasty in your communication to your mother than was agreed upon."

"Well, my dear husband, when I had gone as far as I did in my advice to her, I thought it a very good opportunity to tell her what we had heard. I hope you don't think I have done wrong."

"No, my dear, I think you have done perfectly right; and what you said about slavery and abolition sympathy was most admirable. Although she expressed an unwillingness to alter her conduct towards those children, I cannot help thinking that what you said, and what your father may do, will prevent a repetition of the severity with which those children have been treated. My mind is certainly much less disturbed than it was. I will venture to predict, Ann, that in less than six months from this time, your mother will have given up all those notions, and that your father will own slaves himself."

When they arrived at home, it was quite dark. Mrs. Boswell went into the house, the Doctor remaining in the portico to see some person he could distinguish a few yards off approaching him.

"Your servant, massa," said a spruce young negro man.

"Well, my man, who do you belong to?"

"I belongs to Major Scott, sir; my name's George, sir."

"What's your will and pleasure, George?"

"Massa, I'm most shame' to tell you, sir, what I come for."

"Out with it, George; let me hear what you have to say."

"Massa, sir, you got a gal name' Cecilia, sir. Now, sir, I dun 'tain de 'fection of Cecilia, and she dun 'tain my 'fection, sir; and I want your 'probation, sir, to our bein' man and wife, sir."

"Ah! it's a love matter, is it, George? Well, Cecilia is in the gift of my wife. If she consents, George, and you will bring me a note from your master, giving his assent and saying that you are a good character, George, I will consent to it, too.

"Ann, my dear, come here." When she reached the

portico, the Doctor said, "Here is a young gentleman come to ask your consent to a marriage between your maid Cecilia and himself."

"Doctor, if you are willing, and Cecilia is willing, I shall not object, certainly."

"George, I have told you the terms upon which you get my consent."

"I'll be here to-morrow night, sir, with a note from masser, sir."

"When do you think of having the knot tied, George?"

"The night of de fus' day of June, sir."

"That is the very same night that your young mistresses are to be married; and as Mr. Grattan will be engaged for that night, you must get Parson Peter to come and tie the knot, George."

"Yes, massa, dat's what I 'tend to do, sir. Missis, I's ten thousand times obliged to you, madam; an' so also to you, massa."

George returned the next night with a note from his master, in which he gives him a very good character, and consents to his being married. As the wedding-day approached, there was much gossipping in the neighbourhood as to the splendid preparations which were being made for it. Old Mr. Frazer stopped everybody who passed the cross-roads, to tell what he had heard of the immense cost of the wedding garments, all of which were to be made in Baltimore; of the large amount of the confectioner's bill; of the costly addition to the furniture, and of the various other items of expenditure; of the beautiful presents which had already been sent to the intended brides; that the girls in the neighbourhood all intended to set their caps for the Boston beaux who were expected on with Mr. Benson; that Major Scott was going to give the Yankee ten negroes, and he wondered what he would do with them; that George Preble was going to California, and he wondered what he would do with his negroes; that Mrs. Scott, notwithstanding the great preparations, was almost broken-hearted at the thought of being separated from her daughters; that old Mr. Stephens, not being able to get white people to live with him, was working some of Dr. Boswell's slaves. After emptying his budget, as far as the patience of his listeners would allow, he would conclude by saying, "'Tis astonishing how people will talk of other people's matters! if I was to listen to half they have to tell, when they stop here, I should find but little time to work."

Mrs. Boswell, too, was making preparations for a wedding. Cecilia was a great favourite with her, and she determined that her wedding should at least equal any that report had given her from the annals of negro matrimony. In looking over her wardrobe, she selected her second day's wedding-dress for Cecilia to be married in, reserving her bridal dress for the wedding at Major Scott's. Cecilia would have fallen heir to that, if her wedding could have been postponed but one day longer. Aunt Dinah, Cecilia's mother, was furnished flour, sugar, butter, and eggs, to make a very large pound cake, and with a beautiful wreath of artificial flowers to decorate it. Dr. Boswell's contribution was two hams of bacon and a pig. The poultry was furnished by Aunt Dinah herself. With a little fixing by Mrs. Boswell, the dress was adjusted to Cecilia's dimensions, and pronounced a good fit.

"How do you like it, Cecilia?" asked her mistress.

"Oh, missis, I mighty 'bliged to you, madam; I likes it monstrous well; I's sure I never seed black folks hav' sich a dress as dis, madam, before."

"I am afraid you will be too fine for George, Cecilia."

"George tell me, madam, he got mighty fine suit, madam; Masser George gin him mighty nice coat, almos' new; Missis Scott gin him mighty nice pair pantaloons, dat Major Scott hadn' war much, and Miss Julia mak' him a fus' rate wes'co't wid her own hands, madam."

"I did not suppose Miss Julia could have found time to make up clothes for George, when she has so much to do for herself."

"Oh! as to dat, madam, Miss Julia, and Miss Amelia, too, had der things made up in Baltimo', an' dey been had one millinery dar for weeks, fixin' little things, madam. Missis, George tell me, madam, dat when I married I must 'bey him, as I promised to 'bey him, and he say de Scriptur' say wife mus' 'bey she husban'. A'n't I got to 'bey masser, and not George, missis? I's sure I hearn 'em say dat the Scriptur' say we can't 'bey two massers."

"You will have to obey three masters, Cecilia, instead of one or two, and I must try and explain this matter to you. In the first place, you must obey God (who is your Heavenly Master) above all others. Whatever He tells you to do in his word, you must do. He tells you that you must pray to him, and if your earthly master was to tell you not to pray to God, you are bound to obey God rather than man, and you could pray in secret, and your master here could not prevent it if he wished; but your master here never will wish you to disobey your Master in heaven. There are a great many things for you to do, about which your Master in heaven is silent, and gives no instruction. In every one of those things you must obey your master upon earth. So it is, if your husband was to tell you to do, or to leave undone, what your earthly master had ordered you to do, or not to do, you are bound to obey your earthly master, and not your husband. When your husband tells you, however, to do something which is not forbidden by your Master in heaven, and is not forbidden by your earthly master, and is not contrary to his interest, you are then bound to obey your husband.

"I am confident, from the character we have of George, that he would not give you an order to do anything contrary to the wish and orders of your heavenly and earthly masters. We are told in Scripture that we cannot *serve* two masters; we cannot serve God and Mammon. The meaning of that is, we cannot serve God, by loving him, obeying him, and worshipping him as he wishes us to do, and at the same time serve the world by loving it, and indulging in its sinful practices; because when you love and serve one, you must of course despise and not serve the other. Do you think you understand what I have said, Cecilia?"

"Yes, missis, when George wan' me to do what God don' wan' me to do, and what masser don' wan' me to do, I musn' 'bey George."

"That is a very good understanding of it, Cecilia."

CHAPTER VIII.

THE WEDDINGS.

The morning of the wedding-day Robin came to the house to see his master. The Doctor saw in his countenance some indication of uneasiness of mind, and said,

"What's the matter now, Robin?"

"Masser, you know dey gwine have a weddin' here, to-night, and I's bin told, sir, Major Scott George has 'gaged a fiddler, and dat dey gwine hav' dancin', and I coms to see if you 'lows sich thing 'pon dis plantation, sir."

"Why, Robin, weddings don't occur often, you know, and if they choose to have a little dance, and conduct it well, I don't think it worth while to object to it."

"Well, masser, if *you* willin', nobody else has any right to objec', sir. I thought it was my business to let you know, sir, dey are to be married in my cabin, sir, but I would hate mighty for dem to dance dar, sir. My ole missis had dat big room in my cabin, sir, 'secrated to de worship of God, an' I don' want it 'filed, sir, by de foot of de dancess."

"Robin, you are perfectly right, there; you must tell them from me, that they are not to dance in your cabin. After the ceremony is over, they must go to Dinah's room and dance, if they are determined to have dancing."

"Dinah say, sir, de supper is to be set in her room, and dey can' dance dar."

"There will be a moon, to-night, and it will be very mild: they might have the supper-table set out in the yard. They may make what arrangements they please, but to dance in your cabin, that they must not do. I am going from home, Robin, and shall probably not be back until very late. You must sit up until this wedding-party has cleared out, and see that nothing goes amiss, Robin, in my absence."

"I'll do so, masser, certainly, but I's sorry you gwine from home, masser, when der will be sich a crowd of strange niggers here, sir. I can't be wid um nother, as I doesn' go whar dar's dancin' an' fiddlin'."

"Well, I don't mean that you shall join them, Robin; but if they know that you are up, they will be more apt to keep order."

"I sha'n't lay my head 'pon my piller, 'til you come back, masser."

The invitations were for seven o'clock. The Doctor and Mrs. Boswell left home at six. When they arrived, they found a large company assembled and waiting for them to witness the ceremony. Every countenance beamed with joy, except those of the entertainers. Upon that of Major Scott there was a deep, settled gloom; Mrs. Scott was sitting alone in a corner of the room, a perfect picture of Niobe. The brides and grooms, maids and groomsmen, took their stand about the middle of the room, and Mr. Grattan, in a solemn and impressive manner, went through the Episcopal form. After the greetings and introductions were over, Dr. Boswell found himself seated by a young gentleman to whom he had been previously introduced as a Mr. Hicks, from Boston.

"I have seen, to-night, Doctor," said Mr. Hicks, "what I have never witnessed before."

"Ah! what's that, sir?" said the Doctor.

"The marriage, sir, of two couples at the same time."

"It very rarely happens, Mr. Hicks. I don't recollect ever to have seen it myself."

"I guess, Doctor, I shall see many strange things before I get back home."

"Very probably you will, sir. In a journey of several hundred miles we must expect to meet with sights not familiar. I hope, sir, what you have seen of Virginia, has at least come up to your expectations."

"Why, sir, I have seen but little of Virginia as yet. The travelling is now so rapid, that a person can form no opinion, even of the fertility of the country through which he passes. I am very much pleased with the appearance of this valley as far as I have seen it."

"The country immediately about here, sir, is not a fair sample of the valley as an agricultural country. Between this and the Potomac river we have as fine a country as is to be met with anywhere. There are some portions of the western country, I suppose, much more fertile than any part of our valley; but, taking other things into consideration, there is not, anywhere, a more desirable country to live in than this valley of ours."

"There is one thing, Doctor, which is a great drawback to your country, and would be to any country—I mean slavery."

"I knew very well what you meant, Mr. Hicks; for

Northern people never let us pass without a brush upon that subject, and it is one upon which the North and South differ so widely, that it is hardly worth while, at this day, to enter upon anything like controversy in regard to it."

"I thought the Southern people were always ready and willing (if not able) to uphold their opinions in relation to their peculiar institution, by argument."

"They are undoubtedly able, Mr. Hicks, to uphold and sustain their opinions by undeniable positions, but they consider it perfectly useless to attack prejudices which are held to with a pertinacity which no argument, be it ever so cogent, can upset."

"I think I can prove to any reasonable being, Doctor, that your slavery institution is contrary to Scripture, and contrary to humanity."

"Indeed, Mr. Hicks, I have no desire to enter into an argument, for after it was finished, we should both think precisely as we do now. Suppose we join the ladies, and have some chat with them more appropriate to the occasion?"

"Before we move, Doctor, tell me what interesting-looking young lady that is, in such close conversation with the Parson."

"That, sir, is Miss Evelina Preble, the sister of the young gentleman who was married to-night. I had supposed you had been introduced to all the ladies."

"Not to her, sir. I should be very much pleased with an introduction."

"If you will follow me, I will introduce you, with pleasure."

"An old adage, Miss Preble," said he, after introduction, "says that one wedding makes many; and I suppose that two coming together make *very* many."

"I don't know that there is any truth in that adage, Mr. Hicks; but if there is, I suppose the circumstances (whatever they are) which produce that result from one wedding, are not increased by two happening together."

"I suppose, sir (addressing himself to Mr. Grattan), if many or few should follow this double one, that the minister always holds himself in readiness to act his part?"

"Yes, sir," said Mr. Grattan, "the minister considers himself in the line of duty when performing the marriage ceremony, and it is a duty which falls in with his inclination, to assist in contributing to the happiness of others."

"I am glad to find that the young ladies of Virginia have no particular objection to going North. The success of my friend Benson is certainly encouraging to Northern enterprise in those matters. Who knows, Mr. Grattan, but that some time or other I may have use for your services? I suppose I could command them at any time, sir?"

"Why—why—yes, to be sure, sir, if—if any other lady of Virginia wishes to get—to go to Boston, sir, and calls for my services, why, they will be rendered, sir."

Mr. Grattan spoke this with a flutter of feeling which can be ascribed to no other cause than a sudden recollection of old Mr. Preble's opposition. He had, moreover, heard, that this Mr. Hicks was the son of a very wealthy merchant in Boston. He had no mistrust, however, of the affection of Evelina, but the thought of the old man's objection, added to his great fondness for wealth, caused a momentary rush of feeling of uneasiness, tinctured with a spice of jealousy. Fortunately he was relieved from the embarrassment produced by that feeling, by being thrown into another, less painful.

Mr. George Preble came over from another part of the room, and told him that he had been deputed by his wife and Miss Eliza McKnight, to inquire whether a little family dance, for the amusement of the young people, would be disagreeable to him.

"What do your father and mother-in-law think of it, George?" said Mr. Grattan.

"We have not mentioned it to them, sir; we thought it would be best to obtain your consent first, and to mention it to them afterwards."

"I have no consent to give or withhold, George; if the Major and Mrs. Scott are willing, and a dance is gotten up, I cannot consent to remain here and witness it, but will have my horse brought out, and go home."

"Ah! well, that settles the matter, Mr. Grattan; we can never agree that you should be driven off, to give us an opportunity for dancing."

"Girls," said Evelina, as she joined the party who had sent George to Mr. Grattan, "how could you do so cruel a thing, as to force Mr. Grattan either to go away, or to object to your dancing? Julia, you must have known that your mother would not consent to have dancing in her house; a member of the church to have dancing!"

"I am sure," said Miss Eliza McKnight, "I would not care if Mr. Grattan was to go away. I think it very unkind in him, to prevent our having a little innocent amusement. I never did like, at a party, to sit prim, with my hands before me, and hear nothing but nonsensical talk."

"I guess you won't have any dancing here, to-night, miss," said Mr. Hicks, who had followed Evelina; "I think very hard of the parson myself, for preventing it; but I can't think, Miss McKnight, that you will be subjected to nonsensical talking, here, where there are assembled so many of the elite of Virginia."

"People who have nothing to do but talk, sir, must say a good many foolish things, and then they are apt to make ill-natured remarks about each other's appearance and dress, &c. I wonder if it wouldn't be a more innocent amusement to dance, than to be talking slander, and gossipping in every way?"

"That is not the necessary substitute for dancing, Eliza," said Evelina; "we may carry on amusing, innocent, and edifying conversations. I don't think it follows at all, that because we don't dance we must be talking nonsense and slander."

"*You* may say so, Evelina, because I suppose, of course, you are much amused and edified by the conversation of the Rev. Mr. Grattan."

A crimson blush came over the face of Evelina.

"In my own name, and that of the other gentlemen present," said Mr. Hicks, "I must return thanks to Miss McKnight for the compliment which she in her last remark has paid us, selecting the Rev. Mr. Grattan as the only gentleman in the room whose conversation would be amusing and edifying."

"Indeed, Mr. Hicks, I did not mean that; I meant nothing more than that the conversation of Mr. Grattan would be particularly pleasing and edifying to Miss Evelina Preble. How could you suppose that I meant to cast reflections upon a stranger, whose style of conversation may be both amusing and edifying for aught I know?"

"You have at least, miss, cramped the ease of my conversation, as I shall hereafter be under continual apprehension, lest my remarks should neither give pleasure or edification to Miss Eliza McKnight."

"Oh! sir, you may be as easy as you please, and throw away all apprehension; I'll promise you, sir, to be both amused and edified."

Evelina had gone over to another part of the room, to pay her respects to Mr. and Mrs. Benson, who were sitting together on a sofa.

"That's a very sweet, interesting young lady, Miss McKnight," said Mr. Hicks.

"Do you think her a beauty, sir?"

"She is decidedly very pretty, and I may say she is a beauty; a more intelligent countenance I never beheld."

"I never could think Evelina a beauty; there's something about her which prevents her being a beauty in my eyes. Mr. Grattan no doubt thinks her as beautiful as you do; report says there's a mutual attachment, if not engagement, between them."

"Do you think that report true, miss?" said he, with earnestness.

"I can't say, Mr. Hicks, that it is positively so; but I should think there was good ground for the report. Whenever I have met them in company, they seem to have no conversation for anybody but each other. Whenever you see a young gentleman and lady, upon all occasions, separate themselves from the rest of the company, and carry on long conversations in an undertone, you may be sure there is a good understanding between them."

"That would generally be the conclusion; but in this instance, he being a parson in the neighbourhood, may think it his duty to give instruction to the young members of his congregation; and after Miss Evelina is sufficiently taught, he may select some other one of you for his sofa lectures."

"Indeed, sir, they are not talking about religion all that time, you may depend."

"The parson will be a lucky man, I should think, if he gets that young lady." Miss Eliza McKnight was somewhat disconcerted; and, as the conversation of Mr. Hicks was not very edifying, and by no means very agreeable, she left him. Mr. Hicks sought out Miss Evelina, and found her in conversation with Mrs. Benson. Mr. Benson was on the sofa with them, but not joining in conversation. His thoughts seemed to have gone back to Boston, and he might have been at that moment in his counting-room, surrounded by day-books, ledgers, and invoices. As Mr. Hicks approached, he heard Mrs. Benson tell Evelina that her mammy was going to Boston with her. He looked surprised, for he had never heard the word mammy used in any other sense than as a real mother, and this was the first intimation he had that Mrs. Scott was going to Boston with her daughter.

"I am very much delighted, cousin," he said, "to hear that we shall have the pleasure of your mother's company in Boston."

"Why, my dear cousin, I didn't mean mamma; I meant my old Mammy Betty, a black woman who nursed me, and is so much attached to me that she would not be separated from me for anything in the world; and I would not leave her for anything you could give me."

"I am very much astonished to hear, cousin, that you call an old black woman mammy, and particularly that you are so reluctant to part with her. I thought you Virginians were parting with them every day to traders."

"We never in that way part with our mammies, Mr. Hicks," said Evelina; "and, indeed, we very seldom ever sell to traders any but those who have been made dissatisfied with their situation, and have been induced by the persuasions of abolitionists to leave their masters and fly to the free states. When those are caught and brought back, they are always sold to traders."

"And what will you do, cousin, with your Mammy Betty, when you get her to Boston? You know she will be free then, and they won't let her stay with you a day after you get there. She will be so fond of liberty, she'll leave you directly; and besides I know cousin, here," pointing to Mr. Benson, "won't like to hear his wife call an old black woman mammy."

"When my mammy gets to Boston, sir, she will be free, I know, and she will do for us what little work we will require of her on wages, and I know that all the people in Boston can't persuade her to leave me, sir. Your cousin and myself have talked over this matter, and it's all settled before this, cousin. If my mammy loves me, and I love my mammy, I don't care about the people of Boston laughing at me. The people of Boston had better mind their own business, and let me and my mammy alone; don't you think so, Mr. Benson?"

"My dear, I was just thinking about Boston at that moment—yes, certainly—certainly."

Mr. Hicks took a seat upon the sofa by the side of Miss Evelina, who caught the eye of Mr. Grattan whenever she looked towards the corner, where Mrs. Scott was sitting, he having taken a seat beside the latter.

"Have you a mammy too, Miss Preble?" asked Mr. Hicks.

"Yes, sir, in almost every family in Virginia, where there are slaves, there is some motherly old negro woman who has had the care of the children when they were young, who is very much attached to them, and they to her, and they all call her mammy. Those old negro women are generally very respectable, and sometimes religious. They have very good ideas of propriety of conduct, and are attentive to the behaviour of the younger children. There is always some one of the family of children that this old mammy has had more to do with, or more trouble with than with the others, and that one becomes her pet. Mammy Betty's pet is Amelia; my brother George is the pet of my old Mammy Phillis, and if he goes to California (as he talks of doing), nothing can stop her from going with him."

"I had no idea, Miss Preble, that those feelings of affection which you talked of, existed between slaves and their owners. I have always understood that the relation of master and slave was one of cruelty and oppression on one side, and of hatred, and a constant desire to escape from servitude, on the other."

"Your Northern prejudices against the South, sir, are all founded in error. A large number of those who are called abolitionists, have been made so by false representations of Southern barbarity. Those persons from the North who come here to reside (and in the present day there are not a few of them), have those prejudices removed; for I have heard many of them declare that slavery was a very different thing from what they expected to find it; and very many of those who take up their residence here for life, become slave-owners. Your essayists and novelists, Mr. Hicks, do great injustice to the South by horrid statements of Southern cruelty, having no resemblance to truth."

Before Mr. Hicks could make any reply, a young groomsman who had waited with Evelina, came up and claimed his right to conduct her to the supper-table, to which the company had been just then invited.

The pen of an Anacharsis would be at fault in a description of the delicacies of that board.

After supper, the company returned to the parlour, and Mr. Grattan sought, and soon found an opportunity of conversing with Evelina.

"I should judge," said he, "that your new acquaintance from Boston was quite an agreeable companion, from the length and earnestness of your conversation with him before supper."

"Why, to tell you the truth," she replied, "I had at first conceived for him dislike, bordering on disgust; but upon further acquaintance, I found him more tolerable than I had at first expected. The last part of our conversation was upon a subject which the Yankees never fail to introduce; our slavery at the south; which I endeavoured to defend from the aspersions of abolitionists. I should not think, however, that Mr. Hicks was a thorough-going abolitionist."

"I presume you like him the more for that?"

"Yes, sir, I suppose that helped to remove my prejudices."

"A few more conversations might develop still further excellencies, perhaps." This last remark was accompanied by a manner and look so different from any Miss Evelina had before seen from Mr. Grattan, that she was confounded and hurt.

"I don't know, sir, that I shall ever again have a conversation with him, as I suppose, now that the wedding is over, he will be returning to Boston in a few days. I left Aunt Priscilla very unwell, and I shall return home to-night."

"Not alone, I hope, Miss Evelina? Perhaps you have engaged an escort? If not, would you accept one?"

"I am under great obligations to you, sir, but I have engaged my father as an escort."

"I had really forgotten for the moment that your father was here."

"I had not, sir; and therefore have engaged no other escort."

"A young lady, Miss Evelina, can have no better escort than her father."

"And generally speaking, sir, no better adviser."

Mrs. Boswell advanced towards them, and said, "Where in the world have you kept yourself to-night, Evelina? I don't think we have been in speaking distance before."

"You have been so surrounded, Mrs. Boswell, that I could never get near you."

"Perhaps, madam," said Mr. Grattan, "Miss Evelina derives more pleasure from the company of new acquaintances than from old."

"I think I know Evelina too well, Mr. Grattan, to suppose that she would desert such old acquaintances as you and I, for any new ones she might meet with. I have myself trumped up a new acquaintance to-night, in this Mr. Hicks, from Boston, and I can't say there is much pleasure to be derived from his conversation. Have you been introduced to him, Evelina?"

"Yes, madam, I had an introduction to him a short time after the ceremony was over."

"If you had any conversation with him, Evelina, you must have found him very insipid."

"I did have a conversation with him, Mrs. Boswell, which was somewhat interesting, because it gave me an opportunity of speaking my mind very freely about the abolitionists."

"I think you said, Miss Evelina," remarked Mr. Grattan, "that he was no abolitionist himself; therefore I suppose your invective was not intended for him?"

"Certainly not, sir; as I do not look upon him as an abolitionist."

"Well, Evelina," said Mrs. Boswell, "I think he is a good deal tinctured with abolitionism, as slavery was the subject of our conversation, introduced, too, by himself. The Doctor told me, just now, that he thought so."

"It is very possible, madam, that Mr. Hicks may have expressed himself differently when in conversation with the Doctor and yourself, from what he said to me. Very true, he did enumerate some of the evils he said he had heard belonged to slavery, but he did not say, that in his opinion those evils did exist. He may, however, be an abolitionist, and I may have been too charitable in my conclusions, drawn from what he said."

"Your charity is certainly very commendable, Miss Evelina," said Mr. Grattan.

"What are you talking about, here?" said George, as he approached them. "Lina, papa wishes to see you over yonder (pointing to the opposite side of the room). Mr. Grattan," continued George, "did you ever see a more perfect picture of 'patience on a monument,' than my old chum, Benson? He is the most plodding genius you ever saw—look at him—he is making calculations at this very time, of the probable success or failure of some of his adventures. I'll go and tell him how shameful it is for a newly married man to put on such looks of abstraction." He went to the sofa where Mr. Benson was sitting.

"Why, Bob," said he, "instead of looking as if you had gained a friend and companion for life, you actually look as if you had lost every friend in the world."

"George, you know I was always serious and contemplative when we were at College together. Don't you recollect my nickname—'Old Grum?'"

"Yes, I recollect it very well," said George; "but upon an occasion like this, you should feign pleasure, even if you don't feel it. I think it a compliment you owe your wife, to appear happy at this time, even though you should be sombre for ever after."

"George, Amelia knows that I love her, and that I am very happy; and if she doesn't know it now, she will know hereafter, that I haven't the same way of expressing happy feelings that other people have."

"You have a curious way, Bob, to be sure, of expressing happy feelings by the most doleful look that ever a man put on."

"George, Amelia tells me you are going to California—is it so?"

"I have been thinking about it for some time, Bob, and have come to the determination at last to go. By the by, Major Scott told me, the other day, that he had picked out a lot of ten negroes, in families, for each of us. I have been very much puzzled what to do with mine, if I go to California. I deplore very much the necessity of selling—if I could carry them with me I would, but as I can't, I shall be forced to sell, whether I would or not. I shall, in the sale of them, lessen the inhumanity, by selling in families, and in the neighbourhood, though it should be at considerable sacrifice. What will you do with yours, Bob? I suppose, however, coming from the North, the land of liberty and humanity, you will set all yours free, of course."

"I never was a thorough-going abolitionist, George; and if I were, it could not be expected of me, that when I become entitled by marriage, or in any other manner, to what you Southern people have made property, that I should give it all up. Let me see; ten negroes at the lowest calculation would be worth four thousand dollars. Can you suppose that I or anybody else would throw away that amount of property? When I get them, I must do with them just what Southerners do. Sale and barter are incident to every species of property, and if there is any inhumanity in selling slaves, it attaches to you who have made them property, and not to me who receive them as such; and I must, from the same necessity that you plead, dispose of them as such."

"You will sell them in families, and in the neighbourhood, I hope, as I mean to do?"

"George, I do not think I am bound to mitigate the rigours of your institution, by sacrificing my property. The institution of slavery is yours and not mine, and I am not responsible for the consequences, be they what they may. I shall be under the necessity of selling them, and that being the case, I must sell them for every cent they will bring; and if members of families are separated (as I said before), it is the inevitable consequence of their being made property."

"Well, Bob, that is sophistry that I don't understand, but it lets me into a secret as to pretended northern philanthropy—touch the pocket and it's gone."

"There is no sophistry about it, George; my philanthropy extends to universal emancipation of your slaves; but as long as they remain property, they must be subject to all the incidents of property."

"Or, in other words," said George, "when it is property in the hands of Southern men, it ought to be let go, and abandoned; but when it becomes property in Northern hands, it should be converted into hard cash. How long do you expect to remain in Virginia, Bob? I ask the question to know whether the day I have fixed on for the public sale of my negroes would suit your convenience. I intend to advertise mine for sale at Mr. Frazer's shop on the 15th of this month."

"That will be a long time for me to stay from my business, George; but I suppose I must, and sell on the same day."

"Do you prepare your advertisement, Bob, and I will

prepare mine, and we will have them inserted in the papers, and have hand-bills stuck up at public places."

When left alone with Mr. Grattan, by the departure of George and Evelina, Mrs. Boswell said:

"Mr. Grattan, I think you were very hard with Evelina, and I can't understand why it was."

"Mrs. Boswell," said he, "I will with shame and deep sorrow acknowledge to you that I have suffered a momentary fit of jealousy to come over me to-night. The antipathy which Mr. Preble evinces towards me, did cause me to apprehend that if this Mr. Hicks, who is said to be immensely wealthy, should take a fancy to Evelina, the old man's influence would be exerted in his behalf. I have too high an opinion of Evelina to believe that she could be induced by the wealth of the Indies to break an engagement which, I will tell you in confidence, has been entered into between us; but her advocacy of this Mr. Hicks, added to the other considerations I mentioned, did for a time confirm and heighten that feeling of jealousy, and caused me to make remarks which I am now ashamed of, and sincerely sorry for."

Mrs. Boswell laughingly said, "Evelina, Mr. Grattan, wouldn't marry that Yankee from Boston for all the wealth of California, Australia, and Mexico, together. Upon my word! a real flaring up of jealousy! and for no earthly imaginable cause."

"Pray, Mrs. Boswell, don't expose my folly to any one. If you should, however, hear Evelina say anything of what passed, you may tell her of my deep mortification and contrition, and that I most earnestly crave her pardon for my remarks."

When Evelina went to her father, he pretended some excuse for wishing her to come to him; but the whole truth was, he wished to draw her away from Mr. Grattan; and it was very unfortunate for herself and Mr. Grattan, too, that just by her father stood Mr. Hicks, in conversation with Miss Eliza McKnight. She was so near as to hear Mr. Hicks propose some game for the amusement of the company, to which Miss Eliza sneeringly replied, "No, Mr. Hicks, I should be afraid of scaring away the Reverend Mr. Grattan."

"He might go, and welcome, for me," replied Mr. Hicks.

Mr. Grattan discovered that Mr. Hicks was immediately in her neighbourhood, and concluded that it had been design, on the part of her father, to bring them together. He stood for some time, after Mrs. Boswell left, with his eyes riveted on the spot where Evelina and her father were standing, and saw Mr. Hicks leave Miss Eliza McKnight, and enter into conversation with Evelina. Mr. Preble just then looked at his watch, and said it was nearly one in the morning. There was a general rush from the room by the ladies, to prepare for their departure. Mr. Hicks posted himself near the outer door, and was ready to help Miss Evelina to the carriage. As he was doing so, Mr. Preble very politely told him that he should be very much pleased to see him at the Cottage. All of which was seen and heard by Mr. Grattan.

Evelina and Mr. Grattan went that morning to their respective homes with heavy hearts; the latter with a condemning conscience for entertaining unfounded suspicions, which he could not even then entirely divest himself of; and the former with feelings wounded and lacerated, by imputations unjust, and which she was unconscious of deserving.

On their way home, Mrs. Boswell said to the Doctor; "Could you keep a secret if I were to tell you one?"

"You are bound to tell me, my dear, whether I promise to keep it or not. Wives, you know, have no right to have secrets which they could not communicate to their husbands; however, I will promise not to divulge it."

"Mr. Grattan is quite jealous of young Hicks, from Boston."

"That is impossible, my dear; he certainly cannot, even in thought, do so much injustice to Evelina, as to suppose she would marry that booby, who is to me the most disagreeable stranger I have ever met with. Why, he hasn't an idea beyond negroes and slavery. He almost bored me to death."

"Mr. Grattan told me so himself, but seemed to be very sorry for it, and asked me to beg pardon of Evelina for the surmises he made relative to it."

"I would as soon think, my dear, that Evelina would marry Looney or Brock, as that thick-skulled Bostonian. I am very sorry to hear that Mr. Grattan acted so little like himself."

"The best people in the world will sometimes, my dear husband, do and say silly things, but there is nobody who would regret an imprudent word or action more than Mr. Grattan."

"If he said anything to wound the feelings of Evelina, he deserves a severe castigation of conscience."

They arrived at home about two o'clock in the morning,

and there was Uncle Robin at the door, waiting their arrival.

"Well, Robin," said the Doctor, "has the wedding-party cleared out?"

"Yes, masser, all de strangers dat was here dun cleared out, sir."

"Was everything conducted properly, Robin?"

"Yes, sir. Dey didn' dance, cause dey couldn' git de fiddler; I a'n't been hear any noise, sir; I's bin told dey 'muse' demsel's playin' sell de thimble, sir. All de black people 'pon dis plantation sleep now, but me."

"I did not expect you to sit up, Robin, after everything was quiet."

"Masser, I thought de bes' plan to 'lieve your mind, sir, was to set up tell you com' home, an' let you know dat everything went on well, sir."

"Did you get any supper, Uncle Robin?" asked Mrs. Boswell.

"Yes, Missis, Dinah send me large piece o' cake, and somethin' of every thin' she had for supper, madam."

CHAPTER IX.

WHITE RUNAWAYS.—RELENTINGS.

The next morning before breakfast, Rachel (Mr. Stephens's cook) came over to let Mrs. Boswell know that her mother was sick in bed, and that the Crosbys had taken themselves off to the poor-house to their parents, the evening before, without leave.

"That is just what I have been expecting," said the Doctor, "that they would run off. What talk it will afford the gossips in the neighbourhood! How they are to be gotten back, I can't see, my dear; I think the only plan now, is for us to carry Kate and Molly over and insist that your mother shall keep them, and I will bind out those children to somebody else. They will never stay there, and it is not worth while to be troubled with them any longer."

Mrs. Boswell, in tears, said, "I cannot express to you, my dear husband, my thankfulness for your kindness to my dear parents; I see no other plan than the one you propose, but I am fearful that my mother, even in this extremity, will not consent for the girls to wait upon her."

"There will be no harm in trying the experiment, my dear, and the girls must get ready to go with us."

Breakfast was hurried, in consequence of Mrs. Boswell's anxiety to see her mother. When they arrived at Fredonia, Mrs. Boswell went into her mother's chamber, and found her quite sick. She complained much of the conduct of John and Sally, and wanted them sent for immediately.

"My dear mamma," said Mrs. Boswell, "if we were to send for them, their parents would not let them return, and if we were to force them back, the whole neighbourhood would be up in arms against us. The Doctor has suggested a plan, mamma, which I hope you will agree to. We have brought with us Kate and Molly, who are very good, tractable servants, and if you will try them, mamma, you will find much more satisfaction than you have ever had with those Crosbys, and you can keep them as long as you wish."

"My dear Ann, I am very thankful to the Doctor for his kindness, but I don't think I can consent to be waited upon by slaves."

"Oh, do, for my sake, mamma, give up such prejudices. You have been waited upon by those two little awkward creatures, who looked miserable all the time they were here. We now offer you two girls nearly grown, who have been well trained to housework, who, if you treat them well, will do everything you want them to do, with cheerful countenances, and be as happy here with you as possible. Do, mamma, consent to take them; you will find so much comfort in them."

She made no reply, but was evidently not so determined against taking them as she was at first. Mrs. Boswell opened the door and called the girls in. Kate looked frightened, and seemed to be listening for the horrible words, "poor creatures." If they were uttered, they were inaudible. Mrs. Stephens, however, covered her face with the counterpane. The girls were set to work by Mrs. Boswell, to put in order a room where everything seemed to be out of place, and when it was made neat and comfortable, she proposed to her mother to sit up in an arm chair until the girls could make up her bed. She got up with the assistance of her daughter, and went to the chair, keeping her back to the girls. Mrs. Boswell observed her casting her eyes over the room, and was pleased to discover upon her countenance something like satisfaction at its altered appearance.

She complained of much weakness, and begged that the girls would make haste with her bed. When it was done, Mrs. Boswell assisted her back to it, and when covered up, she said in a low voice, "What comfort there is in a well made up bed!"

"Mamma, won't you have something to eat? I think you would be much better after drinking a cup of good coffee or tea."

"My dear Ann, I don't think there is any preparation made for breakfast. Rachel was sent over to Selma, and I doubt whether there is any fire made in the kitchen, yet."

"Girls," said Mrs. Boswell, "go and get water, make a fire in the kitchen, put on the tea kettle, help Rachel about breakfast, and have it ready as soon as you possibly can."

They were absent but a short time, when Kate came and told her mistress that the kettle was boiling.

"Already!" said Mrs. Stephens; "I did not suppose they had been gone long enough to make the fire."

"Mamma, when servants work cheerfully and willingly, they won't take long to do anything you put them at. I suppose it would have taken those little Crosbys two or three hours to make a tea kettle boil."

"My dear Ann, I don't wish ever to hear those Crosbys mentioned again."

"I am delighted, mamma, to hear you say so, and I hope you will never see or hear of them more."

While this conversation was carried on in the chamber, Mr. Stephens and the Doctor were engaged in a similar one in the dining-room. Mr. Stephens was informed of the arrangement, and readily consented to relinquish all claim to the Crosbys under the indenture. The Doctor determined to leave Mrs. Boswell at Fredonia, and go and see Squire Brown, who he knew had to hire hands for his farming operations, and who he thought would be accommodated by Mr. Stephens's transfer of the indenture. Before he left home, he had told Uncle Robin to bring his horse over to Fredonia. Breakfast was soon brought in, and Mrs. Boswell carried a cup of coffee and some crackers to her mother, who said she had not tasted such good coffee for months before. After breakfast was over, Uncle Robin came to the door, and asked his mistress whether he could see her ma.

"I will ask mamma, Uncle Robin, if she will see you."

The old lady sent him word that she would be glad to see him in the chamber; and Mrs. Boswell, thinking that her presence might be a restraint upon their conversation, went into the dining-room. She had great hopes that Uncle Robin would say something to her mother which might reconcile her to be waited on by slaves.

"Missis," said Uncle Robin, "I's sorry to hear you is sick, madam; how you do, now?"

"I thank you, Uncle Robin; I feel somewhat better since I drank a good cup of coffee my daughter had made for me. How are you, Uncle Robin?"

"Thank God, missis, I's in reasonable health, madam. I think from what dey tells me, missis, you mus' bin made sick by dem little white creturs you had here, madam."

"I think it probable, Uncle Robin, that my sickness was caused by the trouble and vexation they occasioned me."

"Why, madam, white sarvants in dis country an't so good as blacks, anyhow, madam. I don' know how it is whar you com' from, madam, but white folks too proud here, madam, for good sarvants. I wou'dn' give dem two gals masser brung over here, to-day, for cuppen full o' white sarvants, madam."

"Well, Robin, I came to this state, thinking that the slaves here were the most miserable creatures in the world, and that they were always anxious to get away from their masters whenever they could. Now, Uncle Robin, I think I can rely upon what you say; and I wish you to tell me whether they are really happy or miserable?"

"Well, missis, I gwine tell you nothin' but the truth, madam. I does think as de black people bin brung to dis country, madam, dat dey better be slave here den free. I see how it is, madam, wid de free niggers, and wid de slaves, madam; and, if you b'leve me, if my masser wus to say to me dis day, 'Robin, you may be free,' I'd say, 'No, masser, I won' be free; who gwine take care of me, masser, when I gits ole, and pass wuck, masser?' Missis, I never bin see miserable sarvants, madam. Why, sarvants bin happy, madam, eber sence de days of Solomon. When dat queen (what you call her, missis?) went to see all Solomon good things, she tell Solomon he sarvants look happy: so it bin always, madam, wid sarvants who have good massers. If dem people way back North, madam, would but let niggers alone, dey'd be jus' as happy as white folks, madam. Now, missis, don't you think any mo' of dem good for nuttin' Crosby, madam, but try dese gals, Kate and Molly; an' if dey don' mak' your time easy, madam, you may say Robin know'd nothin' 'bout it."

"Uncle Robin, I have had so much more comfort in the short time that these girls have been here, I will try them, if for nothing else than to gratify my daughter, who is so very anxious that I should keep them."

"You gwine do jes what's right, madam, de Scriptur' say, parents mus'n' provoke der children to anger, madam. Now dar's no danger of provokin' my missis to anger, madam, but if you don' keep dese gals, dar's danger, madam, of provokin' my missis to hard thoughts 'bout you, madam, which is nex' thing to anger."

"Uncle Robin, how does your Sabbath school come on? I understand you have one that you superintend; these girls, I suppose, must be sent over to the cabin on Sabbath morning?"

"Why, madam, my Sunday school does com' on right well; I does super'tend it, but dar's always som' white man or 'oman dar, dat's what de law require', madam. I'll be 'bliged to you, madam, to sen' dem gals over 'bout nine o'clock."

"Very well, Uncle Robin, they shall be there in time."

"You' sarvant, missis. I hopes de Lord will raise you up off dat bed, madam, and dat you may live in peace and quiet wid dem gals."

"Good bye, Uncle Robin, you must come and see me again when you have leisure."

Dr. Boswell was hailed as usual by old Mr. Frazer as he passed his door on his way to Squire Brown's.

"I suppose, Doctor, you were at the grand affair at Major Scott's last night."

"Yes, Mr. Frazer, I was there."

"Was it a very superb entertainment, Doctor?"

"Everything was very nice, and good, and abundant, Mr. Frazer, but I saw nothing very superb or splendid."

"Well, sir, from what I heard of the preparations, I thought it would have been a tearing down party. I understand, Doctor, there is another Yankee come into the neighbourhood; I hope he won't take off another of the Virginia girls. I am very anxious to know how that fellow Benson will get along with those ten negroes the Major intends for him; now, I'll lay you a wager, sir, that he sells them off to the traders."

"Indeed, Mr. Frazer, I can't gratify your curiosity, for I know nothing of Mr. Benson's arrangements. You seem to keep up your antipathy to the Yankees."

"Yes, Doctor, I do most cordially despise them all. Why, sir, I have just heard that another gang of negroes have gone off from up the valley; there's nobody's property safe, sir. If something isn't done with these Yankees who are prowling about among us, we shall lose all the negroes in the state, sir. Oh! Doctor, those children went from here this morning; they came here last night about dusk, and asked me to let them stay all night; I asked them where they were going, they said to see their parents, and upon further inquiry I found they had run off. I thought at first I would take them back to Mr. Stephens, but they begged so hard, and looked so miserable, that I had not the heart to do it. I gave them their breakfast this morning, and they are gone to the poor-house. It is not worth while, Doctor, for you to attempt to get them children back; they say they won't stay, unless they are kept constantly tied, and the old man won't let them go back, I know, sir."

"I don't intend they shall ever go back there, Mr. Frazer; I shall make some other arrangements for them."

"What other arrangements will you make for them, Doctor?"

16

"You will hear in good time, Mr. Frazer, after they are made."

"Indeed, Doctor, I'm not one of those people who would pry into other people's matters; what little news I do pick up at this public place, is generally forced upon me. Do you know whether old Mr. Preble has certainly forbidden Mr. Grattan to come to his house, Doctor?"

"No, I have never heard that he had, and if there is such a report in circulation, I don't credit it at all. I believe it to be entirely false, sir."

"Well, sir, I only heard it as a report; I don't vouch for its truth; it is shameful for people to circulate such a report if it's not true."

"True or false, Mr. Frazer, such things ought not to be freely talked of, about a minister of the gospel."

"That's just what I tell people, Doctor."

The Doctor rode off and left him. When he arrived at Squire Brown's, he found him talking with old Mr. Crosby, who had been brought over in a cart from the poor-house (about a half mile distant). The children had gotten there before he left, and he had come over to the Squire's to consult with him about them. The Squire met the Doctor very cordially, but old Mr. Crosby seemed very much disinclined to take the hand which the Doctor held out to him.

"I am come, Squire Brown," said the Doctor, "to see you upon the subject which I suppose brought Mr. Crosby here."

"I come here, Doctor, to see my children righted," said Mr. Crosby, with much vehemence; "they've been treated worse than brutes ought to be treated, sir; and if there's any justice in law, sir, I'll have them righted."

The Doctor very mildly replied, "Mr. Crosby, I am sorry to see you give way to passion; I don't wish your children to go back to Mr. Stephens, but wish this matter settled to the satisfaction of all parties, and want to have as few words about it as possible. I have come here, hoping that Squire Brown would take them off his hands."

"That's just what I would wish," said Mr. Crosby; "I look upon the Squire as a humane man, and one very fitten to have my children, sir."

"Doctor," said the Squire, "you have taken me entirely by surprise; but I will go and consult my wife, and if she thinks she can do anything with Sally, we will take them. I know John will be quite useful to me."

The mildness of the Doctor, and his very acceptable proposal, having subdued the anger of Mr. Crosby, he remained silent until the Squire returned.

"Well, Doctor, my wife thinks she can make Sally useful, and we have agreed to take them. Whatever clothes they have left at Mr. Stephens's, can be sent over to Frazer's shop."

"They were furnished, Squire, with very good clothing when they came, and with some since the first suit; but to satisfy all parties, I will leave in your hands six dollars for their use."

"I always knowed, Doctor," said Mr. Crosby, "that you would do the right thing, and I'm very much beholden to you, sir."

When the Doctor was gone, the Squire said to Mr. Crosby, he was very sorry he had said anything to wound the feelings of such a good man as Dr. Boswell.

"Squire," he replied, "if the truth must be told, I was

as mad as blazes when I first saw the Doctor; but I soon cooled off, and I'm mighty sorry if I wounded his feelings, for he been monstrous good man to me, sir."

"I think it very probable, Mr. Crosby, that the cruelty of Mrs. Stephens to your children gave the Doctor almost as much pain as it gave you; but he was very delicately situated. I don't know how he could, with any regard to her feelings, have hinted at, or advised a change in her treatment. I suppose, after this, the Stephens's will be as fond of being waited on by slaves as any of us. Those Northern people soon get over the notions they bring here with them."

The Doctor went directly to Fredonia, taking care to give spur to his horse as he passed Mr. Frazer's shop. They were all very much pleased to hear that the Crosbys had been disposed of with so little trouble, not excepting Mrs. Stephens, who had the Doctor in her chamber that afternoon, and who behaved more rationally, and more like a lady, than she had done since her arrival in Virginia. It was apparent, that from sad experience and wholesome appliances, the kink in her brain was in the way of being unravelled.

"I hope I see you better, this afternoon, Mrs. Stephens?" said the Doctor, as he seated himself by her bedside.

"Thank you, Doctor, I am much better than I was this morning; Ann's being with me all day has been of great benefit. I feel myself under great obligations to you, Doctor, for the trouble you have taken in settling this disagreeable matter; I will try hereafter to give Ann and yourself less uneasiness on my account. I will confess to you, Doctor, that the prejudices which I imbibed in early life, and which I brought with me to Virginia, are somewhat removed by what I have seen and felt since I have been here; and I think my happiness now depends upon the success of an effort which I am fully resolved to make, entirely to eradicate those prejudices.

"Doctor, I have no doubt that when you have been contemplating the many excellencies in the character of our dear Ann, you have often contrasted hers and her mother's, and wondered at the astonishing difference. Although I do not pretend to equality with Ann in those qualities which adorn her character, yet it is due to myself, Doctor, to say, that you have seen me in Virginia under the trembling influence of a solitary idea, which had almost overthrown my mind, and which had entirely obscured traits of character, much lower in degree than those of my daughter, to be sure, but, I flatter myself, infinitely higher than the perverseness, folly, and childishness, induced by that one idea, would seem to indicate. I must acknowledge, also, that the same influence operating upon a temper naturally excitable, caused great impatience under trials, produced by the very bad conduct of those children whom I foolishly took here, and that I sincerely regret the cruelty which I exercised towards them. Your girls, I promise you, will receive different treatment; for, besides the warm feelings of benevolence which I hope I shall always cherish for persons in their situation, the recollection of your kindness, Doctor, I hope, will restrain any passionate inclination to correct your servants, who are so fortunate as never to receive correction from yourself."

"Well, madam," said the Doctor, "servants as well as children should be taught implicit obedience; and if they require correction, it should be administered in moderation, from a sense of duty, but never in anger, madam."

It was now getting late in the afternoon, and the girls, who had not been present when the conversations took place between Mrs. Stephens, the Doctor, and Mrs. Boswell, about their remaining, seeing their master and mistress preparing to go home, were making similar preparations for themselves in another room. Mrs. Boswell said to them, "Girls, you are to stay here and wait upon papa and mamma."

They both exclaimed, "Oh, missis, we don' wan' stay here, madam; please let us go home wid you an' masser."

"No, you can't go; your master and myself have both told mamma that you were to stay; she has promised to be very kind to you; you must be good girls, mind what is said to you, and keep mamma's room and the dining-room in nice order. You must be over at Selma by nine o'clock on Sunday morning."

"Not 'fore Sunday, missis?" exclaimed Kate, in tears.

"Good-bye," said Mrs. Boswell; "now mind, you must be good girls."

She left them both weeping bitterly.

When they got back to Selma, they found Mr. Henry Stephens there, from Norristown.

"My dear brother," said Mrs. Boswell, "I never was so delighted to see anybody in my life; and so unexpected, too. Why did you take us by surprise? You mentioned nothing of coming to Virginia, in your last letter, which papa received a few days ago."

"No, Ann, when I wrote that letter I had no idea of coming, but business brought me to Baltimore, and I thought I would make you a flying visit."

"My dear brother, I am sorry to hear that it is only to be a flying visit; I hoped you had come to stay with us some time."

"No, Ann, I can only give you one day (to-morrow), the next day I must set out again for home."

"I am truly sorry to hear that, Henry," said the Doctor; "you must think better of it yet."

"It would give me much pleasure, I assure you, Doctor, to remain longer, but important business requires me to be at home in two days from the day after to-morrow."

"Your servant told me when I arrived a few minutes ago, that mamma was sick. You are just from there, I suppose; how is she, this evening?"

"There is not much the matter; she has taken a slight cold, and will be quite well to-morrow, I hope."

"I must go over and see them; how far do they live from here?"

"About a half-mile, brother," said Mrs. Boswell; "come into the portico, and I will show you the house. Supper will be brought in directly, and you can go over and stay with them until bed-time, if you choose, and then come back here; they are not prepared for lodging any one."

After he was gone, the Doctor said: "I can't imagine what has brought Henry on to Baltimore; I thought his business was generally in the direction of New York or Boston."

"I fear, from what papa told me the other day, that Henry's affairs are not in a very prosperous condition.

He was afraid, he said, that the failure of a mercantile house in Boston had shaken Henry very considerably; he does not think him well qualified for being a merchant, and wishes him to sell out and buy a farm."

"I wish he would buy a farm, in this valley near us. There are several farms near this, offered for sale; I will mention it to him."

"My dear husband, Henry will never come to Virginia to live; he is as sensitive upon the subject of slavery as ever mamma was."

"I think it rather unfortunate, my dear, that he should have come here just at this time; he may throw your mother back upon that (to me) discordant note of 'poor creatures.'"

"I hope they will have other things to talk about than slavery."

"A real abolitionist, my dear, lugs in that topic head and heels, neck and shoulders, in place and out of place: it is an eternal ding dong with them. I should not be surprised if those girls are sent back, forthwith."

"I have no fears of that sort. Mamma's confession, to-day, was wrung from her by bitter experience and necessity, and she is not going to throw herself back upon the extremity in which I found her this morning. You can form no idea of the comfortless situation in which she was, when she attributed her behaviour since her residence in Virginia, to partial alienation of mind, produced by that fixed idea. She was right, for she has seemed to me an entirely different human being from what she was in Pennsylvania. If Henry's visit will have the effect you apprehend, it will be unfortunate that he ever came. It will be a sad disappointment to me, if she does fall back again into that dreadful state of mind, and deprives me of the pleasure I now anticipate from her more rational society."

"I too, Ann, have marked the difference between Mrs. Stephens in Virginia, and Mrs. Stephens in Pennsylvania, and I have for some time thought she laboured under partial hallucination."

"I wish I had told Henry not to mention the subject of slavery to her."

"That never would have done, my dear; such a request would have filled him brim-full of the subject, and his vessel would have overflowed at his first glance at Kate and Molly."

Mr. Henry Stephens returned before bedtime, and expressed himself much pleased with his father's and mother's situation.

"Was mamma sitting up, Henry, while you were there?" asked Mrs. Boswell.

"No, Ann, I found her in bed, with two black girls in her room at work. I had a great inclination to say to her that I never expected to witness such a sight as my mother surrounded by slaves who were labouring for her; but I thought if she chose to give in to the practices of Virginians, it was no business of mine. I know one thing, that if the Lord spares me my senses, wherever I am, I shall retain my abhorrence of slavery."

"The Doctor was just saying, brother, that he would propose to you to sell out in Norristown, and come and settle by the side of us in Virginia."

"Although I should like to be near the Doctor and yourself, Ann, I could never consent to that. No, my life must be spent in a free state; I should be the most unhappy man in existence, to live where my eyes would see a slave at work at every glance."

"Then you don't like work, Henry?" said the Doctor.

"Yes, I do, sir; I like to see everybody employed in some work or other; but let them be free, and work only as long as they please, and just on what kind of work they please. I don't like to see people who have no wills of their own, made to be eternally delving in work that they have no interest in."

"Henry, were you ever through one of your Northern factories?"

"Yes, sir, to be sure; I have been in Northern and English factories, too."

"Do the people in those factories, Henry, work when they please, and leave off when they please, and have they an interest in the work they are delving at?"

"Why, Doctor, if they left off from work when they pleased, they would be turned out of employ; they certainly have an interest in their work to the amount of their wages."

"Would the wages of a labouring man in England, or the North, Henry, furnish him with good warm winter clothing, and necessary decent summer clothing, and two abundant meals of bread and meat, for every day in the year?"

"I can't answer that question with certainty, Doctor, but I suppose his wages would be rather scant for that."

"Then, Henry, my slaves have more interest in the work they are engaged in than the labouring people of England, or of the North; for they have, as wages of labour, all those things I have enumerated; and although they work at the will of their master, it is a more lenient will than the will of necessity, which you have acknowledged obliges those free white people to work. Your remarks, however, apply to persons not bound out to masters, as operatives in factories and workshops; what is the situation of those who are?"

"They are kept at work all day and part of the night, I believe; but that depends upon the time at which they finish their tasks."

"Do they get any wages, Henry, which gives them an interest in their work?"

"They are clothed and fed, sir."

"Do you suppose that the clothing and food which they get would amount to half of the annual cost of the articles I told you my negroes get?"

"Not more than half, I suppose."

"My negroes, then, have double the interest, in the work that they do, than that description of operatives, and are required to be engaged a much shorter time at work. When those operatives who are bound to their employers, neglect to finish their tasks, what is the consequence?"

"They are made to do it, sir; and if they don't, they are flogged."

"Henry, I wish you could stay with us, and read two small works, one called 'Helen Fleetwood,' and the other 'The Little Pin-headers;' then go and see the situation of the negroes on my plantation of the same ages with those boys and girls mentioned in those works; and draw the comparison for yourself between their relative situations."

"Doctor, I am against slavery in toto, and it is not worth while for us to argue about it."

"No, it is not, Henry; there are none so hard to convince as those who are determined not to be."

Before Mr. Stephens retired to bed, he told his sister that his father and mother requested that she and the Doctor would come over with him, and spend the next day, so that they might all be together.

"Doctor," said Mr. Stephens, the next morning as they were walking out, "I have a very particular and important business on hand, the transaction of which will be infinitely beneficial to me. My partner in business wishes to withdraw from the firm, and has offered me his interest in our establishment for three thousand dollars, payable in three months, and requires a draft on a mercantile house in Boston, to run for that time. He can get the money on the draft, provided it is well endorsed; and, having heard of your circumstances, he is willing to take you as the endorser. I would esteem it a particular favour if you would lend me your name."

"Are you well enough acquainted, Henry, with the liabilities of your firm to be perfectly satisfied that the purchase will be a safe one? Does not the wish of your partner to sell to you, on what you call advantageous terms, raise something like a doubt of its being profitable to you after you have made the purchase?"

"Not at all, sir; he is anxious to go to Europe on an adventure, from which he expects much more profit than he could possibly reap from our business, were we ever so successful. He is a man in whom I have great confidence, and I am well satisfied there is no liability unknown to myself. I can give you a positive assurance, Doctor, that the draft will be paid at maturity, and there is not, I may say, a possibility of your being made to suffer."

"Under that assurance, Henry, I will endorse the draft." They went into the house, the draft was produced, and endorsed by the Doctor. They all spent that day at Fredonia, where nothing occurred of sufficient interest to relate. Mr. Stephens returned home on the following day. On that day Miss Evelina received a visit from Mr. Hicks; her father paid him marked attention, but she, recollecting his connexion with the distressing incidents of the wedding-night, felt every disposition to avoid his company, and the civility in her deportment, if civility it may be called, not being in accordance with the feelings of her heart, was a painful effort, forced upon her by a sense of duty to her father.

"I hope," said he, "Miss Preble experienced no inconvenience from her late, or rather early, ride from the wedding?"

"No, sir, not the least."

"We should have had a much more pleasant party if we had been allowed to dance. Don't you think so, Miss Preble?"

"I don't know, indeed, sir, how much it would have added to the pleasure of others; but it would not have increased mine at all, as I never dance."

"Well, that's strange. I had somehow or other taken up the idea, that dancing was a universal amusement in Virginia; and I did not suppose that I could be at a party here, where there was no dancing, or that I should have met with a single Virginia lady who was not fond of the amusement."

"It is by no means a general practice in Virginia, sir."

"I declare, miss, I think I've seen the amusements of

the Virginia dance, with the accompaniments of the pigeon wing, the cutting out, and cutting in, celebrated in poetry and song."

"Very probable, sir, as the slaves in Virginia are passionately fond of the dance, with the accompaniments you mention."

"Poor creatures, I guess they get rid of the sorrows of the heart, through the medium of the feet."

"They are very often, sir, advised to use the feet as a medium to escape imagined sorrows."

Mr. Preble was made very uneasy by Miss Evelina's last thrust, and changed the subject, by asking Mr. Hicks how he liked Harper's Ferry.

"Oh! sir, it's a grand display of the sublime; but I must confess that I was disappointed in my expectations, which had been raised too high by Mr. Jefferson's extravagant description of it."

"You should go, Mr. Hicks, to see our Natural Bridge, which is a work of nature far superior in grandeur to Harper's Ferry."

"I should have abundance of time, Mr. Preble, as Benson has determined not to return until after the 15th of the month. I came here as his waiting man, and I guess I must obey his orders, particularly while I am in a land where obedience is enforced by the rod. How far do you call it to the Natural Bridge, sir?"

"It is, I believe, sir, between one hundred and fifty and one hundred and sixty miles."

"Are there stages running from this section to the bridge, sir?"

"Yes, sir, there is a stage running up the valley every day."

"It is very inconvenient to me, Mr. Preble, to stay from home as long as Benson requires I should do. Do you think, Miss Preble, that, as his groomsman, I am bound to stay until he says I may go?"

"I suppose, sir," responded Miss Evelina, "that a groomsman, after the performance of the duty for which he was engaged, is perfectly absolved from all obedience to his master (if you so call the groom), becomes a free man, and has a right to return home when he likes."

"I declare, Mr. Preble, you have put me very much in the notion of going to the Bridge. Miss Preble, don't you think I had as well spend a part of the time I remain in Virginia in taking that trip?"

"I think you said, Mr. Hicks, it would be very inconvenient for you to remain as long as Mr. Benson wishes; I could, therefore, never advise any gentleman to sacrifice his convenience, or his business, to pleasure."

"Oh! as to convenience or business, the loss of a few days will be of but little moment. I meant to ask you, miss, whether if I stay (as I have determined to do), you thought I could derive more pleasure from a trip to the Bridge, than by remaining where I am?"

"I should think a trip to the Bridge would afford you much more amusement, than remaining in this neighbourhood; and as that section of country furnishes much to please strangers, you might spend the whole time which will intervene between this and the 15th in viewing its beauties."

Old Mr. Preble excused himself to Mr. Hicks for being obliged to leave him to be entertained by his daughter, saying that he had an engagement to meet a gentleman at Mr. Frazer's shop, and that the hour appointed had nearly arrived, expressing a hope that Mr. Hicks would repeat his visit to the Cottage, if he determined not to go to the Bridge.

Mr. Hicks thanked him, and said he was perfectly excusable in not neglecting his appointment.

"Miss Preble," said he (taking a nearer seat), I assure you I had no serious thought of going to the Bridge; there's attraction for me in this neighbourhood far beyond any that a sight of the Bridge offers."

"I am at a loss to understand, sir, how this neighbourhood, which you have not generally seen, and in which you have not been three days, should have for you attractions superior to a work of nature, which is acknowledged to be one of her grandest efforts."

"Nature, miss, produces works upon a smaller scale, which, if they fail to excite astonishment and wonder, are eminently qualified to engage the affections of the heart."

"The works of nature, sir, whether upon a large or small scale, are calculated to engage the affections of the heart for nature's Great Architect, but not for the work itself."

"Nature's Great Architect, miss, has made some works after his own image, one of which presents itself at this moment, in the person of Miss Evelina Preble, as worthy of every affection of *my* heart."

"Mr. Hicks, I esteem it but a poor compliment to a lady's understanding, her prudence or discretion, to be addressed in such language after an acquaintance not yet of three days' length; and I am constrained, sir, to take my leave of you." She left the room with a dignified air. Mr. Hicks was in considerable difficulty to decide whether he should ring the bell for a servant to send and implore Miss Evelina to return, stay until Mr. Preble returned, and lay his case before him, or go back immediately to Major Scott's. He decided in favour of the latter course, and in the road leading by Mr. Preble's outer gate, he met the Rev. Mr. Grattan. As they passed, there was a slight recognition from each. That accidental meeting caused much uneasiness to both; it was conjectured by Mr. Grattan that Mr. Hicks was from the Cottage, and by Mr. Hicks that Mr. Grattan was on his way there. This last conjecture, however, was without foundation, as Mr. Grattan was on a parochial visit to a member of his congregation, who lived beyond the Cottage.

Dr. Boswell had rode that morning as far as Mr. Frazer's, with Mr. Stephens. Mr. Frazer saw him as he was passing, and in a very earnest manner said, "Doctor, get down; I've got something to show you; it is worth seeing, I can tell you." The Doctor alighted, and as he was going into the house, Mr. Frazer directed his attention to two advertisements, tacked to the side of the house, one on each side of the door. The Doctor read the first one he came to, as follows:

"Will be offered for sale at the shop of Joel Frazer, on the 15th instant, ten likely slaves, for cash. These slaves consist of three families, and not being sold for any fault, they will be set up in families. No bid of a trader will be taken, nor of any one residing out of the county.

GEORGE PREBLE."

He read the other advertisement, as follows:

"Will be offered for sale, for cash, on the 15th instant,

before the door of Joel Frazer, ten likely negroes. They will be set up singly, and sold to the highest bidder.

ROBERT BENSON."

"That's just what I told you, Doctor, that that Yankee would sell his negroes. And see, too, Doctor, how he's going to sell them; not like George Preble, in families, in the county, but to anybody and everybody. Now mind what I say, Doctor, if he don't get from twelve to fifteen hundred dollars more than George gets for his. Give me old Virginia, Doctor, any day, for humanity. I won't swear in your presence, Doctor, but I was just going to curse that Yankee."

"Mr. Frazer," said the Doctor, "he couldn't well do otherwise than to sell his negroes, as they could not be carried to Boston."

"To carry out his abolition principles, Doctor, he ought to set them free; that's the real truth of the matter."

"You could not find many Northern people, Mr. Frazer, who would do that; they would take them from the South in a body, but they hold fast to slaves, or their value, when they become possessed of them."

"I understand, Doctor, you got the Crosbys off Mr. Stephens's hands. They have a fine master now, sir; Squire Brown is a first-rate man."

The Doctor, finding that Mr. Frazer was getting upon a subject which had occasioned him great uneasiness, and which he wished never to hear mentioned again, left him. On his way home he overtook the Rev. Mr. Grattan returning from his visit, and carried him to Selma, to dinner. Mrs. Boswell said to the Doctor, when they arrived, that she had been over to Fredonia, where she found her mother busily engaged with the girls, at work on a flower bed in the garden, and that she had never seen her in better spirits at any time.

"A great change has come over your mother, my dear, since she has gotten partially rid of that kink in her brain. Mr. Grattan, I suppose you have heard something of Mrs. Stephens's vagaries upon the subject of slavery, since she came to Virginia? I believe it has been the common talk of the neighbourhood for some weeks."

"Yes, sir, I have heard that she was very sensitive upon that subject, and felt much concerned that a lady so closely connected with your family should have her peculiarities made a topic for neighbourhood gossipping. I was disposed to make every allowance for what I considered the result of prejudices, founded upon misapprehension of what slavery really was in Virginia, induced by the very false representations made of it. I felt confident, that when she had been long enough in Virginia to judge for herself, those prejudices would be removed: and that any unfavourable impression which might be made on the public mind, would pass off, and be forgotten."

"The indulgence, sir," said the Doctor, "of those anti slavery prejudices, to the extent to which she carried them, does certainly impair the intellect. Mrs. Stephens in Virginia has appeared to me entirely different from Mrs. Stephens as I knew her in Pennsylvania. I am happy to inform you now that her views upon that subject are undergoing a change, and that there is every prospect of her becoming entirely reconciled to a relation which she once, through ignorance, abhorred. It is a source of great satisfaction to us, that her character, which, among strangers to her former self, may have suffered loss, is about to be restored to a proper appreciation of its worth."

"I assure you, sir," said Mr. Grattan, "it gives me, also, great pleasure to hear it."

"I see from George Preble's advertisement, Mr. Grattan, that he has made up his mind positively to go to California."

"What advertisement do you allude to, sir?"

"I saw an advertisement to-day, of George's, advertising ten negroes for sale on the 15th."

"George is certainly to blame in taking his wife to such a distance from her father and mother; and, moreover, the inhumanity of selling slaves, who are guilty of no fault, should have at once banished all thought of it," said Mr. Grattan.

"George is about to sell his in a manner attended with as little inhumanity as possible; he advertises them in families, and restricts the sale to persons living in the county. Benson advertises his, without any restriction, to be sold separately."

"That, sir, places sympathy, and a real tender consideration for those persons, in the latitude to which it in truth belongs—the South. The North has set up pretensions to such feelings; but those pretensions, as evidenced in the case of Benson, prove false when interest is at stake. I am astonished, Doctor, that Major Scott should have given them negroes, under the circumstances in which they were placed."

"I have conversed, sir, with Major Scott upon that subject. He said that he wished to give his children something at their marriage; that he had no money, and no other property but negroes to give them; that he had been all his life opposed to selling negroes, but that he was perfectly reconciled at the mode of sale proposed by George; and he and George were both of opinion that Benson would undoubtedly sell in the same way. Mr. Benson's manner of selling will cause him great pain, I know. The Major and his wife are destined to suffering which should not be wantonly increased."

"Indeed, Doctor, when I think of the bereavement which hangs over them, my sympathies are highly excited. Mrs. Scott, I know, will bear the separation with true Christian resignation; but I fear the Major will not have sources for consolation to which she resorts."

"Mr. Grattan," said Mrs. Boswell, "have you seen Evelina since the wedding?" and, with an arch smile, added, "I wonder if the Boston beau has been to the Cottage, yet?"

"To your question, Mrs. Boswell, I can answer, no, that I have not been to the Cottage since that night; and I can put a stop to your wonder, by saying that I met Mr. Hicks this morning just from the Cottage, as I supposed."

"Had you any conversation with him?"

"No, madam, we passed each other in the road. I was about to rein up my horse, to speak to him, but I observed he put spur to his; and our recognition was scarcely perceptible."

"Mr. Grattan," said the Doctor, "you may put your mind at ease upon that subject. I have known Evelina from her childhood; and I know that she never would consent, under any circumstances whatever, to take such a man as Hicks as a companion for life. They would be two of the most uncongenial souls that ever got together."

"Mrs. Boswell, you have been divulging, I see, to the Doctor, some of our secrets."

"Why, you know, sir, I promised to obey my husband in all things, and when I asked him that night on our way home, if he would promise to keep a secret, he said I was bound to tell him whether he promised or not; and I looked upon that as something like an order, and obeyed."

"I can assure you both, that I have heartily repented of the folly of that night," said Mr. Grattan.

"If Mr. Hicks has any idea of Evelina, the meeting must have disturbed him more than it did you, as he must have concluded that you were on your way to the Cottage. But I can't think that he has any such intention, as I overheard Miss Eliza McKnight tell him, that Evelina's affections were engaged, or something to that effect, and Miss Eliza had her own reasons for making that communication, no doubt."

"Why, my dear, you never told me of that before," said Mrs. Boswell.

"My dear, those things make so slight an impression upon my mind, that my memory scarcely ever brings them back, after the occasion has passed, and I perhaps never should have thought of it again, but for the present conversation. I think Miss Eliza McKnight would have no sort of objection to catch Mr. Hicks, herself."

Charles came into the room to let the Doctor know that Uncle Robin wanted to see him.

"Well, Robin, what's your will?"

"De people all seems dispose', sir, to hear de Rev. Mr.

Grattan speak a word, dis evenin', sir, an' as we not very busy, I thought I'd com' to ax you leave, sir."

"I will ask Mr. Grattan, Robin, and if he has no objection, I shall have none." He went back and proposed it to Mr. Grattan, who cheerfully consented, and Robin was told to summon the negroes to attend at his cabin, at four o'clock. After dinner, the Doctor and Mrs. Boswell accompanied Mr. Grattan to Uncle Robin's cabin, where they heard a discourse from which they, as well as the slaves, might derive benefit.

When Mr. Grattan was taking his leave, Mrs. Boswell informed him that the brides and grooms, and some other friends, would be at Selma on the next day; that she had intended to invite him by a written invitation, but there was no necessity for it now, and she hoped he would be of the party.

"It is not my habit, Mrs. Boswell, to go to large gatherings, except when duty calls, and I hope the Doctor and yourself will excuse me."

"We should be much pleased to have your company," said the Doctor, "but you are perfectly excusable not to break through, even on our account, a rule which I cannot but think very proper for a minister to adopt."

CHAPTER X.

THE WEDDING-DINNER.

A LOVELY morning ushered in the day, and gave promise that the wedding-dinner would be well attended. The sun had not risen above the horizon, before breakfast was over, and Mrs. Boswell was engaged in finishing preparations for a splendid dessert, which she had commenced two days before.

When it was all ready for the instruction of Charles and Cecilia, every dish was placed in its proper position upon a large table in the pantry, and they were told to place them in that order, when brought to the table in the dining-room. She said she had been often put out of patience with servants, for misplacing dishes, and by the confusion produced by every one around the table attempting to bring their irregularity to order; evincing, not unfrequently, as much ignorance as the servants themselves. There was an empty dish at the head for the plum-pudding, which was to come in hot. The Doctor was called in to admire it, after the arrangements were completed. "Well, my dear," said he, "that does credit to Norristown. I have only one objection to make; your pyramid is so high there is some danger of its falling."

"Not the smallest; it can't fall, it is too well proportioned," said Mrs. Boswell.

Mr. Hicks, notwithstanding the stern rebuke which he had received from Evelina, determined to go over to the Cottage, just in time to accompany her and her father to Selma. When he got there, Evelina was at her toilet. The servant who waited in her room, was sent into the parlour for something she had left there, and when she returned, she said to her young mistress, that she had heard her Pa tell Mr. Hick that he would have his horse put in the stable, and dat Mr. Hick was gwine in de carriage. Miss Evelina went immediately to take counsel, where she always resorted for that purpose, to her Aunt Priscilla. In a voice indicating a feeling of horror, she exclaimed:

"My dear aunt, what do you think? Papa has asked that man to go to Selma in the carriage with us."

"What man, my dear?" said Miss Priscilla Graham.

"That man Hicks, from Boston, whose conduct here, yesterday, I told you of last night."

"My dear, you shan't go with him, if I can prevent it."

"Well, shall I send papa word, aunt, that I have a headache, and can't go?"

"No, my dear, that would be false; and I am astonished that you should have proposed it."

"Indeed, aunt, I did not mean to tell a falsehood; my head does ache very severely."

"My dear child, although your head may ache, still such a message as that would be false. You would be assigning to your father, as the cause of your not going to Selma, a headache. Now you know, Evelina, that notwithstanding the headache, you would have gone to Selma, but for this Mr. Hicks being invited to go in the carriage."

"My dear aunt, I proposed it without reflection; I did not mean, I assure you, to tell an untruth. What shall I say to papa keeps me from going?"

"My dear, we could make no excuse but the real one, which would not be deceptive; and I must tell your father plainly, if he insists upon knowing the cause of your not going, that I do not wish you to ride in the same carriage with Mr. Hicks. Evelina, my dear, do you go into the next room, and I will send for your father to come up here. Mary, go and ask Mr. Preble to come up into my room, if he pleases."

Mr. Preble followed Mary when she returned.

"Mr. Preble," said Miss Priscilla, "I am sorry to give you the trouble of walking up stairs; I wish to inquire of you, whether this Boston gentleman is to go to Selma in your carriage?"

"I have invited him to do so, madam; he has consented, and his horse has been put away."

"I am very sorry for it, Mr. Preble, as it will prevent Evelina from going."

"Why so, madam? I can't see why it should prevent her from going. I invited Mr. Hicks, because I supposed it would be more agreeable, this hot day, to go in the carriage, than to ride on horseback."

"Mr. Preble, such a favour as that is not expected by a stranger; nor is it customary to extend it to an entire stranger, as Mr. Hicks is, to you and your family."

"Miss Priscilla, I do not think that is a sufficient reason by any means for Evelina's refusing to go. This gentleman has been brought here by a dear friend of my son, and we are to presume that if he was not a fit associate for us, that Mr. Benson would not have introduced him here. And, as it is my wish that he should go in my carriage, Evelina has no right to object."

"Evelina says not one word against Mr. Hicks going in your carriage, sir; but, as he is to go, she prefers staying at home, and I think, sir, for a very good reason."

"Well, madam, I have not yet heard anything like a good reason for her not going; and I have a right to lay upon her the commands of a father, and make her go."

"Mr. Preble, you certainly have that right, but I hope you will not exercise it, sir, under the circumstances of this case; and I am forced, reluctantly, to tell you what those circumstances are. You left Evelina and Mr. Hicks together, yesterday, in the parlour; and in your absence, he, an entire stranger as he was, professed attachment for her. I think, sir, it was an insult offered your daughter, for a stranger to suppose that she was so entirely devoid of prudence and discretion as to form a matrimonial engagement with him almost at first sight. Evelina, sir, received his proposal in such manner as every female who has proper respect for herself ought to have done, by immediately leaving the room. And if she were now to go in the same carriage with him to Selma, he would consider it encouragement to renew his addresses. I hope, sir, now that you know the whole cause for her declension, you will not force her to go."

"Well, madam, it does seem to me that you and Evelina have made much fuss about nothing. I think that the highest compliment a gentleman can pay a lady is to address her. I know very well what is the real cause of Evelina's not wishing to go with him. You may tell her from me, madam, that, although I shall not force her to go, it will avail her nothing in regard to another matter." He then took his leave; and in a few minutes he and Mr. Hicks were on their way to Selma.

"I am very much surprised and mortified, Mr. Preble," said Mr. Hicks, "that your daughter declined going to the party, to-day; and I fear, sir, that I have been the innocent cause of her not going, by accepting your polite invitation to take a seat in your carriage, as I guess she might apprehend that our being seen together, in your carriage, might have given umbrage to another individual."

"I don't care, sir, who it gives umbrage to; I gave you the invitation, and now say to you that you are welcome to the seat you now occupy."

"Mr. Preble, your kindness emboldens me to introduce a subject which is nearest my heart. From the moment I first saw your daughter, I have cherished an ardent affection for her; and when you left us together, yesterday, I could not resist the violence of my attachment; and I will candidly confess to you that I made it known to her. Perhaps it was too hasty in me to do so; but I hope, sir, you will excuse me, on the ground that the ardour of my attachment overstepped the cold rules of custom, and that I became the avowed lover of your daughter only a short time in advance of the period which those rules would have sanctioned as a fit time for making the declaration. Having made known to you, sir, the state of my heart, I will now ask your permission to continue my suit."

"If you and Evelina, Mr. Hicks, can come to an agreement upon this subject, I shall be satisfied. I have formed one determination in regard to my daughter's marrying, and that is, that I will never force her to marry any one contrary to her own wishes, and that she shall never marry any one contrary to mine."

Mr. Preble having been kept at home later than he intended, by Miss Priscilla Graham, they arrived at Selma after the company had assembled, and many were the expressions of regret and astonishment at the absence of Evelina. To Mrs. Boswell's inquiry of her father why she had not come, the old gentleman was at a loss at first to give answer, but said something about her Aunt Priscilla being a curious old lady. The conversation in the carriage had given such life and spirits to Mr. Hicks, that it was observed by the whole company; and the conjecture with some, was, that his trip to the Cottage that day, must have given rise to something more than ordinarily agreeable. Some conjectured that Evelina's absence was owing to her thinking that it would look too particular for her to ride in the same carriage with a suitor; others, that she was afraid to let Mr. Grattan see her by the side of Mr. Hicks. There were some few, however, who knew Evelina well, and thought she had acted in strict accordance with her known prudence and delicacy of character.

"Upon my word," said Miss Eliza McKnight, "you seem to be upon the high ropes, to-day, Mr. Hicks. No wonder, when you have been more highly favoured than I have ever known a stranger to be."

"How's that, Miss Eliza? your remark wants explanation."

"Why, sir, to be set up in Mr. Preble's carriage—perfectly at home, sir,—entertaining the old gentleman, no doubt, with future prospects of happiness for yourself and his daughter! There's Evelina staying at home, too, thinking it wouldn't look entirely prudent for her to be seen going abroad in the carriage with her intended. It may be she was afraid some one else might have been here to-day, who might have thought his right to ride in the carriage was prior to yours, sir."

"Your conjecture was ahead of the fact, Miss McKnight. I wish it may be realized, however, at some future day."

The lady bit her lips in evident displeasure, for she had hoped to have drawn from Mr. Hicks a declaration that he had no intention of addressing Miss Preble. His conversation thus failing to be as pleasant as she wished, she took a vacant seat, leaving him standing in the floor.

George Preble occupied a seat next Mrs. Boswell. The latter remarked that she sincerely regretted his sister's absence.

"Evelina," he replied, "was perfectly right not to come; and as soon as I saw that man Hicks get out of my father's carriage—knowing the prudence and delicacy of my sister as well as I do—I was satisfied she was not there. It is no longer a secret that she is actually engaged to Mr. Grattan; and what would have been thought, if she had to-day accompanied, in her father's carriage, this man who has been pestering her with his visits, and who is already supposed to be her lover?"

"Although, Mr. Preble, I regret Evelina's absence, I must say that I admire her the more for not coming, under those circumstances. She has acted just as I think she ought to have done. Why did not Major and Mrs. Scott come?"

"I thought they were coming, madam, until the carriage

came to the door. They then both said they had no disposition to go into company to-day. Just look over yonder, Mrs. Boswell, at Benson. What does he look like? We gave him a most befitting nickname at College—'Old Grum.' He has a most peculiar turn of mind; he seems to be always absorbed in his own contemplations, and I fear greatly (between ourselves), that he has, in an eminent degree, one trait of character I did not suspect until within a few days past—a money-loving, penurious disposition. His advertisement of his negroes has staggered me. I can never fully recover my former regard for him."

"Were I his bride, Mr. Preble, I should be very much concerned at his sombre appearance. I should be always uneasy lest people should think him unhappy in his marriage relation—that he had been disappointed in his wife, or something of that sort. I suppose, however, it is small concern Amelia gives *herself* about it."

"Very possibly; if she can hug and kiss old Mammy Betty five or six times a day, it is the summit of her happiness."

"Betty is to go with them, to Boston, I understand. Indeed, Amelia told me so herself."

"O! yes—she is to go. Amelia would sooner part with Benson, than with her; though Benson had rather carry the old dame to Boston in his pocket, in the shape of banknotes, than in human form."

The Doctor, seeing how completely Benson had cut himself off from the lively social intercourse of the company, here took a seat by him in his hermitage of a corner, and inquired if he had seen much of the neighbouring country.

"No," he replied, "I take a little walk every day for exercise; but have not been on horseback since I came to Virginia."

"Well, sir, if you are fond of extensive landscape views, you would be highly gratified by a ride over the river into the mountain, from some of the heights of which you would have a splendid view of this whole valley."

"I have been so much accustomed, Doctor, to expanded water prospects, that I don't take much to land views. Moreover, the sight of vessels coming in and going out, loading and unloading, so expressively reminds one of the extensive commerce of the world, that he scarce retains a taste for other spectacles. Boston harbour now, sir, at this very moment, presents a business-like appearance which is delightful. I can enjoy it even in memory."

"But, my dear sir, when you happen to be so far removed from that scene, you might, methinks, let memory go to sleep for a while, and enjoy other scenes for the sake of variety."

"It is not my nature to take pleasure in variety. What my mind takes to, it dwells upon. For instance, I could take pleasure in thinking upon trade and its incidents, and would not care to have it shut out by any other topic."

The Doctor gave up his contest with trade and its incidents, and strolled to the side of Mrs. Benson. That lady's fixed allusion was to her intention of carrying her mammy to Boston with her. She expressed a fear, that, as Mr. Hicks had told her, the people of Boston would laugh at her for applying such a term to an old black woman, adding:

"Would you care, if you were in my place, Doctor?"

"No; I should let them laugh on, and call her 'mammy' still."

"That's just what I mean to do, Doctor; and I know besides, that all Boston can't take her from me."

"No, indeed; I'll go security for that."

"How delighted the dear old creature will be to see the big houses, and the ocean, and the ships! How happy we shall be together, there!"

"I hope you may. You may need her lively and cheering company, there, as Mr. Benson seems to be generally absorbed in his own reflections."

"Oh! he's always thinking of business. I can hardly ever get a word out of him."

"I think you will get along very well with each other —he with his trade and its incidents, and you with your mammy."

"Well, I'll promise I'll let his trade alone, if he'll let my mammy alone."

"If you will stick to that determination, madam, you will both be as happy as the days are long."

As the Doctor passed from Mrs. Benson's side, he caught the eye of Miss Rosa McKnight, who beckoned to him to come to her, where she was entertaining Mr. Sebastian.

"Doctor," said she, in an undertone, "Mr. Sebastian mentions a rumour that Mr. Benson has advertised for sale ten negroes, given him by Major Scott. I cannot credit it, that a gentleman living in the very heart of abolitionism, should do such a thing. Have you heard anything of it?"

"I have seen, Miss Rosa, more than I have heard. I

have seen his advertisement, and he as certainly intends to sell those negroes on the 15th, as that you are sitting in that chair. And what is still worse, he intends to sell them in a manner that will be accompanied with all the horrors of separation."

"Well, I never could have imagined, that after all the fuss Northerners make about slavery, a Yankee from Boston would sell negroes. I think it probable that is all Mr. Hicks is after in his attentions to Evelina Preble—getting hold of some of the old gentleman's negroes, to sell."

"I do not know whether he has been often to see Miss Evelina; but I think her sufficiently attractive in herself, to secure the visits of young gentlemen, with no help from slaves."

"She may be all that, Doctor, for what I know."

The host's next tour was one more decidedly of duty—to introduce his father-in-law, who had just entered the room. After the presentation, Mrs. Boswell inquired of her father what had detained him, and why her mother had not come also.

"You know, Ann," he responded, "your mamma never goes into company."

"Oh, papa, it would have been so fine an opportunity to make mmama acquainted with her neighbours."

Charles announced dinner, and never in the valley of Virginia had been seen a more abundant, appetizing, or tasteful display of viands than graced the board at Selma on that bridal occasion.

The Doctor's first toast was the health and happiness of the brides and grooms; and at the second round of the bottle, he looked significantly at Mr. Benson,—"Here, sir, is to trade and its incidents;" then turning to Mr. George Preble—"To California and its gold, sir." The dessert was then brought on, and to the no little annoyance of Mrs. Boswell, Charles and Cecilia, in their great anxiety to follow the pattern set for them, had forgotten some of the localities. For instance, a dish of custard glasses was placed before Mrs. Boswell instead of the plum-pudding, and the pudding before Mr. Hicks, on the side of the table; another custard dish before Miss Eliza McKnight, who sat opposite Mr. Hicks. They both observed, from Mrs. Boswell's manner in pointing towards certain dishes, that something was wrong in the arrangement; and Mr. Hicks pushed the pudding to the middle of the table, to range with the pyramid which sat before him; and Miss Eliza followed suit with the custard, completing the range with the pyramid on its lower side. After a good deal of disturbance, many directions, and officiously tendered assistance, the material discrepancies were adjusted. There were some minor ones, however, which Mrs. Boswell was content should remain, as the consequences of further effort at harmony might be still more vexatious. The slight unadjusted derangement, however, did in no way impair the flavour of the delicacies which were left somewhat out of appropriate locations. Mr. Hicks was heard to say that he could eat just as much plum-pudding carved in the middle of the table, as if it was carved at the head. The beauty of that board at Selma was in a short time marred by empty glasses, empty plates and dishes, half-destroyed cakes and puddings, &c.

As the company was returning from the dinner-table to

the parlour, Mr. Hicks proposed to Miss Eliza McKnight a walk in the garden, which she caught at with apparent delight. Uncle Robin generally spent his forenoons in attending to the operations of the plantation; it was his custom, however, to work the garden in the afternoon. Mr. Hicks and Miss Eliza went towards him as soon as they saw him, Miss Eliza pointing him out as the "pious old man who owned the cabin."

"How do you do, my old friend?" said Mr. Hicks.

"Thanky, masser, the Lord's goodness spares me yet, sir."

"Don't you get tired of work as late in the day as this?"

"No, masser, I wucks at my lesur, sir; I can't say I's ever tired."

"Would you not like to work for yourself, old gentleman, and not for a master, as you do now?"

"Why, sir, I is wuckin' for myself when I wuckin' for my masser, sir; dese close I got on, de dinner I just dun eatin', I wucks fur when I wucks for my masser."

"But wouldn't you like to be free, and work for yourself only, old gentleman?"

"Masser, I can't wuck always, you know; if de Lord spar' my life, I gwine git too old to wuck, some time or other, sir; and what I gwine do den, if I wus free, sir? and when I gits too old to wuck, my masser gwine take care of me, till I die, sir."

"Wouldn't you like, old man, to be raised from the degraded condition of a slave to the level of a free white man?"

"Masser, if you b'leve me, sir, niggers can't never be raised, in dis country, as high as white folks, anyhow."

"Why not, old gentleman? if you set them free, and give them an opportunity to get property and learning, why can't they be made like the white man?"

"Well, masser, jes look at it a little while, sir: my name is Robin Strange; now, sir, s'pose Robin Strange was free man, bin to college, have fine edication, fine plantation here 'pon dis river, sir, got one carriage to ride in, sir; an' Robin Strange hear dat Mister Dr. Boswell was gwine have one fine weddin' party of white gentlemen an' ladies; an' he, Robin Strange, put on he ruffle shut, hab he carriage got, an' ax heself to go an' dine dar, too. When Robin Strange drive up to de door, sir, you think Mister Doctor Boswell gwine meet him at de door, help him out of he carriage, and say, 'I mighty glad to see you, to-day, Mr. Strange?' No, sir; jes' soon as he see one black man in dat carriage, he ider tell him heself, or he sen' him word, sir, dat he don't en'tain black people at he house, an' he mus' go back home; an', sure 'nough, Mr. Robin Strange go back home, sir, wid flea in he ear. Is dis bein' on a level wid white folks, masser? *Here* 'tis, masser (running his finger over his hand and face); dis here colour, sir, mus' war out 'fore you can make niggers equal to white people, sir."

"Is it possible, old man, that you would rather be a slave than to be free?"

"Masser, I tells you de plain truth when I say yes. Dis, sir, is no country for free black man; Africa de only place for he, sir. I 'vise de young ones, sir, whose massers want um to go to Africa, to go dar; but I too old, sir, to go to Africa. My masser been say to me, over an' offen, 'Robin, you may have your freedom, an' you wife an' children, too, if you'll go to Africa.' I say, 'No, masser, I don't want to leave you, sir; an' I's sorry you willin' to part wid me, sir.' "

As they were returning to the house, Miss Eliza said: "I declare, Mr. Hicks, Uncle Robin is a right queer old man, isn't he? and didn't he say some things that were right true?"

"No, indeed, miss, I could have upset everything he said, if I had had time."

"Well, you people from the North, Mr. Hicks, know a great deal about these things. I always thought that if I was to go to the North, I should be an abolitionist. Now, there are some people, if they were to go to the North Pole, would like to carry slaves along with them; I mean their notions about slavery. There's Evelina Preble, so fond of slaves and slavery, that I do not think she would ever consent to live anywhere but in a slave state."

"Miss Evelina Preble is so sweet and angelic a creature, that she might almost persuade an abolitionist to come and live in a slave state, if he could get her on no other terms," replied Mr. Hicks.

Miss Eliza McKnight had thought that Mr. Hicks's invitation to a walk in the garden, was a good omen for her; but that last reply was overwhelming. When she got into the house, she told her sister Rosa and Mr. Sebastian (who had come with them), that it was time for them to be going home.

The company all left in good time for getting home. As Mr. Stephens was taking leave, Mrs. Boswell said, "Papa, I will not trouble you with any bundle, for mamma, as I have already sent her some of all the good things we have had, to-day. You and she must come over, to-morrow, and help the Doctor and myself to eat what is left."

A short time before Mr. Preble and Mr. Hicks were expected back at the Cottage, Evelina said to her Aunt Priscilla, "Aunt, I suppose we shall have Mr. Hicks here with papa, to-night, as his riding-horse was left here. What would you advise me to do, aunt; shall I go down to supper or not?—I dislike very much to go into his company, again, and I don't think I can treat him with common politeness, if I go."

"My dear Evelina, I would advise you to go; your father was a good deal nettled at your not going to Selma, and I think you should avoid, as much as possible, giving additional cause of offence, particularly at a time when you stand so much in need of his kind consideration for you. He will, no doubt, invite this gentleman to stay all night, and if he stays, I think it will be treating your father with disrespect not to assist him in entertaining his company."

"Well, aunt, if you think so, I will go down and make an effort not to be rude to this man, whom I think I despise more than I do anybody else in the world."

Mary then told them that the carriage had returned, and that the gentlemen were in the parlour. Shortly afterwards, Mr. Preble sent for Evelina to come down. She obeyed the summons without going to her toilet. Instead of endeavouring to improve her appearance, she would rather that night have frightened Mr. Hicks away by her uncomeliness, than to have been in his sight a perfect Hebe. But her loveliness, "when unadorned," was "adorned the most;" and Mr. Hicks thought as she entered the room, that he had never seen her look so bewitching.

"You can't think," said he, "Miss Preble, how much pleasure you have missed in not making one of the party at Selma, to-day. I do not think that I have ever been at a more agreeable dinner party."

"I have no doubt, sir, that every effort was made on the part of your entertainers, to make it agreeable to their visiters."

"Your absence was very much regretted, Miss Preble, by your friends; and many inquiries were made of me as to the cause of your not being there, which inquiries I was entirely unable to answer."

"I think it rather strange, sir, that they should have made the inquiries of a stranger, and not of my father, who ought to have been presumed to know better than yourself, what had kept me at home."

"I believe they made the same inquiries of him, miss. Did they not ask you, Mr. Preble, what had prevented your daughter from going, to-day?"

"Yes, sir," said Mr. Preble; "but I am sure I was as unable as yourself to assign any good reason for her not going."

"I heard some conjectures, miss, by one of your female friends, as to your reasons for staying at home. Miss Eliza McKnight had her notions upon the subject, but I am not at liberty to say what they were."

"I have not the smallest inclination, sir, to hear the conjectures of Miss Eliza McKnight upon a subject which she could have known nothing about."

"I guess Miss Eliza is rather a cute one, from what I have seen."

"I do not exactly know what you mean by cute, sir; but if she formed any conjecture (coming near the reality) of what kept me at home, she must have more sagacity than most people."

"I'll tell you what she had sagacity enough to find out, miss; she says you are very much of an anti-abolitionist—that she does not think you would ever agree to live in a free state."

"In *that*, sir, I will give her credit for just as much sagacity as she is entitled to, for having discovered, and truthfully related, what my feelings are upon that subject."

"If you were to go to a free state, miss, and experience the real happiness resulting from the fact that every one around you was just as free as yourself, your prejudices would be soon laid aside, and you would be astonished that you could ever have enjoyed anything like happiness in a country where there are so many human beings in a state of bondage."

"Those persons, sir, who have been born among slaves, and have enjoyed happiness among them, and know how happy the slaves are, too, had better remain where they are, instead of seeking for a larger amount of happiness where it may not be found. And on the other hand, persons who have found their happiness in countries where slavery does not exist, had better content themselves to remain—their views and feelings being suited to that state of things."

"Your views, miss, would produce an entire stoppage of matrimony between citizens of the free and slave states.

I should certainly conjecture, from that remark, that you thought my cousin Amelia had done very wrong in marrying Bob Benson."

"I have expressed no opinion, sir, and mean to express none upon that particular occurrence. They have exercised their pleasure upon the subject, and it is not for me to say whether it is right or wrong."

"Suppose you were to marry a gentleman who, after marriage, wished to reside in a free state; would you not think it your duty to submit to his decision, and go wherever he wished you to go?"

"If I were to marry a gentleman, resident of this state, and his interest called him to a free state, I should, of course, sir, not object to his removal, although it might be very much against my inclination."

"I have known many instances of that kind to occur, miss. Ministers, for instance, often receive calls, and accept them, too; and leave slave-holding states for the free. A minister's wife, I presume, would not hesitate, when his interest called him to a free state, cheerfully to obey the call?"

"I presume not, sir, if she loved her husband as I suppose all good ministers' wives do; and, if a wider field of usefulness lay before him in a free, than in a slave state, it would be sinful in his wife to wish him to disobey the call."

"Distinguished ministers, who occupy country parishes in the South, are very apt to receive calls from our Northern cities; and from the reputation of our friend, the Rev. Mr. Grattan, I guess it is not improbable that he may receive a northern call, some time or other."

"The Rev. Mr. Grattan, sir, will be faithful in discharge of his duties to any congregation who might be so fortunate as to obtain his services."

Evelina could stand such conversation no longer, and left the parlour. Her father had been reading a newspaper, during the latter part of the conversation above detailed; and when Evelina retired, his paper was laid aside.

"Have you a father living, Mr. Hicks?" said he.

"Yes, sir; my father is an importing merchant in Boston. He owns several ships, and has some important adventures now upon the ocean."

"His business, then, I suppose, is profitable?"

"Yes, sir; he is engaged in the East India trade, with a partner residing in Salem; and they have been very successful. I suppose my father, sir, can't be worth less than half a milllon of dollars."

"A large family, I suppose?"

"No, sir; I have only two brothers, and one sister, who married a wealthy merchant in Salem. I guess he's almost as wealthy as my father. One of my brothers is doing a good business for himself; the other is a youth, at school; and, when I get back, I expect to join my father in business; so you see, sir, we are a thrifty family."

"Very, indeed, sir."

"Mr. Preble, the subject upon which I was talking to you, to-day, on our way to Selma, is one that I have much at heart; but I very much fear I shall have to abandon it, as I should rather infer that Miss Evelina's affections are engaged. I hear from various sources that there is a good understanding between herself and the Rev. Mr. Grattan, and the manner in which she speaks of that reverend gentleman confirms the reports."

"She shall never marry Mr. Grattan, sir, as long as my head is above ground."

"I am very much at a loss, sir, to determine what course to pursue; my affection for your daughter is a very sincere one, but then there is no use in cherishing it, if it is not reciprocated."

"As I told you this morning, Mr. Hicks, I never will force her to marry against her own inclination; and I again repeat, that she shall never marry against mine."

"Does your daughter know of your determination, Mr. Preble?"

"Yes, sir, she is fully apprised of it."

"Suppose you again speak to her on the subject, Mr. Preble, and perhaps when she finds that it will be folly for her to cherish a passion for an individual whom she can never marry, her affections may be transferred to another."

"I will think about it, sir. In the mean time, it would be well not to be too precipitate, and to give her time to become better acquainted with you."

"I think you are right, sir; as Miss Evelina herself has frequently spoken of our being strangers to each other."

The next morning Miss Evelina was at her seat at the breakfast table, where the conversation carried on between Mr. Hicks and her father was not of sufficient interest to relate. After breakfast Mr. Hicks ordered his horse, and rode over to Major Scott's. George Preble brought his wife over that morning to see his Aunt Priscilla, for the first time since his marriage.

"My dear children," said Miss Priscilla, with one hand

upon the shoulder of each, "I hope the Lord will bless your union to the temporal and eternal happiness of you both. I trust you have entered upon this interesting relation of husband and wife, with a fixed determination to perform the duties imposed by that relation, and that there will be a union of effort to promote each other's spiritual as well as temporal welfare. George, my dear, the pleasure which I derive from your marriage with Julia is very much marred by the prospect that we are so soon to lose you both; and my old heart bleeds at thought of the country to which you are going, and the debased state of society in which you are to mingle. Wherever you are, my children, the prayers of your poor old aunt will ascend to heaven for your happiness, and especially for your protection from the contaminations of sinful associates."

"Aunt," said Mrs. Preble, "your solicitude for our welfare, and your prayers for our protection, will, I trust, come in aid of what I hope is the natural disposition of both George and myself, to avoid evil, and that we shall be preserved from those contaminations which you so much apprehend."

"My dear, we should not trust to any natural disposition to good which we may imagine we possess; we are all by nature poor sinful creatures, and it is only by the grace of God that we can be kept from indulging the sinful instigations of the carnal heart."

"My dear aunt," said George, "you should not look only on the dark side of the picture which your imagination has painted, but turn it over and look at the bright side too—portray George Preble and his wife, after an absence of five years, returned from California with happiness and wealth."

"Ah! George, there you have coupled two things—happiness and wealth, which, so far from being inseparable, are rarely found to unite. My dear child, how can an enfeebled poor old creature like myself, form, in imagination, the outlines of a picture, five years before its representations are to be realized? When you return five years hence, that picture (pointing to her own likeness) may be the only remembrancer of one who never ceased, during life, to mourn your absence."

Evelina, whose heart was too full for her to join in the conversation, was in tears on her aunt's bed, and when this last sentence reached her ears, her grief became violent.

"Come, Lina, you and aunt must cheer up; we don't intend to go for two months, yet."

"George," said Miss Priscilla, "Evelina has been considerate enough to keep from me your intention of selling your negroes, but Mary brought me your advertisement, and I was really shocked to learn that you were going to sell negroes when there is no necessity for doing so."

"My dear aunt, there is a necessity for my selling; I can't carry them to California."

"But, George, necessity we make ourselves, is no excuse for doing an improper act; the plea of necessity should only be used when that necessity is the result of circumstances over which we have no control. This very necessity which you talk of, should have prevented your going to California."

"Well, aunt, it's too late now; the people have been informed that my negroes are to be sold on the 15th, and I can't disappoint the public; the sale must go on. I have endeavoured to divest it as much as possible of the horrors attending the public sale of negroes."

"Those horrors, George, can't be altogether gotten rid of. I have also seen Mr. Benson's advertisement, and he will make no effort to mitigate the horrors of his sale."

"Aunt, I am entirely outdone with Benson; I did not, until within a few days past, understand his real character. I am much concerned that my college acquaintance with him should have brought him here, and caused him to be so nearly connected with us; but I couldn't help it, his first trip to Virginia was entirely voluntary, I never thought of inviting him to come to see me; the fact is, I had forgotten there was such a human being upon earth, until the day I returned from that memorable trip and found him here. He has brought, too, another Yankee here, for whom I feel a thorough contempt. What brings him so often to the Cottage, Lina? he seems to be domesticated here, riding to parties in papa's carriage, and staying with you all night."

"Indeed, George," said Evelina, "you must ask him and papa what brings him here, and what caused him to stay last night; I had nothing to do with it, and if I had my way, he should never darken our doors again. You can't contemn him more thoroughly, George, than I do."

"I never for a moment believed that it was any of your doings, Lina; and as soon as I saw him get out of the carriage, yesterday, I knew very well why you were not there, and approved highly of your prudence. I know of but one way for you to get rid of that chap."

"What is that, George? for I should rejoice to find out a way."

"Well, I am very certain that pa won't part with any of his property during his life, especially his negroes; now, if pa would just tell him so, he'd be off in a minute. That fellow, you may depend, has his eye upon negroes, he wants to make just such a speculation as Cousin Bob has made, and if he could get hold of them, you would see just such another advertisement as Cousin Bob's."

"George," said Mrs. Preble, "you should not be so severe upon the Yankees, you should recollect how closely we are now connected with Cousin Bob, as you call him."

"Now, Julia, you know you have no better feeling for Cousin Bob and Cousin Hicks than I have; indeed nobody seems to take to Cousin Hicks but Eliza McKnight, and if her father had a few more negroes, I think Cousin Hicks would take to *her*, a little more than he does."

"She evidently seemed pleased with his attention, yesterday," said Mrs. Preble; "and when they returned from their walk in the garden at Selma, she looked as if something had disconcerted her."

"I observed Hicks," said George, "in conversation with old Uncle Robin, and have a great curiosity to know what he was talking about. He is very unguarded in his remarks about slavery, and it is very probable that he was talking with him upon that subject. Uncle Robin would be too hard for him there."

George excused himself to his Aunt Priscilla for their short visit, alleging business of importance which would call him to town, after his return to Major Scott's. In their absence, Mr. Hicks had reached the Major's, where he found his cousin Bob alone in the parlour, ruminating as usual.

"Cousin," said he, "I have on hand a little love matter I've never told you of. Isn't Evelina Preble a sweet creature? I have a strong notion of addressing her. The old gentleman and myself have talked the matter over, and I think he's right well pleased at the prospect of having me for his son-in-law."

"What! did you begin with the old man first, Dick? that really is business-like. What did he say he would give her, Dick? when you begin with the old folks, it should be a matter of trade, sir, trade."

"There wasn't one word said about that, but I guess the old chap was right willing to hear something about my affairs, for he made many inquiries about father's property, the number of children, &c."

"Then he's willing for the adventure, without putting in any capital. Ah! Dick, that's the old one exactly. I heard George say, when I was in Virginia before, that his father would never part with one cent's worth of his property, during his life. We, you know, Dick, go for mutual risk and mutual profit in trade."

"Well, cousin, did you in your own case take care that there should be a pledge of capital before you made the adventure?"

"No, but in my case it was different; there was every reasonable expectation, which was not dashed by the knowledge of any peculiar fondness for property's remaining in hand during life. In trade, Dick, we sometimes embark in speculation, upon reasonable probabilities—never against them, however."

"Upon my word, cousin, you haven't made trade your study for nothing. I'll see into this matter a little further, before I embark in a partnership adventure where capital and risk are all on one side, and probabilities adverse, too. I'll go to-morrow, and see the old fox again."

CHAPTER XI.

ABRUPT LEAVE-TAKING.

ON the same day Mr. and Mrs. Stephens walked over to Selma, to spend the day. The latter was in fine spirits, and looked upon the poor creatures, whom she had heretofore shunned, with as much calmness and composure as if she had been with them all her life. In the afternoon, she proposed to her daughter a walk to the cabin she had heard so much about; and, after admiring Uncle Robin's sanctum, their walk was continued through the whole line of Cabin Row. When she had completed the inspection of all the cabins, she declared she had never, before, any idea that slaves were made so comfortable. On their return, they passed through the garden where Uncle Robin was engaged in his afternoon work.

"How are you to-day, Uncle Robin?" asked Mrs. Stephens.

"Thank you, missis, Robin still spared, madam; he mighty glad to see you, missis, lookin' so well. How dem gals been behave deselves?"

"Those girls have behaved themselves remarkably well, Uncle Robin, and have been a great comfort to me. The difference between them and the Crosbys is very great, to be sure, and I feel much indebted to you, Uncle Robin, for removing from my mind some of my prejudices against slavery."

"Missis, if I bin de poor instrument, madam, in de hand of de Almighty, to brung you to see things right, you must give de praise to Him, madam, and not to dis poor cretur' Robin. Missis, when you did fus' com' here, I did pity you mightily, madam; I did see dat you was under great mistake 'bout we slaves. Is what I bin hear 'bout people in your country true, madam? dat dey car' picturs about, an' show 'em to eberybody, wid niggers tied up by de heel, an' head down, an' oberseers whippin' dem wid ox yoke; an' some oder picturs, wid niggers tied down to de floor, an' der foot roastin' at de fire; an' some more, too, wid niggers' hands sco'tched wid de brand? I s'pose dem picturs, madam, if der's any truth in what I bin hear, make you feel so bad when you fus' com' here; an' I did wan' tell you so bad, madam, dat I bin neber see sich things in Fugginney, an' I neber hear talk of sich things tell I hear 'bout de picturs way back North, madam. I bin hear, too, missis, dat der's some folks who tells de people, dar, dat massers in dis country, when der niggers runs away, puts out a noration, dat dey will give four hundred dollar' to anybody who will bring one o' der run-away niggers to um, dead or 'live, madam. Now, missis, does you thinks der's any such a foolish masser in dis worl' who gwine giv' four hundred dollar' for de 'struc-tion of he own property?"

"Well, Uncle Robin, I have heard of pictures repre-senting the cruel treatment of masters to their slaves, but I don't know that I ever have seen one. I have heard, however, a great many untruthful statements, and those statements had something to do with my bad feelings, I have no doubt; but the story about the four hundred dollars was too absurd to be believed."

"Dat's jus' what I s'posed, madam; de Lord will bring dem people to judgment, madam, for slanderin' der neighbers."

"Uncle Robin, did you get the cake I sent you yesterday evening?" asked Mrs. Boswell.

"Yes, missis, an' I thousand times 'blige' to you for recollectin' Robin, when you had so many gentlefolks to tend to, madam."

"Good-bye, Uncle Robin," said Mrs. Stephens; "you mustn't forget your promise to come to see me."

"No, madam, I gwine try an' com' ober some o' dese times."

On the following day old Mr. Preble and Mr. Hicks were in the parlour together, at the Cottage.

"How do you think those negroes, advertised for sale on the 15th, will sell, Mr. Preble?"

"I think Mr. Benson's, sir, will sell very well; but George will make a great sacrifice of his, by confining the sale to persons residing in the county. I don't think George ought to do it. The fact is, Mr. Hicks, when people sell slaves, they might as well get for them as much as they are worth. George is under no sort of obligation to let the people of this county have his property for less than its value. When slaves are sold, it's just one of the consequences of their being made property by law; and unless the law is altered, I don't see that it is incumbent on one single individual to be making an effort to mitigate the rigours of the law, and depress the value of property in his own hands, below what it is in the hands of other people. Benson will get at least twelve hundred dollars more for his lot than George will get for his."

"It was very liberal in Major Scott, sir, to divide his property into three equal lots, and give to his sons-in-law as great an amount in value as he retained for himself. I suppose it is not very common in Virginia, for a parent to divide his property before his death, and give it to his children?"

"No, sir, by no means; parents generally spend large portions of their property in educating their children, and when that is done, they very wisely think that their children should not come in for the balance until their deaths. I have spent a good deal of my property upon the education of my children, and I am determined not to give them any more until my death. I shall leave George this plantation, and Evelina some negroes. As long as she remains single, she of course will be genteelly supported here, but she must look to it when she marries, and take care that she marries a man able to support her."

Mr. Hicks was not anxious to conduct the conversation further, and took his final leave of the Cottage. He left so abruptly that old Mr. Preble was fearful he had been too explicit, but he could not bring himself to making any promise of property before his death. Although he would have been willing that Evelina should marry Mr. Hicks on account of his reputed large fortune, he had no great anxiety that she should marry at all, as George was about to leave him for five years. Had he known, therefore, that Mr. Hicks would not repeat his visits to the Cottage, it would have given him no very great concern. It was expected that he would give the wedding-parties a dinner, but the old man had his notions of economy, which were adverse to all expenditures not absolutely necessary; he was, moreover, heard to say that the uneasiness of Evelina and Miss Priscilla, at the expected departure of George, forbade anything like hilarity at the Cottage.

CHAPTER XII.

THE SALE.

THE 15th of June at length came round. The departure of twenty slaves very early in the morning from Major Scott's, was attended with violent grief and lamentation. Although they had been selected in families, there were many dear relatives and friends left behind. Mrs. Scott confined herself to her room, not wishing to witness the scene; the Major went to and fro like a maniac, lamenting his folly in having been instrumental in producing such anguish. Mrs. Preble, like a perturbed spirit, was wandering from room to room, without any apparent motive. Mrs. Benson, with her arms around the neck of old Mammy Betty, gave vent to her feelings in the exclamation: "Oh! Mammy, I'm so glad you are not one of them." The lamentations in the yard and cabins were truly piteous. George and Mr. Benson followed the wagons, and they were all at Mr. Frazer's before ten o'clock. The crowd they found there was great, and still increasing. George's lot of slaves were placed on one side of the road, separated into families; Mr. Benson's on the other. The crier took his stand on a box in the middle of the road. Mr. Bosher and four other soul-drivers (as they are called) were present, and confined themselves to that side of the road where Mr. Benson's negroes had been located; they were very minute in their inspections, examining their limbs and various parts of their bodies, opening their mouths and examining their teeth, pulling off hats and bonnets, and making, in their own peculiar slang, remarks about bald heads, gray hairs, scars, &c. There was a woman in Mr. Benson's lot with an infant in her arms, who seemed to be in agony of grief, and to every trader who came up to examine her, she said: "Oh! masser, do pray, masser, if you buy me, buy my poor little baby an' my husband wid me; t'other chilons may go, sir, but I can't part wid my poor little baby an' my ole man, sir."

Her master walked by, and she implored him most piteously to set up herself, her husband, and her poor little baby together; but he said he had informed the public that they would be set up separately, and he couldn't now alter his arrangements.

It was so arranged that George Preble's lot was to be first sold. The crier read the terms of sale, and put upon the block, Peter, his wife Chloe, and two children, one a boy of fourteen years of age, the other a girl of twelve. They hung for some time on a very low bid; at length one dollar more was bid, and the hammer fell. "Give your name to the clerk, sir," said the crier to the last bidder; and the name of John Stephens was given. Chloe went up to George, who was standing near, and said, "Masser, I can't go to dat man, sir."

"Why not?" said George; "I should think you would rather live with him than anybody else, so near your old home."

"Masser, I don't know nothin' bout him, sir, but I bin hear he wife mighty cruel, sir."

"Oh! that's all nonsense; you *must* go to Mr. Stephens, and you will be well treated, I know."

Old Mr. Frazer was staggering about in the crowd, and when he heard that Peter and his family had been purchased by Mr. Stephens, "Well," said he, "wonders will never cease; did I ever expect to live to see the day when a Pennsylvania abolitionist would come to Virginia to buy niggers?" Many similar remarks were made in the crowd; and Mr. Stephens, to avoid further notice, had his lot put into a two-horse wagon, and was soon off for home. George's other two families were sold, at prices corresponding with the first, to persons residing in the neighbourhood. Mr. Benson's negroes were then set up singly; the competition between the five traders ran their prices up very high. With commendable feelings of humanity, Mr. Bosher purchased the woman with her young child and her husband, and promised not to separate them.

The crier announced that the sale was over, and that Mr. Benson's lot had sold for fifteen hundred dollars more than George Preble's.

"Hurrah for old Virginia humanity!" said Mr. Frazer. "George, you stay among us, old fellow, and we'll send you to Congress."

"And where will you send Mr. Benson?" cried a voice in the crowd.

"Kick him to the devil," responded Mr. Frazer.

The excitement in the crowd was so great against Mr. Benson, that George told him he thought it would be dangerous for him to remain longer. He took the hint, and left for Major Scott's.

Mr. Stephens had informed his wife, before he left home, of his intention to purchase Peter and his family. He said he had heard that they were excellent servants, and that Chloe was a good cook. She made no objection, and when they arrived was prepared to meet them very composedly.

"Well," said she, "who would have thought, Mr. Stephens, that we should be owners of slaves? But it's not much to be wondered at, seeing that slavery is so different a thing from what we supposed it to be when we left Pennsylvania. This is Chloe, and this is Peter (turning to each); and what's the name of this girl?"

"She name Sally, madam," said Chloe.

"And the boy, what's his name?"

"He name John, madam."

"Indeed! Mr. Stephens, I had rather they should have been named anything else in the world; I wished never to be reminded again of those wretched little Crosbys."

"Well, my dear, I suppose you could change their names, if you like. Were they ever christened, Chloe?"

"Yes, sir, dey bin christian by de minister wid dem names."

"It is too late to change them, now. I think their being named Sally and John very little matter, my dear."

"Oh! I don't care much about it, Mr. Stephens."

Such an accession to their numbers reminded them of the necessity of sending Molly and Kate back home.

They were directed to get their clothes, to go back to Selma, and say to their master and mistress that Mr. and Mrs. Stephens sent their best love and thanks for their kindness, and that they were sent back because they had no further use for their services. Mr. Stephens had that morning borrowed Dr. Boswell's two-horse wagon, but had not hinted to the Doctor what he wanted with it. The truth was, he was somewhat ashamed to let the Doctor know that he intended to purchase negroes.

"What in the world has happened, now?" said the Doctor, when the girls delivered the message. "I suppose your mother, Ann, has heard of this sale, and it has metamorphosed those girls into poor creatures again."

"Why doesn't mamma want you any longer, Kate?" said her mistress.

"De dun brung heap o' servants of de own dar, madam, de dun got Major Scott Peter, an' Aunt Chloe, an' Sally, an' John, madam."

The Doctor and Mrs. Boswell looked at each other with astonishment.

"My prophecy, Ann, has had its fulfilment in a much shorter time than I expected."

"Suppose we walk over, after dinner," said Mrs. Boswell, "and see this wonder of wonders, my father and mother surrounded by slaves of their own."

They went over in the afternoon, and were met by the old people with countenances which would be vulgarly called sheepish.

The Doctor, in a playful manner, said, "I understand, Mr. Stephens, you have been buying some of these 'poor creatures' at last."

"Oh! Doctor," said Mrs. Stephens, "don't be too hard upon us, we have only given you an evidence of the thorough change in our feelings and sentiments; and as for 'poor creatures,' let the expression become obsolete with *us*, at any rate; let us remember it as a thing that was, and that is now gone for ever."

"Well, madam, it belonged to you, and you can make what disposition of it you please, even to bury it for ever."

The new purchase was brought in for the Doctor to pass judgment upon the bargain. He pronounced them very cheap.

"What are the names of your children, Chloe?" asked the Doctor.

"De gal name Sally, an' de boy John, sir."

"Mrs. Stephens, I should think you would like those two *names* to become obsolete, and to be buried alongside of 'poor creatures'."

"It will be a hard trial to me, Doctor, to have those names always sounding in my ears, but I hope after a while to forget those detestable children they now remind me of."

"Doctor, what shall I do with Rachel?" asked Mr. Stephens. "We have no use for her now, as Chloe will be our cook hereafter."

"She is free, you know, and she can go where she pleases. Give her some little matter to release you from your contract with her, and she can get employment elsewhere without any difficulty."

CHAPTER XIII.

A TRIP TO BOSTON.

ARRANGEMENTS had been made by Mr. Benson to leave for Boston, on the day after the sale: he, his wife, Mr. Hicks, and Mammy Betty, left Major Scott's early in the morning of that day for the depot. Mrs. Scott and the Major had suffered so much in anticipation of that event, that the reality was rather a relief than otherwise. Amelia promised, when she left, to pay them a visit at the end of twelve months; to which Mr. Benson consented conditionally, if trade was slack in the following June. We will follow them to Boston; nothing of importance occurring in their journey, except that an effort was made in Philadelphia to prevail upon Mammy Betty to leave them. Old Mr. Benson's house was on State street, at which they arrived in the afternoon of the fourth day from Virginia. Amelia was received by her father and mother-in-law, not with that warmth of affection with which a Bostonian daughter-in-law would have been received in Virginia, but with as much kindness and politeness as the old people were capable of manifesting. Mr. Benson, Sr., was the prototype of Mr. Benson, Jr. Trade and its incidents, with him, never gave way to any protracted exhibition of kindness or politeness; and, in a few minutes after his first introduction, he was in his counting-room again.

Mrs. Benson the elder was a middle-aged lady, cold and formal in her manners, extremely neat and precise in her dress, the style of which was that which prevailed in New England a hundred years before; she was unquestionably of Pilgrim descent, and, to all appearance, not many generations distant from Pilgrims of the olden time. She and her son conducted Amelia to the parlour, and Mammy Betty, not knowing where else to go, followed them. Mrs. Benson the elder eyed the latter with intense curiosity.

"Robert," she said, "who have you brought here with your bride? I trust you haven't brought a slave along with you, my son?"

"Mother, you know there can be no slaves in Massachusetts; this old woman was a slave in Virginia, but she is now free, and as she is very fond of Amelia, having nursed her, I consented to her coming with us; we should have to hire a servant at any rate for our chamber, and she will answer very well as Amelia's chamber cleaner, at lower wages too than we could possibly get a white one."

"You are so accustomed to black waiters, child, that you don't want to be waited on by white ones, I guess?" addressing herself to Amelia. "Moth—moth—Mrs. Benson," said Amelia, "I have no dislike to white servants, madam, but my old Mammy Betty and myself are so fond of each other that we couldn't bear to be separated."

"Is it possible, child, you call her mammy? That's like the poor people here, who, when they say mammy, mean mother."

"In Virginia, madam, all the children call their black nurses mammy."

"Well, child, it does sound mighty strange; the people here will laugh at you, child, but I guess it won't be long before this old woman you call mammy will take herself off from a person who has so long held her in bondage."

"No, missis," said Mammy Betty, "I'll never leff my 'Melia, madam, while my head hot; ebery body in dis big town, madam, can't 'duce me to leff my 'Melia."

"Well, old woman, if you stay here, you'll have to keep Amelia's room very nice, and bring her water, and in the winter keep her in fire."

"Missis, madam, I kin do all dat, if so be dat de wood ant too far to brung, madam."

"How curious she talks, child; is that the way the slaves in Virginia all talk? You needn't be afraid, old woman, of having too much to do—the wood and water won't be very far off. Amelia, child, I hear the bell ringing for supper; come along with me."

"Whar mus' I go, missis?" said Mammy Betty.

"Why, you don't expect to go with us to supper, I hope? we don't eat with blacks in this country."

"Dey don' do so nudder in Fugginny, madam."

"Do you go up those stairs, and turn into the first right hand room, that's Amelia's room, and I will send you some supper. Does she know which is her right hand, child?"

"Oh, yes, madam," answered Amelia.

When supper was over, the old lady carried her daughter-in-law up into the room which had been prepared for her, and which had all the comforts and adornments of a bridal chamber. Mrs. Benson the elder opened a door into a small apartment, and told Mammy Betty that, although it had been intended as a closet to Amelia's room, she might occupy it as a bedroom.

Mr. Benson, Sr., and his son repaired to the counting-room when the ladies left the supper-table. "Robert," said the old man, "how did you make out in Virginia; any cash, my son?"

"Oh, yes, sir, I got property which I converted into cash; the old gentleman gave me ten negroes, which I sold for about four thousand dollars."

"Upon my word, Robert, it won't tell well in Boston, that you have been selling slaves in Virginia; but as that was your wife's dowry, and you were not allowed to bring them here, I don't see how you could have done otherwise."

"No, sir; if we come lawfully into possession of what is property in the South, in our hands it must carry along, and be subject to all the incidents of property; and sale and barter, you know, are its incidents."

"I see, Robert, you have brought an old woman with you; what are you going to do with her?"

"I have just told mother of our arrangements in regard to her; she is an old woman much attached to Amelia, and Amelia to her; she will live with us on very moderate wages, and will do all the work of a chamber servant."

"But she is old, and can't be useful many years; what will you do with her when she is past work?"

"My father-in-law, Major Scott, will take her back at any time; and at some future period, when she seems to be failing, Amelia and I can take her back to Virginia, and leave her there. Well, father, how has trade gone in my absence?"

"It has been as brisk as it usually is in the summer season; there's every promise of a good fall business."

"Any shaking, father, within the last month?"

"Yes, the firm of Coots & Co. like to have gone; we are clear of that concern, however; I saw the danger ahead, and prepared for it. Benson & Son are off their paper, but I think they will recover from the shock and keep up."

Their conversation about trade and its incidents was kept up until a late hour. Mrs. Benson saw but little of her husband during the day; her mother-in-law was not very agreeable to her, and she was perhaps less so to the old lady; consequently, she spent most of her time in her own room, where she enjoyed the company of her mammy more than she would have done even that of her husband. In the afternoon of the third day after their arrival in Boston, old mammy Betty came suddenly into the chamber and threw herself on the floor, frightened almost into a state of insensibility, exclaiming, "Oh, my 'Melia, my 'Melia, I don' see jus' now in de street one crazy man, an' if you b'leve me, he jump at me jus' like he gwine seize me."

"Well, mammy, don't be frightened; he can't hurt you now."

"Oh, my 'Melia, he's great big nigger man, he hardly got any clothes on, an' when I fus' see him he was bent almos' double, coughin."

"Mammy, I don't reckon he's mad, it's some poor old beggar; he didn't intend to hurt you."

"Yes, he did, 'Melia; if he had cotched me he'd a tare my very life out o' me."

The old woman had to go into the street every afternoon for water; the next time she went she came running back, if possible more frightened than before; she hastily put down her pitcher, and wringing her hands, cried, "Oh, my 'Melia, I don see dat mad man 'gin; he follow me to de do', and jus' miss ketchin' me by my frock; he now at de do' if you b'leve me."

"Well, I will hoist the window, and see what he wants."

She hoisted the front window, and saw a black man standing before the door, half bent, and coughing. He had a few rags around him.

"What do you want here, my man?"

"Missis, I seed one ole black 'oman go in at dis do', an' I knows her, madam. Please, missis, ax her to come down here; I wan' talk wid her. I wouldn' hut her, missis, for anything in de worl'; I loves her too much, missis, to hut 'er. Ax her please come down."

After a great deal of persuasion, she consented to go, provided her 'Melia would hoist the window again, and look out while she was talking with him.

As soon as she reached the door, the man threw his arms round her neck, burst into tears, and said, "Mammy Betty, don' you know Tom?"

"My goodness!" said she; "is dis my masser boy Tom? Oh! Tom, I's so glad to see you."

"Mam Betty, how you lef' my poo' mammy an' daddy? Mam Betty, I ain' bin see any peace sence I lef' my masser house. Oh, Mam Betty, if I was but back dar 'gin, how happy I would be! I mos' gone in 'sumption, Mam Betty; I bin 'blige to sleep out 'pon de ground, and I shill neber git shut of dis cole I bin cotch. Tell me, Mam Betty, what brung you to dis place?"

"Tom, you daddy an' mammy was bofe well; and dey was moughty sorry when you lef'. I com' here, Tom, wid my 'Melia, who dun marry one man in dis very house, Tom."

"Was dat my Miss 'Melia dat hice de winder?"

"Yes, Tom; she dun gone from dare, now."

"Oh! Mam Betty! Mam Betty! what shill I do? I does wan' go back so much to Fugginny, to see my daddy an' my mammy, my masser and my missis, an' all de black folks. Oh! Mam Betty, ax my young missis to sen' her pa word I's here, an' dat I does wan' so much to go back to he plantation. Oh! Mam Betty, if I could but lay dis poo' achin' head 'pon my mammy bres, how happy I should be! Poo' Tom gwine neber see he daddy an' he mammy 'gin. Oh! Mam Betty! Mam Betty! Mam Betty! what is I to do?"

"Tom, you does 'stress me mightly; I wishes I could do somethin' fur you. I'll ax my 'Melia to git you som' clothes, Tom."

"Mam Betty, I almost starve', an' mos' naked, but I don' wan' anything to eat or to war. All I now want in dis worl' is to go back home, and die 'pon my mammy bres."

"Tom, what becom' o' Harry?"

"Harry dun ded, Mam Betty. When we fus' com' here, we gits som' wuck 'pon de street; an' Harry an' one white man begin to quarrel, an' de white man say, 'If ebery master had he due, you wou'dn' be here now,' meaning dat Harry was one runaway; and Harry, thinkin' he was free, strike de white man, and he tak' up one bar o' iron an' hit Harry 'pon de head, an' kill him, Mammy Betty."

"Tom, does dey let white man kill niggers, here?"

"Dey try him fur it, Mam Betty, but t'other white mens swar Harry was gwine kill him; an' dey let him off.

Dese very folks who tell Tom he was runaway, if my masser was to come here fur me to-morrow, would swar dey know'd I was born free."

Tom was too much distressed by his cough to say more. Mammy Betty told him he must meet her at the door the next afternoon about the same time. She returned to the chamber, told Mrs. Benson who he was, and what had passed between them. Mrs. Benson said she would write to her pa after supper.

At the supper table, Mrs. Benson the elder said to her child, "What is the matter with the old woman? I met her running up stairs very much alarmed, as I thought."

"She saw in the street, madam, a negro man, and supposed he was crazy; but she afterwards found out, that he was a man who had run away from my pa, some months ago. Poor fellow, he is in a mighty bad way, and wants to get pa to come for him; and I'm going to write to pa this night, and ask him to come."

"Amelia," said Mr. Benson, Sr., "I shouldn't like that any owner of a runaway slave should be informed by any member of my family where he might find and recover him; and I had rather you wouldn't write."

"He belongs to pa, sir, and don't you think pa ought to have him?"

"By no means; your father had no right to hold him in bondage; and as he has escaped, it would be cruel to give information where he was."

"My Mammy Betty says he's mighty low in consumption; he can't work, and I think it would be more cruel to let him stay here and starve to death, than for my pa to come after him, and take care of him until he dies; at my pa's house; he would be with his father and mother, too."

"But if he gets well, child," said Mrs. Benson the elder, "after your father got him back, he would make him work as a slave again, and that would never do."

"He's never going to work any more, from what my Mammy Betty tells me." Saying this, she left the table, and returned to her room.

"Mammy, these people say I mustn't write to pa about Tom; but I will write, no matter what they say."

Mr. Benson, Jr., was in the habit of writing letters on business after he retired to his chamber at night, and Mrs. Benson found pen, ink, and paper at hand. She wrote a letter to her father, from which we extract that portion which relates to Tom.

"My good old Mammy Betty saw your man Tom in the street, and he begged her to ask me to write and request that you would come for him. Please, pa, come."

The next morning the old woman carried the letter to the post-office; and when she returned from the office, she said to Mrs. Benson:

"My 'Melia, I does wish poo' Tom had one blanket, som' baker bread, an' som' tea, an' som' sugar."

"I wish he had, my dear mammy; but I haven't one cent of money."

"Oh, I hab plenty, my 'Melia; Mas' George an' my Julia giv' me heap when we did côm' 'way."

She paraded the foot of an old yarn stocking, and with much delight exhibited two dollars and fifty cents; she put it carefully back in the stocking, which she wrapped in a piece of newspaper, and went out upon a shopping expedition, in which angels might have participated. In about an hour she returned, and the display of her purchases gave her 'Melia and herself more heartfelt satisfaction than is experienced by the votaries of fashion, after lavish expenditure upon jewelry, silks, and velvet. She had only fifty cents left, which was put away carefully in her box; that day she spent in restless anxiety for the hour of meeting with Tom to arrive. In the afternoon she told Mrs. Benson she would go into the kitchen and make Tom some tea, and put it into a bottle for him to carry to his home; where that was, she had not yet learned from Tom. When she was about pouring the boiling water into the tea-pot, Mrs. Benson the elder came in, and said, "What in the world are you about, old woman?"

"I dun buy som' tea, madam, for dat poo' half-starved cretur, Tom, my masser black man who run away from masser. Nobody in dis town seem to take any pity 'pon him, and I mus' do what I kin for him, 'cause he bin my feller sarvant in ole Fugginny, an' I knows he mammy an' he daddy, madam."

"If he's so poor and so sick and half starved, as you say he is, the town authorities had better send him to the almshouse."

"Does dey sen' black folks to dat sort o' house, madam?"

"Yes, everybody that's sick and poor and naked."

"I's sure, den, madam, dey ought to bin sen' Tom dar, long time ago."

"Your masser, as you call him, hadn't ought to have held him in bondage; you see what's come of it, old woman."

"Madam, if Tom had stay where he was, dis thing never wou'd bin com' 'pon him; he'd bin well now, madam, an' look mighty diff'rent from what de poo' cretur look now."

When her tea was ready, she carried it up into her chamber, put it into a bottle, and carried the bread, tea, and blanket to the door, where she found Tom waiting for her.

"Well, Tom, how you do to-day, my chil'?"

"Mam Betty, I gwine mighty fas'. I does feel poorlier to-day den I bin feel yit; and de misry in my bres' is more den I can 'scribe."

"Tom, here's som' good tea, and som' good baker bread, and one good blanket for you, chil'; an' I hopes you'll feel better, 'fore to-morrow."

"Mam Betty, I doesn' thinks I shill eber feel better in dis worl'."

"Tom, does you eber pray to de Lord to pardon you sins? does you eber think of leavin' dis worl', and whar you goin' to when you die?"

"Mam Betty, I does try heap to 'member what I bin hear Mr. Grattan say in my masser house, an' what I bin hear Uncle Robin say in he cabin, over at Dr. Boswell; but, Mam Betty, I's bin so sinful, I fears de Lord ain' gwine pardon me."

"Tom, did you neber hear Uncle Robin say dat de blood of Jesus Christ can 'stroy the biggest sins, dat you mus' pray to him to take he blood an' wash you wid it?"

"Yes, Mam Betty, I bin hear 'im say so, an' I try o' nights to pray; but den I begin to think 'pon my daddy an' my mammy, an' den I does forgit all 'bout prayin'."

"Well, now, Tom, dat de very thing dat ought to make you pray dat the Lord will let you meet you daddy an' mammy in Hebbin."

"Mam Betty, does you thinks I bin sin when I run away an' lef' my masser?"

"Yes, dat I does, Tom; de Lord say servants mus' 'bey der masters; an' in de room of 'beyin' you masser, Tom, you bin runaway from him; and besides, Tom, de Lord giv' you good sitiation, an' you lef' it, an' brung all dis 'pun you. Don' you call dat sinnin', Tom?"

"Oh! Mam Betty! Mam Betty! I is so sorry for what I bin do! Does you thinks de Lord will pardon me, Mam Betty?"

"Yes, Tom, if you pray to him to take dat sin, an' all you oder sins, an' wash 'em wid de blood of he son. Where'bouts does you stay o' nights, Tom?"

"One hos'ler, Mam Betty, giv' me leave to sleep 'pun de hay in he stable-loff; an' I is gittin' so weak, Mam Betty, I's feard dat I can't git here 'gin. I wan' show you whar de stable is; an', if I don' com' back here to-morrow evenin', you mus' com' an' see me."

She went with him to the next cross street, and he pointed out the stable in which he lodged; when they parted, she said, "Tom, I'gwine hav' som' mo' tea ready fur you to-morrow evenin', an' you mus' com' if you kin; an' 'member, Tom, what I bin talk to you 'bout."

"I'll try, Mammy Betty; an' I mighty thankful to you, seein' you is de only frien' I got in dis worl'."

Tom came the three following afternoons, and received his tea and bread, but Mammy Betty discovered at every visit that he was getting weaker, and his cough more troublesome. On the fourth afternoon he was not at the door; she concluded that he was worse, and determined to go to the stable. When she got there, she inquired of the hostler if that was the stable in which a sick negro man slept; and being informed that it was, she requested to be permitted to go up and see him; he pointed to a ladder, which she ascended; although it was early in the afternoon, it was quite dark in the loft; in a low voice she said "Tom!" no answer being returned, she was much alarmed; she repeated, "Tom!"

"Is dat Mam Betty?"

"Yes, Tom, 'tis me."

"Oh, Mam Betty, I is so glad to see you. I is too weak to go up an' down dat ladder, an' I couldn't go to see you. Cum here an tak' hold o' my han', Mam Betty."

She followed the direction of his voice, and took hold of his hand; it was hot and wet with clammy perspiration.

"Tom, I brung you som' tea an' bread."

"Oh, Mam Betty, how good you is to po' Tom; but I can't eat anything now. Mam Betty, when you call me I was 'sleep, and dream I seed my daddy an' my mammy; an' I thought mammy say, 'What make you go 'way from us, Tom?' an' I say, 'Mammy, I bin mighty sorry eber sence I leff you;' and den she say, 'You dun com' back, Tom, an' say you mighty sorry, an' now I tak' you to my arms, an' I is so glad to see my poo' boy, 'gin.'"

"Tom, dat's jest de way wid you Farder in Hebben: if you tell Him you sorry, and dun com' back to Him, He'll tak' you in He arms an' say He so glad to see you com' back 'gin, jest like you mammy in dat dream."

"Mam Betty, I bin pray heap sence I see you, an' I

MAMMY BETTY HANDING TOM HIS BLANKET AND TEA.

Page 250.

hope de Lord dun wash my sins in dat blood you tell me 'bout. Mam Betty, is Miss 'Melia bin hear from her pa, yit? Oh, Mam Betty, all I want now is to git back an' die in my daddy an' mammy house. I's 'fraid poo' Tom gwine die here pun dis hay; an' when *you* gone, no frien' here wid 'im. Oh, Mam Betty, if my daddy an' mammy was jus' but here to close dese eyes, I could die in peace. Oh, Tom, Tom, what mak' you do so? to lef you daddy and mammy, and com' here to die in dis lof'."

The old woman had told Mrs. Benson that she was afraid Tom was worse, from his not meeting her at the door; and said if she found him very low, she should like to stay with him all night. Mrs. Benson with great reluctance consented, and throwing her arms round her neck, gave her a kiss at parting. As soon as she felt the cold clammy sweat of death upon his hand, Mammy Betty had determined to stay with him; she sat by him the whole night, and talked much to him about his God and Saviour; about midnight he seemed inclined to sleep; a still, solemn darkness reigned in that loft until the dawn of day. The old woman became alarmed—she took his hand—it was cold in death. There he lay, a corpse, with his blanket around him, a monument to Northern philanthropy, entwined in the drapery of Southern barbarity. We will direct the hand of Mammy Betty while she sketches an inscription in her own language. "Poo' Tom! dey didn't treat you as dey promise to do; if you had bin know you own good, you wouldn't bin here now." It is hoped that the hostler, for his own comfort's sake, informed the town authorities that there was a dead body in that loft, and that it was decently disposed of.

Mammy Betty restrained the violence of her grief until she arrived at home. As soon as she entered the chamber, she threw herself into a chair, and in a flood of tears, exclaimed, "My 'Melia, my 'Melia, poo' Tom dun dead." Mrs. Benson, not ordinarily very sensitive, appeared to sympathize deeply with her mammy at the death of Tom.

In a few days after that event she received a letter from her father, from which we extract that portion which was responsive to Tom's application.

"My dear Amelia:

"I received this morning your letter requesting me to come for poor Tom, which I must decline doing for several reasons: in the first place, I know it is highly probable that the people of your town would not suffer me to bring him back to Virginia; in the next, my neighbours would be up in arms against my keeping a negro who had run away to a free state, and been recovered; and after the trouble and vexation attending his recovery (if it was effected), I should be obliged to sell him to a trader. I am truly sorry to hear of his nakedness and cough; enclosed are twenty dollars, with which you must get him clothing, and whatever is necessary to make him comfortable."

"Mammy Betty," said Mrs. Benson, "now that Tom is dead, you must have back your two dollars out of this note, and I will send the balance back to pa."

"My dear 'Melia, when I did buy dem things for Tom, I neber 'spect anybody was gwine pay me back de money. I ain gwine take it, 'Melia, dat I aint."

"My dear mammy, pa's got plenty of money, and you have but a very little left; and you *must* take it."

"No, dat I won't, my 'Melia; you s'pose I gwine take pay for de little I gin poo' Tom? Neber, no neber; poo' Tom dead now, an' de poo' feller welcome to what I bin giv' 'im."

"Well, Mammy Betty, you can do as you please; but if pa knew that you had spent two dollars for Tom, and that I had not paid you back, he would not like it, I know."

"He ant 'bliged to know anything 'bout it; jest sen' back he money, and say nothin' to anybody 'bout what I bin do for poo' Tom."

"Old woman," said Mrs. Benson the elder, as she unexpectedly entered the chamber, "I have just heard that you were out all night a few nights ago; and I am come to let you know that we don't suffer our servants to be out prowling about the streets at night."

"Missis, madam, I ain' bin prowlin' 'bout de street; I did stay out, madam, all night, but I stay in one hay-loft wid a poo' dyin' feller sarvant, madam. I's sure I wouldn't lef my 'Melia, an' my own bed, for sich a place as dat, but dat I thought 'twas my duty, madam, to be wid him when he fetch he last bref."

"I don't see why it was your duty to be there with him, when there are so many other people in this town who might attend to the sick."

"Yes, missis, der's plenty oders mought bin tend to him, madam, in dis town, but from der lettin' Tom go 'bout as he did, an' die whar he did, dey can't be willin' to do much for black folks here, madam."

"There are plenty of houses here in town, old woman, where they would have taken him in, if he had applied."

"Missis, if I had bin knowd dat, I'd a ax you to take

him in, some o' dem ebenins when he was standin' here at the do', madam."

"We are not fixed, old woman, for taking in such people. I wouldn't have a dirty negro man to be staying in my kitchen for any consideration. I'm sure I shouldn't be able to eat a meal while such as he remained there."

"Madam, I reckon dar's heap o' tothers in dis town, ain't fixed for takin' in sich a poo' naked cretur' as he wus."

"Well, old woman, there was certainly no necessity for his going off to a stable, and dying there with the brutes. Was there nobody with him when he died, but you?"

"Madam, I hope Tom Lord an' Saviour, who wus born in one stable, wus wid Tom when he die dar."

"I wish from my heart, old woman, there was no such thing as slavery in the world; it is really horrible to think upon the misery it produces."

"Well, missis, I neber seed sich misry as poo' Tom's, tell I com' here, madam, an' if all de folks 'way down home, yonder, wus to set all der niggers free, we'd hab plenty o' Tom misry, madam."

CHAPTER XIV.

CRUEL MERCIES.

MRS. BENSON the younger was visited by many of the Boston ladies who were in that circle in which the Benson family moved. We regret that she was so poor a sample of Virginia refinement and cultivation. Many were the remarks which were made about her simplicity, and her calling an old black woman mammy; but it was generally allowed that she was good enough for that plodding, sombre, disagreeable-looking creature, Bob Benson.

The months of July and August were mostly spent by her in receiving and returning visits, and in long conversations in her own room, with her dear Mammy Betty. Occasionally, Mrs. Benson the elder would come with her work, and spend some time in her chamber, and she returned the old lady's visits with as much punctiliousness as she did those of other visiters.

About the first of September, when she was returning from a morning call, she was overtaken without umbrella, by a shower, and before she reached home was completely drenched. That night she complained of hoarseness and sore throat, and her mammy thought she had a slight fever when she retired to bed at a much earlier hour than usual. When Mr. Benson, Jr., came up to bed, the old woman said she thought her 'Melia was right sick. "Oh! she'll be well in the morning," he replied. Mammy Betty retired to her closet, not to sleep, however. About the middle of the night she went to her bedside, and called her in a low voice: "'Melia—my 'Melia!" "I'm not asleep, mammy," she answered, "my head aches so bad, and my temples throb so I can't sleep."

"Well, my chil', I'll set by you, wid my han' 'pun you head; may be dat will do you som' good."

She remained by her until the day dawned, when she left the room to get her water, and some wood to make a little fire, as it was a damp drizzling morning. When she returned, Mr. Benson had dressed himself, and gone down to his counting-room as usual.

"How you do now, my chil'?" she inquired.

"Oh, Mammy Betty, I'm mighty sick; I don't think I ever felt before as I do now."

"You eyes does look mighty red; does de pain you, my chile?"

"Yes, mammy, I'm in pain all over."

"My 'Melia, you ought to hav' one doctor to see you."

"Oh, no, mammy, I hope I shall get better after a while."

After the old woman had made a little fire, she went down and told Mrs. Benson the elder, that she thought her 'Melia was mighty sick, and asked her to go up and see her. She went up immediately, and finding her much more unwell than she had expected, sent the old woman down to ask Robert to come up. When he came into the room, she said,

"Robert, indeed I think Amelia is very sick; she should take some medicine, but you know we don't keep medicine, and if we did we don't know what kind to give. Don't you think we had better send over for Dr. Reid?"

"Yes, mother, if you think her very sick, I will go over myself for the Doctor."

He soon returned with the Doctor, who examined the symptoms of her disease, and pronounced her quite sick. He gave her some medicine, and said he hoped she would be better after a while; that he would be back again, towards the afternoon. Mr. Benson, Jr., took a seat by his wife's bed, remained about an hour, and then returned to his business, leaving his mother and her mammy to take care of her.

The medicine which she had taken was all thrown off her stomach in a very short time after it was administered.

When the Doctor returned, towards night, he found her much worse, and repeated the dose which he had given in the morning. He told Mrs. Benson that the fever was increasing in violence, that she was a little flighty, and that if the last dose did not produce a change for the better, she would have a severe spell. Mammy Betty overheard what he said, and it was with much difficulty she could be restrained from breaking out into violent grief. The Doctor told her that her young mistress's recovery depended in a great measure upon her being kept quiet. With much exertion she suppressed her grief while in the chamber. She often went, however, into her closet, shut the door, and gave vent to her tears.

Mr. Benson, Jr., was informed by the Doctor that his wife's situation was dangerous. As soon as he heard it he left his business, went up into the chamber, where he remained all the afternoon, assisting in nursing her. She had a restless, sleepless night, and on the following morning the Doctor pronounced her in imminent danger. Her fever raged with such violence as to take from her all consciousness. It caused exquisite torture to Mammy Betty, to find that her 'Melia did not know her. During the day the Doctor proposed that her father should be telegraphed, thinking that she might possibly live until his arrival. Old Mr. Benson went to the office and sent a despatch to Winchester, with a request that a messenger should be sent with it to Major Scott's.

Dr. Reid, at the suggestion of Mr. Benson, Jr., called in an assistant physician of high reputation, who confirmed the opinion before expressed by Dr. Reid, that her case was hopeless. Mammy Betty, now that she could no longer disturb her 'Melia, indulged in violent grief. She could be persuaded to take scarcely a mouthful of food, and no persuasions could induce her to take rest. She sat every night in a chair by the bed, wringing her hands, and weeping bitterly.

In the afternoon of the fifth day from the telegraphic despatch, Major Scott arrived. His daughter was still living, but in a state of insensibility. When he entered her chamber, Mammy Betty threw her arms round his neck, screaming, "O, masser, my 'Melia gwine die." It was with difficulty he could disengage himself from her. He walked up to the bed, kissed his daughter's forehead, and sank into a chair by her side. Understanding that the family had been sitting up for several nights, Major Scott proposed they should take rest, and that he should be suffered to watch over his daughter that night. Mrs. Benson and her husband, who both required rest, retired early. Mr. Benson, Jr., remained, and occasionally took a little sleep on a trundle bed which had been brought into the room for his convenience. Mammy Betty and her master watched the whole night; in the morning there were no favourable symptoms. She lingered until the morning of the ninth day, when she expired.

Mammy Betty's grief was beyond all description. She threw herself upon the bed near the corpse, and in agony exclaimed, "My 'Melia! my chil'! talk to you mammy; let you poo' mammy hear de soun' of dat voice once mo'. My darlin' chil' gone and lef' me here by my poo' lone self. What is I to do? what is I to do, now my poo' chil' gone?" Mr. Benson, Jr., was deeply distressed. Major Scott paced the room, in anguish of soul too deep for utterance. While those around him were bewailing their individual bereavement, his heart was stricken by his own, and the sorrows of a far distant mother and sister.

Mammy Betty was carried and laid upon her own bed. The violence of her grief subsided into a deep settled melancholy, bordering on insensibility to everything around. At four o'clock the next day, a respectable procession followed the corpse to its final resting-place, where another frail tenement of clay was consigned to its kindred earth.

Major Scott, on his return from the funeral in a hack with Mr. Benson, Jr., expressed his intention of leaving Boston in a steamship, which he understood would get under weigh for Philadelphia, from the harbour, about ten o'clock. He told Mr. Benson it was his wish to carry Betty back to Virginia.

"I would wish you to do so, sir," he replied, "as I suppose she would like it above all things; but, Major Scott, it must be done with as much secrecy as possible, or she might be prevented from going."

"I don't exactly understand you, Mr. Benson; who would think of preventing her from going?"

"If she were your own servant, Major, it is doubtful whether you would be suffered to take her; but, as she is known to be free, the difficulty will be greatly increased, from an apprehension that you, a Southern slave-owner, were about to carry a free negro from Boston to make a slave of her in Virginia."

"But, sir, I suppose free people of colour here have a right to go where they please; and if she proclaims to the mob, who were attempting to take her, not only her willingness, but her great anxiety to go, would they not let her exercise her own choice?"

"I have understood, Major, that in some instances, where that willingness to go has been declared to the mob, they said the assent had been obtained by trick and deception, and that they did not regard it as any positive evidence of the inclination of the free person to go away."

"Well, sir, what precaution had we better take to avoid these difficulties?"

"Why, I know of no other than to take her to the steamship in a hack, as secretly as possible."

"We will engage, then, the hack we are now in to be at your door about nine o'clock to-morrow morning."

When they returned, Major Scott went up into Mammy Betty's closet. A cold shuddering came over him as he passed through the chamber which had been once his daughter's, and from which he had seen her corpse taken but a short time before. He found the old woman in a doze, perhaps the first she had taken for several days and nights.

"Betty! Betty!" he called.

"Who dat call me?"

"Don't you know me, Betty?"

"Is dat my masser, my 'Melia pa? Yes I does know my 'Melia pa: what dey gwine do wid my 'Melia? where dey gwine car' her to?"

"I am come to know of you, old woman, whether you wish to go back with me to Virginia?"

"Yes, masser, I go if dey let my 'Melia go."

"Old woman, don't you know that your Miss Amelia is dead, and that she can't go back to Virginia?"

"If dey don' let my 'Melia go, masser, Betty no go nudder, masser."

The Major, finding that her mind was wandering, either from want of rest or from excessive grief, postponed further conversation with her until the morning, when he hoped she would be more rational after a good night's rest. He returned below, and requested Mrs. Benson to have her removed to another room, and something given her to eat.

The next morning, early, he went to the room to which she had been removed, found her awake, and quite rational.

"Old woman, will you go back to Virginia with me?"

"Yes, masser, dat I will, I neber gwine stay here, sir, now my 'Melia gone."

"Well, you must get up and have everything ready by nine o'clock."

"O, my masser, I is so glad I gwine from dis place! I bin see nothin' but trouble an' sorrow here, masser. Poo' Tom he die, an' 'stress me mightly; but dis las' blow, O 'tis too hebby, too hebby for me to bear!"

"It is indeed heavy, very heavy to us all, Betty; but it has come, and we must bear it."

"Masser, I hope de Lord will 'nable us to bear it, sir."

"I hope so indeed, Betty."

After breakfast, the hack was soon at the door; Major Scott and Mammy Betty took a cordial leave of old Mr. and Mrs. Benson. Mr. Benson, Jr., went with them in the hack to the steamship; when they approached, they saw a crowd on the deck of the ship, and many persons on the wharf. The Major, Mr. Benson, and Mammy Betty went immediately on board. Just as they got there, a tall stout man, wearing the badge of office, stepped up and asked, "Is this Major Scott of Virginia?"

"Yes, sir, my name is Scott."

"I am a constable, sir, of the city, and have a precept from Judge Thorndike, commanding me to take from your possession, and bring before him, a free negro woman called Betty, information having been given his honour, on oath, that you, Major Scott, are about to convey this said negro woman Betty to Virginia, with the supposed intention of making her a slave."

"I have no intention of doing any such thing, sir. The woman is free, and is very anxious to go back with me to Virginia, where all her relations reside, and she will be as free there as here; I can't let you take her, sir," taking hold of Mammy Betty as he spoke.

The captain of the ship came up, and addressing himself to Major Scott said, "Stranger, you'd better mind what you are about; this is an officer of the law, and if you resist him we shall have the devil to pay here. You must give up this woman, sir. I shall be made to suffer as captain of this vessel if I take her away." The words "look out," were sounded with the bell; the crowd rushed to the wharf, the officer dragging away Mammy Betty, the vessel was off in a moment, and Major Scott and Mammy Betty were separated for ever. She uttered an unearthly shriek, and not another sigh or groan escaped her. She was led by the officer to the Judge, who said to her, "Old woman, were you willing to have gone with Major Scott to Virginia?"

With a shriek she fell dead at his feet; the word Virginia had fallen as a flash of lightning upon her heart, and riven its last chord. Another monument was there

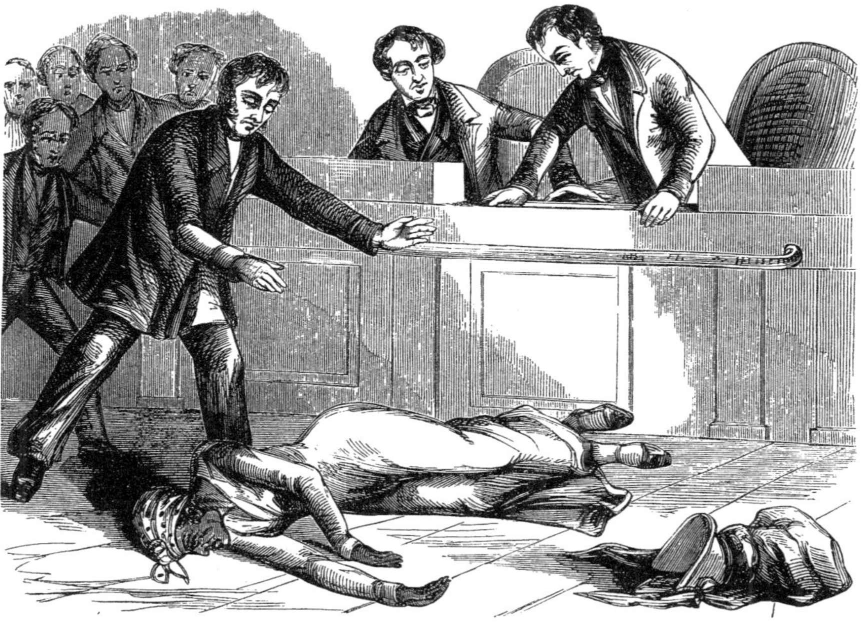

WITH A SHRIEK, SHE FELL DEAD AT HIS FEET.

Page 264.

erected to Northern philanthropy, upon which we will inscribe from Holy Writ, "Thy prayers and thine alms have come up as a memorial before God," and "the tender mercies of the wicked are cruel."

Great was the excitement in the crowd; many were heard to say, that that occurrence was only one of the many evils of slavery. A South Carolinian, however, who had been spending the summer in Boston, and was in that crowd, thought differently; and fearlessly expressed his thought, that it was the result of an officious meddling with Southern rights, miscalled philanthropy.

CHAPTER XV.

RETURN TO VIRGINIA.

READER, the sorrows of our coloured friends in Boston are over. Poor Tom, we trust (though houseless here), has found a mansion in the skies not made with hands; and ere this has welcomed Mammy Betty to a participation of his joys. We will leave their remains to the protection of mother earth, and retrace our steps to Virginia, where our hearts (stricken with sorrow for the miseries we have witnessed) will find consolation in a better state of things. The sacredness of grief must not be intruded upon by a visit to Major Scott's; we will inform the reader, however, that George Preble, upon hearing of the death of Mrs. Benson, abandoned all thought of going to California. It was settled between the Major and himself, that he and Julia should reside with her parents; that he should have the management of the Major's estate during the life of himself and wife.

We will go to the Cottage, where we shall find Doctor and Mrs. Boswell; the one attending upon Miss Priscilla Graham, who is ill, as her physician; the other as assistant nurse with Miss Evelina Preble.

"Have you heard," said the Doctor, addressing himself to Miss Evelina, "that the abolitionists in Boston had taken poor old Mammy Betty forcibly from Major Scott, after they had gotten on board a steamship? My heart bled for the old creature, when I heard it. Can you conceive of a more forlorn situation than hers? in deep grief for the loss of her soul's darling Amelia, anxious as she must have been to return to her relations and friends here, and now cut off from all comfort, and all prospect of ever seeing any of them again, in the midst of strangers, too, who care nothing about her, and who may treat her just as we heard they had treated Tom; Oh! it is too bad! too bad!" Mrs. Boswell and Miss Evelina were both weeping over the fate of poor Mammy Betty, and made no reply.

"What did you say was too bad, Doctor?" asked Miss Priscilla, who had overheard his last sentence, though pronounced in a whisper. He went up to her bed, and repeated what he had said. She put her hands upon her forehead, over her eyes, and remained silent for some time, when she said, "The ways of Providence, Doctor, are inscrutable; 'his ways are not our ways;' he makes good to come out of what to us appears evil. Perhaps poor old Betty, who had acted the part of the good Samaritan, and had bestowed the widow's mite, may have had some other idol, after the loss of Amelia, to draw her affections from her God and Saviour, and this blow may have been sent to sever her last tie to the things of earth, and to secure for her Maker and her Redeemer her entire, undivided affection."

"No doubt, madam, Providence has some good design in all its dispensations. But I had rather you would not talk any more, Miss Priscilla, as your fever is now rising, and the excitement of talking might increase it."

"Doctor," said Mrs. Boswell, "can't we devise some plan for getting the old woman back? I've got twenty-five dollars that I would most cheerfully put into a joint fund for that purpose." "I will give as much," said Evelina;—"And I will give fifty," said Miss Priscilla, who overheard again what they were saying.

"Ladies," said the Doctor, "I don't know how your charity is to be brought to bear upon this subject, unless we could prevail upon the abolitionists of Boston to sell her to us; and indeed, if they are all like Bob Benson, we may not even find that a very difficult matter."

"But, Doctor," said Miss Evolina, "although no amount of money could effect her restoration to her friends, her situation there might be rendered much more comfortable, by sending a fund there, to be laid out for her benefit."

"That's well thought of, Miss Evelina; I will make inquiry as to a proper individual to whom to intrust the fund, and we will send her on some money as soon as we have found out to whom to direct it. She who spent nearly her little all upon poor Tom, should not be forgotten when she stands in need of charity herself. Mr. Grattan will be here this afternoon, Miss Evelina, will he not?"

"Yes, Doctor, he comes every afternoon, to read and pray with Aunt Priscilla."

"I suppose Mr. Grattan must know, or have heard of some Boston minister, who would be the very person to send this fund to."

The report which old Mr. Frazer had told Dr. Boswell was in circulation, viz., that the Rev. Mr. Grattan had been forbidden to visit at the Cottage, was entirely without foundation. His visits there had not been very frequent after the wedding at Major Scott's, up to the time of Miss Priscilla's sickness, since which time he had been there every afternoon, at the particular request of Miss Priscilla, who, although she needed no instruction upon the doctrines of Christianity, derived comfort from his conversation and prayers. The little matter of misunderstanding between himself and Miss Evelina had been adjusted to the entire satisfaction of both.

To the Doctor's inquiry when he arrived, whether he knew personally, or by name, any minister in Boston, he responded that "he knew intimately, the Rev. Mr. Scholfield, a minister of the Congregational church, a man of great piety, and peculiarly fitted, by an uncommonly benevolent disposition, for the proper expenditure of any fund which might be intrusted to him for charitable purposes."

It was determined forthwith, that the fund, which was increased by contribution from the Doctor and the Rev. Mr. Grattan, should be forwarded to him.

Miss Priscilla Graham's fever raged with considerable violence that afternoon, and the Doctor advised Mr. Grattan to hold no conversation with her. She asked him herself to read a chapter in the Bible, and pray. He inquired of her whether she would wish read any particular chapter. She said they were all good, very good, precious; but that she was particularly fond of the third chapter of John. When he had finished reading it, she repeated in an audible voice: "He that believeth on the Son, hath everlasting life," and then exclaimed, "Lord, I believe, help Thou mine unbelief." Mr. Grattan then offered up a short prayer. When it was finished, Dr. Boswell and himself went down into the parlour. The Doctor informed him that Miss Priscilla's symptoms were unfavourable; he had but little hope of her recovery, as she was very old, and her system had been much shattered by frequent spells of illness.

"I do not think, Doctor," said Mr. Grattan, "that I have ever seen any individual better prepared for entering the world of spirits, than Miss Priscilla. Hers, I understand, has been a life of piety and devotedness to her Lord and Saviour; she knows and feels the reality of that new birth spoken of in the chapter she selected; she has given a beautiful exemplification of it through life, and if her mind is spared she will give a crowning testimony at her death."

Old Mr. Preble, who had been taking his evening walk, joined them in the parlour; his manner towards Mr. Grattan was cold and chilling.

"Have you seen Major Scott since his return, Mr. Preble?" said the Doctor.

"No, sir; I saw George to-day, who says they are in great distress; and he believes their distress has been greatly increased by their disappointment at not seeing the old woman Betty return with her master."

"That must have been a great shock to Mrs. Scott and Julia; I think, Mr. Preble, the conduct of the Bostonians was outrageous in that affair; I can't see upon what ground they acted in taking her away from the Major. She was acknowledged to be free by the gentleman who carried her to Boston, and by her former master, and was anxious to return to Virginia. I did suppose they would let free people go where they pleased."

"Thinking, Doctor, as the Bostonians do upon the subject of slavery, I don't well see how they could have acted differently; and besides, sir, admitting that she was free, I don't think the law of our state would allow Major Scott to go to Boston and bring a free person of colour here."

"Well, sir, if such is the law of our state, I can't exactly see how it concerns the Bostonians; we don't want their assistance in enforcing the laws of Virginia. We should be very thankful to them if they would enforce the constitution of the United States, and a law of Congress passed some years ago in relation to slavery."

While the above conversation was carried on in the parlour, a much more interesting one was held in the room of Miss Priscilla Graham. As soon as the Doctor and Mr. Grattan left, she called Miss Evelina to her bedside, and said, "Evelina, my dear, I think it my duty to inform you, that it is my firm belief that I shall not hold out many days longer. I have a feeling I cannot describe, which convinces me that my death is rapidly approaching. It is scarcely needful for me to tell you, Evelina, that death has no terrors for me; I shall meet it, not with indifference, but with joy. You know very well, my dear, that every feeling of my heart, every action of my life, had reference to that event; and now that it draws near, it seems that I am about to exchange faith and hope for never-ending fruition. The only cloud which passes over the sunshine of my last days upon earth, is the thought of leaving you; but that is dispelled when I reflect that I shall leave you under the protection of your Heavenly Father, whose ability to guard you from evil and lead you in the right way, is infinitely beyond any effort that your poor, frail aunt has ever been able to make in your behalf. My child, I shall leave you with a firm, unshaken confidence that you will put yourself under the protection and guidance of that Father, by a strict obedience to his revealed word; that you will continue prayerfully to make His precepts and His statutes your study, your delight, and your counsellors.

"Evelina, my dear, your situation at present is a peculiar one. Your aspirations after worldly happiness are drawn from a source which we both unite in believing is calculated to insure it. But your earthly parent thinks otherwise; and you are now exercised by an embarrassing and difficult conflict between duty and inclination. Such being the circumstances in which you are placed, I have thought that the advice of one to whom you have always appealed in difficulty might be needed, and would be thankfully received by you.

"As long, my dear, as your father objects to your union with Mr. Grattan, my advice to you is not to marry him. So far your duty should carry you. If your father, however, should require you not only to give up Mr. Grattan, but to marry another, on whom your affections were not placed, your father, I think, would stretch his authority over you too far, and you would not be bound to obey. In that case, the duty you owe yourself, a proper consideration for your own happiness, and the happiness of him to whom you would be required to give your hand and not your heart, are paramount to parental authority."

"My dear aunt," said Miss Evelina, "I trust the Lord will prolong for years a life so necessary to my happiness as yours; but, if it should be his pleasure to take you from me, I hope your example and admonitions will be blessed to one for whose spiritual and temporal welfare you have always evinced a mother's solicitude."

"I have a great deal more to say to you, Evelina, but my strength fails me for the present, and I must postpone it to another time." She was so weakened by the exertion she had made, that the ladies thought it advisable to send for the Doctor to come up. He found her very much prostrated, and said that many more such efforts as he was told she had made, would hasten an event which he feared must soon take place. When Miss Evelina heard the opinion of the Doctor, her fears were much more aroused for the situation of her aunt than by the old lady's own foreshadowings of her death; and she left the room to mourn in solitude. Miss Priscilla had an uncomfortable night. The next morning the Doctor thought her end rapidly approaching. Mr. George Preble and his wife were sent for; they arrived about eleven o'clock, after which time none of the family left her bedside, each one catching an indistinctly-uttered parting benediction. Her last words were distinctly heard by them all, "Come, Lord Jesus, come quickly;" "I know him in whom I have believed." Her spirit took its flight to the mansions of the blest, about four o'clock in the afternoon.

Miss Evelina's grief was deep, though silent and unobtrusive. George had always felt for his aunt a filial affection, and was more violent in his expressions of sorrow than his sister; but his was destined to give place to a natural buoyancy of spirit, before hers had reached its height.

Notice was given throughout the neighbourhood, that her funeral sermon would be preached by the Rev. Mr. Grattan. In life she had been the friend of all, particularly of the poor labouring whites, and of the blacks, both free and in bondage. Mr. Grattan preached to a large congregation, from the text, "Mark the perfect man, and behold the upright; the end of that man is peace." He said that as his funeral sermons were intended for the living, he rarely adverted to the deceased, but in the present instance he took pleasure in dwelling upon the excellencies of a character so transcendently adorned by all the Christian graces; and that the highest possible good he could wish for the living souls around him, was an imitation of her virtues.

After the funeral, Dr. Boswell was furnished with the key of her desk, and requested by old Mr. Preble to see if she had left a will. He found a paper neatly folded up, sealed, and endorsed "My will, to be opened after my death." It was opened in the parlour, in the presence of the family and a few remaining friends. It was written entirely in her own handwriting, and was dated about twelve months before.

She left her slaves (seven in number) their freedom,

provided they would go to Liberia, and in that event fifty dollars to each. If, however, they preferred not to go to Liberia, they were left to her "dearest niece, Evelina Preble." The balance of her property, amounting to about seven thousand dollars, was left to Miss Evelina.

At the earnest solicitation of Doctor and Mrs. Boswell, old Mr. Preble and his daughter went over that night to Selma, and the Cottage doors were closed upon gloom and solitude. Miss Evelina, as soon as she got there, retired to her room, and as she was silent and indisposed to conversation, Mrs. Boswell left her and joined the gentlemen in the parlour.

"What a beautiful discourse Mr. Grattan gave us this afternoon, Mr. Preble," said she; "I have heard sermons from the same text, but I don't think I ever heard one I liked so well as that."

"Yes, madam," he responded, "it was a very good sermon, but I don't think it was anything very uncommon. Miss Priscilla was everything that he made her out to be, madam."

"From what I know of Miss Priscilla, and from what I have heard from those who knew her better than I did, I would say his was a very just tribute. It would be impossible to exaggerate the excellencies of Miss Priscilla Graham's character. Mr. Grattan was well acquainted with her, and spoke from his own knowledge of her worth. Miss Priscilla also had a very high opinion of Mr. Grattan, for I have frequently heard her express herself in the most affectionate manner of him; indeed, I don't know how anybody can be acquainted with Mr. Grattan, and not love him."

"I can't say that I know much of Mr. Grattan, madam, although he is frequently at my house. It has so happened that we have had very little communication; he's very distant and reserved towards me."

"I have always thought him remarkably affable, Mr. Preble."

"He does seem so, madam, with everybody but myself."

"I have observed," said the Doctor, "that he is reserved towards persons who don't make an effort to bring him out in conversation, which proceeds, I suppose, from his diffidence, fearing lest he might obtrude his conversation upon persons who evince no disposition to be sociable with him. Now, sir, if, the next time you meet with him, you make anything like an advance, you will find him very willing to enter into conversation upon any subject whatever, and that he is well informed upon all subjects."

"I can't say, sir, that I have any great desire to overcome his reserve towards me. I shall always be polite to Mr. Grattan, but I suppose our intercourse will never be more cordial than it is at present."

Mrs. Boswell had purposely given the conversation the turn it took, hoping that Mr. Preble might say something about Evelina and Mr. Grattan, which would afford the Doctor and herself an opportunity of urging him to give over his opposition to their union; but, as he avoided any mention of the subject, they felt a difficulty in introducing it, and their conversation took another turn.

The next morning Mr. Preble returned home, leaving Evelina to remain some days at Selma. She confined herself to her room until the afternoon, when she walked into the garden, where she met with Uncle Robin.

"My young missis," said he, "I mighty glad to see

you, madam. Dey tells me you take on mightly 'bout de death of you aunt. Now 'tan' wo'th while to do dat; wou'd you wish dat angel, dat now is, who leanin' 'pun de bosom of her Lord an' Saviour in Hebbin, to com' back to dis bad worl', where you know she bin feel nothin' but pain an' misery in her ole age? Don' you know, young missis, dat she now enjoyin' happiness which our eyes neber see an' our ears neber bin hear of?"

"I hope and trust, Uncle Robin, that she is now in the enjoyment of that happiness in Heaven."

"Madam, I don' hope 'tis so, I know 'tis so, jus' same as I know you standin' dare; an't God's word true, madam? an' don't dat word tell us dat de righteous shill inherit de kingdom of Heaven, an' dat dey dat believe on de Son o' God shill be saved? an' Missis, who ever been righteous if Miss Priscilla Graham wan't? and who ever bin believe 'pun de Son o' God, if she didn't? tan't only hope, madam, wid me 'bout you aunt happiness; I know it; de truth of God's word pledged fur it; dese thoughts ought to make you 'joice instead of cryin' 'bout it."

"But, Uncle Robin, though I know she is happier in heaven, I can't help grieving for the loss of the society of one I loved so dearly."

"Now, my young missis, I tell you how you mus' git ober dat; you stribe to walk in de footstep of you aunt, follow de good lessons she bin gin you, an' bum by you'll go to Hebben too, an' be in her 'ciety not for short time, but for eber and eber. Misses, is you bin hear 'bout poo' Tom, how he bin die yonder in Bosson, in one hayloft?"

"Yes, Uncle Robin, I've heard all about it, and how kind old Mammy Betty was to him; poor old Mammy Betty, I wish she was here with her friends."

"I does wish so, mightly, madam; if dat boy Tom had mine de tex' o' de scripturs, which say, 'Put ye not you confidence in de guide,' he'd neber bin gone dar to die; he'd bin here now, dat he would. My missis, tan't wo'th while for we to pine at what de Lord order, madam; He does make de wickedness of man tell o' He glory; all dese things wuck out somethin' we don' 'speck."

Dr. Boswell received that afternoon, through the post-office, a letter from a mercantile house in Boston, informing him that a draft which had been drawn by Mr. Henry Stephens, of Norristown, Pennsylvania, dated the 2d of June, and endorsed by him, had been protested, and that the holder looked to him for payment. Mrs. Boswell was not present when the letter was received, and he determined to say nothing to her about it, fearing that she might be made uneasy at the prospect of his being involved in difficulty for her brother. He wrote to Mr. Stephens immediately, informing him of the protest, and urging him to pay the draft without delay. Although he had been assured by Mr. Stephens that it should be paid at maturity, the receipt of the protest caused him much alarm, lest he should be made to pay so large a sum of money, for which he was not at all prepared. His crop of the present year had been exhausted in paying off his store accounts, and the balance of a debt of his father's, which last had taken also the money received for his two boys; he knew of no way of paying the draft than by selling slaves, to which he was very much opposed. He cheered himself, however, with the hope that Mr. Stephens would be able to take up the draft; and that if he himself was made to pay, he might be enabled so to arrange the payment with the creditor as to save his negroes. He waited in much anxiety for an answer from Mr. Stephens; at length it came, and he was informed by him that he had found out, after his partner left for Europe, that he had involved the firm to an amount greatly beyond its solvency; he said it pained him very much to have involved so dear a friend; that he was entirely innocent of any intention to deceive; that he himself had been duped and ruined by a swindler. If the reader has ever been tortured with the apprehension of having to pay three thousand dollars of security debt, he may form some idea of the feelings of Dr. Boswell, after reading that letter. There are few readers, however, who would have borne such a blow with like equanimity, or with fewer hard thoughts of the individual who had brought it upon him.

While he was pondering upon the ways and means of liquidating so large a debt, the sheriff of the county was announced, who informed him, that he had a writ from the clerk's office of the superior court of law, at the suit of Hicks and Son, of Boston, holders of a draft which had been drawn by Henry Stephens of Norristown, and endorsed by him. The Doctor inquired who was the attorney for the plaintiffs, and the sheriff, upon examining the writ, found the name of Melchezedek Squashum endorsed on it. The Doctor was quite alarmed when he saw who were the plaintiffs in the suit; he had hoped that through the influence of their attorney they might be induced to give him time, so as to avoid the disagreeable necessity of selling negroes, particularly if an appeal should be made to their humanity; but the conduct of Mr. Hicks while he was in the neighbourhood in June, and that of his Cousin Bob, gave no promise of a favourable result from such an appeal. He determined, however, to see Mr. Squashum, and make the appeal through him.

The Doctor had never been personally acquainted with Mr. Squashum, but from what he had heard of him, his calculations of enlisting his sympathies in behalf of his servants were not very sanguine. Mr. Squashum was originally from Vermont, and had been in Virginia about fifteen years. He came here as a book agent, and having been instructed by his employers as to the general scope of the works he offered for sale, in a written summary of their contents, which he had committed to memory, he had taken up an idea that he was really a man of literature, determined to abandon his calling, and betake himself to the study of the law in Virginia.

In about two years he obtained a license and rented an office, which last act generally precedes, and is in anticipation of the coming in of fees sufficient to satisfy the landlord. Mr. Squashum had a peculiar tact at impressing others with a belief that he was a man of business; he was for ever talking of his success in the recovery of doubtful claims, and of his cunning and astuteness in the management of difficult cases; in short, he was the prince of pettifoggers, a class of lawyers who are obnoxious to their more respectable and high-minded brethren of the craft, but often run ahead of them in pocketing fees.

Whenever he thought a purpose beneficial to himself could be subserved, he was in words a thorough-going abolitionist; consequently much of his business came from that respectable portion of the community denominated Friends. It was strongly suspected, when he travelled through the country as book agent, that he tampered with slaves, being seen frequently where he could have had no other business than to hold conversations with them. His wit, of which he imagined he had a considerable fund, was lost upon every one but himself, as he rarely enlisted another to join in his incessant giggle. Such was the man to whom Dr. Boswell introduced himself as he entered his office.

"Take a seat, sir, take a seat; sit down, sit down," said Mr. Squashum, in his usually hurried, consequential manner.

"I am come to see you, sir," said the Doctor, "upon the subject of a lawsuit you have brought against me for a client in Boston."

"Boswell did you say your name was? Boswell—let me see—let me see; I must turn to my memorandum-book. Ah! true, here it is; "writ ordered versus Boswell ads. Hicks and Son, Boston, trading under the firm of Hicks and Son, Boston: a, d, s, means ad sectum, ad sectum, sir, at the suit of—we lawyers, sir, can't keep in our heads the number of suits we bring; we must refer to our memorandum-book—well, what of it, sir? I suppose the writ has been served, and you have come to pay the money, I hope. Ha! ha! ha! quick work, quick work, sir."

The Doctor being a man of education, smiled at the "tum," and replied:

"No, sir; you must be aware of the difficulty of a farmer's raising so large an amount, coming upon him so unexpectedly, too. So far from bringing the money, sir, my business with you is to solicit your aid in getting indulgence for some months after your judgment is obtained. I have parted with my crop of wheat of the present year, and my only dependence for paying this debt is my growing crop, which I suppose can't possibly be ready for market sooner than about twelve months hence; your judgment will be obtained much sooner than that, and if I don't get a stay of execution, my negroes will have to be sold by the sheriff, as the balance of my personal property would bring but little. I have never, sir, sold a negro, except for some flagrant offence, and it would occasion great uneasiness to myself and family, to have them sold by the sheriff. I am emboldened in making this application to persons like your clients, who profess great sympathy for slaves, and whose chief objection to the institution of slavery is its constant liability to a severance of the ties of nature by sale. I ask in their behalf, indulgence only for a few months. I hope the humane feelings of your clients will induce them to grant so trifling a request, and I shall esteem it a favour if you will lay my proposition before them."

"Ha! ha! ha! that's good, sir, that's good; Southern people calling upon the North for humanity towards their slaves! humanity had better begin in the South, sir. Ha! ha! ha! they'd better do the thing right at once—set them free, sir, set them free. No, I can't advise my clients to do any such thing; it's a very dangerous thing to meddle with judgments and executions. You may pick some flaw, some flaw hereafter, and my clients may lose the whole debt, sir."

"You are but little acquainted with my character, Mr. Squashum, if you suppose I would take advantage of any informality or mistake in the proceedings, to get rid of the payment of a debt I justly owe, sir."

"I don't know anything about that, but the safest plan is for the execution and the judgment to be contemporaneous—yes, sir, I say contemporaneous. Why, sir, the credit in this transaction was given to your name because it was known you held slaves, sir. It's property, sir, and must follow all the laws of other property. Ha! ha! ha! advise my clients to jeopardize their debt, out of humanity to property—yes, sir, I say, to property—ha! ha! ha!"

"I have been entirely misinformed, sir, as to your views and feelings in relation to slavery. I have always understood you were an abolitionist, and that you professed much sympathy for persons held in bondage."

"My philanthropy, sir—my philanthropy embraces the whole human family. I should rejoice to see every human being upon earth as free as air—yes, sir, I say as free as air."

"I should suppose, sir, that, having a desire to see every human being as free as air, if you could not accomplish that desire, your philanthropy would extend to ameliorating the condition of every human being who was not free; and that, sir, is just as far as I wish your philanthropy to go; when you can't accomplish your grand desideratum of setting them all free, to lessen as much as possible the miseries of those that are not so. It was to effect such an object as that, sir, that I came here to-day."

"I will not advise my clients, sir, to do any such thing; and I now tell you, once for all, sir, that the execution will be contemporaneous with the judgment. Ha! ha!

ha! very laughable, indeed, that the South should just have waked up to the evils of making human beings property. Ha! ha! ha! it's too ridiculous!"

The Doctor left him in disgust, and determined to make the appeal to Hicks and Son, himself, by letter, which he wrote and sent to the Post Office after returning home.

CHAPTER XVI.

SUCCESSFUL INTERCESSION.

MISS EVELINA PREBLE, after remaining a few days at Selma, had returned to the Cottage. George and his wife, hearing of her return, went over with the intention of staying with her until she had become accustomed to a home made dreary, and distressingly gloomy to her, by the death of her Aunt Priscilla. George loved his sister sincerely, and her present forlorn situation excited his warmest sympathy. He knew that she was ardently attached to Mr. Grattan, and was apprehensive that his father's opposition to their union might have a serious effect upon her health, which was naturally delicate.

He had never conversed with his father upon the subject, and although he had a great desire to do so, his resolution failed him whenever he had proposed to himself to make the attempt. Mr. Preble's manner was distant and austere to every one, but particularly so towards his children, who, when young, had stood very much in awe of him, and now that they were grown, could not approach him with the ease and familiarity of friendship. George, however, determined that this visit should not end before he expressed to his father his views fully upon the engagement between Mr. Grattan and his sister; he had frequent opportunities for doing so, as his sister never left her own room, and his wife spent most of her time there too. On the fourth day of his visit to the Cottage, his father and himself were left together in the parlour. In a tremulous voice, he said: "Father, I have for some time had a desire to converse with you upon a subject in which I feel great interest, and which ought deeply to interest us all. Our dear aunt has left us, and we all feel very sensibly her loss, but none half as much so, as our poor dear Evelina; she has lost one who was her mother, her companion, her adviser; her situation then is calculated to excite our warmest sympathy and compassion. I have apprehended, father, that this bereavement, coming upon her at a time when she had been suffering under other causes of inquietude, might prove of serious injury to a constitution naturally feeble; and that the time might not be far distant when you would be called on to mourn the loss of an only daughter, and I an only sister. To avert such a calamity it behooves us to put forth every effort to restore her to the enjoyment of tranquillity and happiness. Your very apparent dislike to the Rev. Mr. Grattan, your cold, distant, and forbidding conduct towards him, has, I presume, prevented an announcement from him of his engagement with your daughter, which fact, I now take upon myself to say, does now exist. Mr. Grattan is a gentleman of unquestioned piety, most respectably connected, and one eminently calculated to make an impression upon a heart like Evelina's; and I know, sir, that he has made so deep an impression on her heart, that, if their union is forbidden, the consequences may be deplored by us, when it is too late."

"Well, George, you know that I could not give or withhold my consent until it was asked; and if it had been asked, George, I will candidly say to you that it would have been withheld. Mr. Grattan, I understand, has no property with which he could support Evelina but a small salary, which you know is very precarious; and you have often heard me say, that my property does not pass from my hands during my life. Under such circumstances, George, how could they get along, and how could they expect my consent to be given?"

"Father, you have forgotten that Aunt Priscilla left Evelina, at the lowest calculation, seven thousand dollars. The interest of that, and Mr. Grattan's income, ought to support them very comfortably; besides, situated as you are, I should think it would be the first wish of your heart to have your only daughter to live with you; and instead of residing here alone, to have the company of so pleasant a companion as Mr. Grattan. If they were to live with you, sir, and not encounter the expenses of housekeeping, they might lay by a portion of their income every year. I, father, shall have an abundance of this world's goods for my purposes, and rather than that Evelina should be made miserable for the balance of her life, I will agree to give up to them every cent's worth of property you may intend for me."

Mr. Preble's heart of stone was somewhat softened by the noble generosity of his son.

"Well, George," he said, "I'll think upon this subject, and we will talk more about it at another time."

George was highly delighted at his father's last remark. He knew his character perfectly—he knew that when determined upon a particular course of conduct, that determination was expressed in a positive, impatient manner, bordering on violence; and from the mild stand to which he had brought him, he augured a favourable result. During the day he went into Evelina's room, and George thought he looked upon her with more commiseration than he ordinarily manifested for the sorrows and afflictions of others. Words of condolence never passed his lips upon any occasion, but he did say to Evelina, while sitting in her room, "that he had supposed the good counsel she had so often received from her aunt, would have enabled her to bear with more fortitude her loss."

Dr. and Mrs. Boswell rode over to the cottage that afternoon to see Evelina. George was particularly pleased to see the Doctor at such a crisis; he saw that it was necessary that the wavering of his father's mind should be turned to some advantage at once, before the old gentleman's apparent sympathy for his daughter should be succeeded by the coldness and indifference so natural to him; and that his present irresolution should not be suffered to give place to his rigid inflexibility of character.

He was unwilling himself to renew the morning's conversation with his father so soon; but the arrival of Dr. Boswell determined him to call in his assistance at a time so propitious. He told the Doctor what had passed between his father and himself, and requested him to use his influence with the old man. The Doctor had for some time been disposed to converse with Mr. Preble upon that subject, and readily consented. George soon left them together.

"Mr. Preble," said the Doctor, "I hope you will not attribute to me any officious intermedding with your family concerns, when I address you upon a subject which might seem exclusively to belong to your own family circle; and I trust, sir, I need offer no other apology for doing so, than a warm and sincere friendship for yourself, and for every other member of your family. I have known for some time, Mr. Preble, that there was an engagement between your daughter and the Rev. Mr. Grattan; and I fear, sir, from what I have heard, that their union will not be sanctioned by you. I may not be fully aware of your reasons for withholding your assent; but be they what they may, you will pardon me for saying, that from my intimate acquaintance with that reverend gentleman, I must presume they are based upon no just foundation. I know of no individual in the circle of my acquaintance, to whom you could intrust with more safety the happiness of your daughter, than to him: he is a clergyman of piety, refinement, and cultivation; his family connexions are as respectable as any in Virginia. I have reason to believe, Mr. Preble, that your daughter is ardently attached to him, and that her happiness for life depends upon their union. I hope, sir, you will suffer me to convey the glad tidings that your opposition is withdrawn?"

"I must say, Doctor, that this match is not according to my notions of suitableness; but, as you all tell me that Evelina's happiness depends upon it, and as the poor child is so much distressed at her aunt's death, you have liberty to say that my consent will be granted, provided that Mr. Grattan will let himself down so far as to ask it in person."

"That he will do, sir, most joyously I can assure you."

Mrs. Boswell whispered it to Evelina; and they took their departure, anxious to communicate it to Mr. Grattan, whom the Doctor sent for as soon as he got home. They found Mr. and Mrs. Stephens at Selma; they had come over to spend the night; and Mrs. Stephens, finding them absent, went into the garden to see her old friend, Uncle Robin.

"Well, Uncle Robin, you see I pay you a visit every now and then, and you never think of coming to see me."

"Missis, I always moughty glad to see you, madam; an' I's bin thinkin' o' goin' ober to—what you call it, madam? Freedom Place—ah! dat's it—for som' time, but I does hab so much to do in de mornin's tendin' to de plantation, an' in de ebenin's fixin' my garden for de winter, dat I ain' bin had time, madam."

"Uncle Robin, our place never was called Freedom Place; in my folly I called it Fredonia, but I want to change that name, now. I wish you would think of some pretty name for me."

"Missis, Robin got moughty poo' head, madam, for dem things. Lem me see—lem me see—s'pose you call it Satefaction, madam?"

"Uncle Robin, I don't think that would sound so well."

"Well, missis, I bin tell you poo' nigger head ain' moughty good for givin' name to gentlefolks' greathouse, madam."

"Suppose I call it Felicity, Uncle Robin? that means happiness."

"Madam, if you is happy dar, I would call it Flissity."

"I think, Uncle Robin, I never enjoyed more happiness in my life than I do now."

"Well, madam, dat's jist what I tell you sometime back; der's much more flissity, madam, in habin' black folks to wait 'pun you dan white folk, anyhow."

"Then you think Mr. Stephens was right, Uncle Robin, in purchasing slaves?"

"Sure I does, madam. It does seem to me, missis, dat som' folks was born to wuck an' wait 'pun t'other som' dat wa'n' born to wuck. Now, missis, jest look at you small han' an' arm, an' den look at my Elce han' an' arm, an' tell me, missis, which you think was born to wuck; ebery-body mus' say Elce. Well, dat bein' de case, whar de moughty difference whether dem dat's born for wuck hab black face or white face, madam? an' if de black face gib you mo' flissity dan de white face, you shou'd bin hav' um. Dat's what make me say Mas' Stephens right in buyin' nigger, madam."

"But, Uncle Robin, some people think it wrong to hold human beings in a state of slavery. I once thought so."

"Well, now, missis, I gwine ax you some questions, an' I gwine answer dem, too, as I go 'long, an' if I don' an-swer right, you stop me, missis. Was you wait 'pun by whitefolks where you com' from? Yes. Did de make you fire an' bring you water? Yes. Did de cook for you? Yes. Did de clean out you chamber? Yes. Did de wuck in you garden? Yes. Did de do all sort o' plantation wuck? Yes. Did de clean Mas' Stephen' boot an' shoe? Yes. Did de do, missis, whateber you tell um to do? Yes. Is I right, madam, when I bin say 'yes?'"

"Pretty much so, Uncle Robin."

"Well, den, missis, dat's jist what de niggers do in dis

country, an' I don' see de moughty difference between um, madam."

By this time the Doctor and Mrs. Boswell had returned, and Mrs. Stephens went back to the house.

"Ann, my dear," she said, "I have had a long talk with Uncle Robin, and I don't think I ever leave him without being edified by his conversation."

"Mamma, you will find but few people like Uncle Robin, for strength of mind; I mean in his sphere. I am particularly struck with his very homely but forcible illustrations. If he had been well educated he would have made a considerable man, no doubt."

"There are but few people as good as Robin, in this world," said the Doctor. "Mrs. Stephens, I suppose your shrubbery is coming on finely, at Fredonia."

"Oh, Doctor, pray never let me hear you call it Fredonia, again; Uncle Robin and myself have just changed its name to Felicity. I was a good deal diverted at his calling it Flissity."

"Well, madam, that's about as close as Robin ever comes to correct pronunciation. I don't know but that Flissity is the most euphonious of the two. I think I could have given you a better name still."

"Doctor, let me hear it; I am not particularly fond of Felicity, and if you can give me a name more appropriate, I may adopt it."

"How would you like Crosbia, madam?"

"Oh, Doctor, Doctor, don't tease me any more with those Crosbys, if you please! Any word in the English language, no matter how beautiful, if it had the letters C R O S following in regular succession, would be shocking to me."

The Doctor was told that Mr. Grattan had arrived, and went into the yard to meet him.

"Well, my friend, I do from my heart congratulate you."

"For what, Doctor?" said Mr. Grattan.

"That you are to marry one of the most charming creatures upon earth—Miss Evelina Preble."

"Why, is it possible, Doctor, that you have just heard of our engagement? I thought you had known that a long time ago. Before you offer your congratulations, you should recollect that engagements and matrimony are two very different things, and that one does not necessarily follow the other, as I very much fear it will be in my case. I understand that old Mr. Preble is violently opposed to it, and neither would Miss Evelina or myself wish to act counter to his wishes."

"Then, sir, you don't wish to be congratulated until after your marriage, I see."

"If Mr. Preble, Doctor, were to withdraw his opposition, I might then be congratulated as the most fortunate and the happiest man in existence."

"I now, sir, renew my congratulations to a gentleman who is made the most fortunate and the happiest man in existence, by the communication that Mr. Preble has withdrawn all opposition, and I have authority for making that communication from Mr. Preble himself."

They reached the parlour door, and there was no opportunity for further explanation, nor had Mr. Grattan any idea to whom he was indebted for so great a blessing. From the devotional appearance of his manner, it was apparent that his first impulse was to return thanks to that Being from whom all blessings flow.

Mrs. Stephens had not been to any place of worship for many months, never since she left Norristown, and she told her daughter she would like to hear Mr. Grattan lecture that night. When Mr. Grattan had heretofore lectured at Selma, it had generally been in Uncle Robin's cabin; but, as Mrs. Stephens was afraid to turn out at night, it was determined that the lecture should be delivered in the dining-room; and Charles was told to inform Uncle Robin and the other servants, most of whom came in and were seated around the room. Mrs. Stephens looked upon them that night, not as poor creatures, but as beings surrounded with comforts and gospel privileges.

After the lecture was over, the Doctor and Mr. Grattan were left together, and the latter was informed of the manner in which old Mr. Preble had been brought over. Many were the praises lavished upon George for his noble conduct. Mr. Grattan determined to go the next morning to the Cottage, to perform the condition imposed by the old gentleman.

On the following day there was a general breaking up of the party at Selma. Mr. and Mrs. Stephens returned to Felicity (as we shall hereafter call it), Mr. Grattan went to the Cottage, and the Doctor and Mrs. Boswell paid a visit to Major Scott's, the first since the affliction in their family. They found them alone, George and his wife being still with Evelina. Mrs. Scott was much more composed than they expected to find her. George's determination to remain, in consequence of Amelia's death, had in a great measure reconciled them both to that event. The Major gave them a minute account of Amelia's illness, Mammy Betty's violent grief, and of the manner in which she was forcibly taken from him. Much sympathy was expressed, and many tears shed at the relation of her sufferings. Major Scott said that he was determined to make another effort to get her back to Virginia, no tidings as yet having reached him of her death. As Mr. Grattan was much beloved by all his parishioners, his love-matters became the subject of conversation. The communication made to the Major and Mrs. Scott, of old Mr. Preble's consent having been obtained, gave them much pleasure. It seemed to be generally agreed that their union should take place at once; but Mrs. Boswell was of opinion that Evelina would not consent to be married until some months had elapsed from the time of her aunt's death. When the Doctor and Mrs. Boswell were returning home, they called at the Cottage, where they learned that Mr. Grattan had been kindly received by the old gentleman, that he and Evelina had had a private interview, the result of which was that they were to be married sometime during the next spring.

CHAPTER XVII.

COLLEGE FRIENDSHIPS BETTER THAN NORTHERN HUMANITY.

As the time approached for the Doctor to receive an answer to his letter to Hicks & Son, in the regular course of mail, he became very anxious; and in about fifteen days from the date of his, he received the following:

"Sir:

"Your communication has been received, and its contents noted. Your proposal fills us with astonishment, and was indeed calculated to excite our risibility, at a proposition coming North to enlist our sympathy in behalf of Southern property. Why, sir, you could not have foreseen the injurious consequences of such a proposition to the South itself! it is calculated to destroy Northern confidence in Southern responsibility. Your wealth consists in slave property, and, in our dealings with the South, credit is given you upon the availability of that sort of property, in enforcing our contracts. Now, if a call is to be made upon our humanity, to arrest the progress of those measures which we resort to for the recovery of our claims, we must either disregard the call, or we must cease to deal with the South altogether. Our attorney, Mr. Squashum, has his instructions, and will proceed in this matter in a manner most beneficial to the interest of his clients. Your obedient servants,

"HICKS & SON."

The Doctor felt much chagrin and mortification at reading this letter; having made a determination (as soon as he found out he would have to pay this debt) never to become security again for any one, he felt himself therefore precluded from asking a favour of any friend which he could not reciprocate; and determined to make no effort for procuring the money from the banks, or any other like source. He saw that the sale of some of his negroes was inevitable, and determined that the sale (when it was made) should not be a voluntary and private one, but should be forced by execution.

The winters and springs in this region of country being cold and dreary, the roads unfavourable for country visit ing, the incidents of that of 1849–'50 are consequently few, and not worth relating. The reader is informed that Mr. Squashum attended the June court, obtained a judgment against Dr. Boswell upon the protested draft, and made his memorandum for the clerk to issue an execution as soon as the court should rise.

As the circumstance of his indebtedness for her brother could no longer be concealed from Mrs. Boswell, the Doctor made to her the communication; she was much distressed, and wept bitterly; after her grief had somewhat subsided, the Doctor proposed that she should assist him in selecting such negroes for sale as would produce the least possible severance of natural ties. Four young unmarried men, and as many unmarried young women, were selected, as sufficient to raise the amount of the execution. The sheriff came in a few days, and informed the Doctor that he was not authorized by law to levy his execution on slaves, if there was other personal property sufficient to pay the debt, unless he instructed him to do so. The instructions were given, and the slaves left in the Doctor's possession until the day of sale. After the sheriff was gone, Uncle Robin came to the house to see his master.

"Masser," said he, "I understands dat a moughty 'stressin' thing gwine take place here 'mong us, sir."

"Yes, Robin; a security debt has come against me from Boston, and I shall have to sell at least eight young negro men and women. It has already caused me great sorrow of heart, and I don't know how I can bear it when the time comes for them to be sold."

"Masser, when trouble an' sorrow does com' 'pun us, sir, we mus' pray de Lord to 'nable us to b'ar it, an' be thankful too, masser, dat 'tis no wus wid us den 'tis. Der's one thing, masser, I can't see into; dese people from 'way back North, hears folks say dat you's a rich man, 'case you got heap o' slaves, an' dey comes here to git you in der debt, an', arter a while, dey sells you slaves to make der money, an' den dey turn roun' an' 'buse you, and says de Lord gwine punish you for habin' slaves. Now, masser, dat ane right, to force 'pun you dis thing, an' den make you bear all de blame on it."

"It certainly is not right, Robin, for them to do so."

"Masser, Robin sometimes use to take pun heself to 'vise you pa 'bout things, an' he hopes you'll scuse him for speakin' he mind to you, sir. As dis thing dun com' pun you, masser, de bes' way is not to take on too much, but to do de bes' you kin to git out o' dis trouble, an' try neber to git into anoder like it. De wise man in de Bible say, 'He dat is surety for stranger, shill smart for it; an' he dat hates suretyship is sure.'"

"Robin, your advice is certainly very good, and I will try to follow it."

"Masser, der's one thing I wan' you to try an' do, sir."

"What's that, Robin?"

"When dese gals an' boys is sold, sir, I wan' you to try an' keep 'em from goin' to de soul drivers, to be car'd to Orleens. I bin hear 'em say, sir, dat when dey gits 'em to Orleens, dey cars 'em to a great big wa'rhouse, where de folks from de Red country round Orleens comes to buy niggers, an' dat dem folks beat de deble an' all he imps for badness, sir. Dey tells me, sir, dat dey wucks hard all de year to make truck to sell in Orleens to git money, an' when dey gits dar money, sir, dey goes to dis big wa'rhouse an' gives monstrous big price for niggers, jist to car' 'em home an' make de t'other niggers dey got dar, whip 'em to death, sir."

"Why, Robin, you are not blockhead enough to believe that, I hope?"

"Masser, 'tis moughty hard to believe, sir, but dey tells me it come moughty straight, sir, from people who bin dar an' see it."

"Robin, those are lies raised by people who never were within a thousand miles of New Orleans, for the purpose of making money."

"Masser, you don' say so, sir; why dem people sartinly don' read der Bible. De Proverb say, 'De gittin' of treasure by a lying tongue is a vanity tossed to an' fro of dem dat seek death.' Masser, der's one nother thing dey bin tell me 'bout dat Red country, which I couldn't b'lieve 'fore you tell me 'twas all lie. I hearn 'em say, sir, dat de only chance niggers have dar to run away from dar massers, is to make der massers b'lieve dat der great-hous' is haunted; dey says, sir, dat white folks dar, and der blood houn' too, mighty fraid o' ghosts, and when dey git frightened dey don' care any mo' bout niggers, sir, an' dey gits off. Now, masser, what make me know 'twasn't true, was, dat I knowd white folks got too much sense to be 'fraid o' ghosts, an' none but woolly-head niggers, sir, 'fraid o' dem things."

"Well, Robin, you are right there, white people would be much more apt to impose ghost-stories upon negroes, than negroes upon white people; but, as I said before, it's all false from beginning to end."

The day of sale at length arrived. The Doctor carried the negroes to the Court House, and delivered them to the sheriff. The crowd was unusually large; each individual seemed to be acquainted with all the circumstances under which the sale was to be made; the sympathy for the Doctor and his negroes was great; there was a general agreement that no one would bid for them; even Mr. Bosher declared that he would not bid. One of the men was put upon the block, and was cried a long time without a bid; at length there was one of five hundred dollars, at which he was proclaimed to be sold to Mr. Melchezedek Squashum.

"That's the way you squashes them, is it, Mr. Melkeesidic?" cried old Mr. Frazer, who was half seas over, as the saying is in Virginia.

There was a gentleman in that crowd from the county of Augusta, whose name was Banks, who had come down to purchase negroes for his own use. He and Dr. Boswell met in the crowd.

"Why, John," said he to the Doctor, "is this you, my old college friend, and are these your negroes they are selling? I had no idea of it. John, it reminds me of old William and Mary to see you. But why are you selling your negroes, John?"

The Doctor told him the circumstances.

"Well, sir, not another shall be sold. I have the money; you shall have the amount of the execution, and we will get back the negro that has been sold."

"My friend," said the Doctor, "you are very kind, but I fear you will put yourself to great inconvenience to wait until I can make the money."

"Never mind that," said Mr. Banks; "pay me in two years, and that will answer my purpose." He then turned to Mr. Squashum, and told him that he would pay the amount of the execution for Dr. Boswell, and that the Doctor could take back home all his negroes.

"Not too fast, sir, not too fast; I've bought one of them, a great bargain, great bargain, sir; can't give him up for less than six hundred dollars."

"I don't wish to have many words with you, Mr. Squash; I will give you five hundred and fifty."

"Well, sir, it's a bargain, it's a bargain."

The execution was settled, the fifty dollars extra paid Mr. Squashum, and the Doctor and Mr. Banks took their leave for Selma.

A few days after the sale, the nuptials of the Rev. Mr. Grattan and Miss Evelina Preble were witnessed at the Cottage, by Dr. and Mrs. Boswell, Mr. and Mrs. George Preble, and the old gentleman.

Our narrative closes about the time when quiet and tranquillity was restored to the South by the passage of the Compromise Acts. Mr. Bosher said to Dr. Boswell, that "He must now seek some other employment, as he could no longer grab runaway negroes flying."

THE END.

www.ingramcontent.com/pod-product-compliance
Lightning Source LLC
LaVergne TN
LVHW010541100826
845148LV00001B/261

* 9 7 8 1 4 2 5 5 7 6 3 2 5 *